Vampire Council:

# Hunted

PATRICK KAMPMAN

Published by Dark Fiction

ISBN: 098359225X
ISBN-13: 978-0-9835922-5-9
E-Book ISBN: 0983592268
E-Book ISBN-13: 978-0-9835922-6-6

# CREDITS

Cover Design by Deborah Grieves
cynnalia.deviantart.com

Edited By Sarah Kampman

Layout by Russell Godwin
argo-marketing.com

# DEDICATION

To my friends and family, for giving me the support
to make this all possible.

## ACKNOWLEDGMENTS

I would like to thank Sarah Kampman for doing such a wonderful job editing my pile of words into something coherent, Deborah Grieves for yet another awesome cover, and Russell Godwin for laying it all out.

# Chapter 1

Ryan arrived early, as usual. He was punctual and thought ill of those who weren't. Time was precious when you had little left, and Ryan knew his own time was short. Sooner or later his luck would run out.

He was satisfied to see she had also arrived early. He didn't have her description; only a name, time, and location where they were supposed to meet. Even with that limited information she was easy to spot.

She sat alone at the bar nursing a Mai Tai, a drink that was a couple of decades out of fashion. Despite an air of self-assurance, her tension was obvious. Her posture was stiff under the little black dress, a manicured nail tapped the side of her glass, and she periodically scanned the bar, eyes darting nervously among the patrons waiting for their turn to be seated. Her gaze rested on Ryan for a moment before moving on in dismissal.

She was older than Ryan's own twenty-nine years; he placed her somewhere in her mid-thirties. She was slender, with shapely but not excessively muscular arms and legs, and dark shoulder-length hair cut in a style that said boardroom rather than nightclub.

When she turned for her next scan of the room Ryan got a better look at her. She was beautiful. Her brown eyes crackled with life despite being burdened by obvious worry. By the confident way she held herself Ryan knew she was unused to being at a disadvantage, and he imagined the unfamiliar situation bothered her.

Ryan didn't allow himself relationships. It was one of his rules. In his business, relationships could only end in tragedy. Every so often he encountered a woman who made him regret his choice. Take this one, for example. On a purely superficial level Ryan could see spending his life with her: she was beautiful, classy, self-confident, and knew how to dress.

Of course, she was probably a bitch. Her type usually was. The main advantage to Ryan's "no relationships" rule was that he never had the opportunity to be disappointed by one.

Ryan glanced up from his menu and took a harder look at the lady he was supposed to protect. He stripped aside the surface qualities and found a tired woman on the run. Her dress was slightly disheveled; her makeup was rubbed thin in some places but not others. He guessed she probably put it on some time ago and had no opportunity to touch it up, possibly even sleeping with it on.

Ryan was surprised he had missed those things on his first pass. He normally did a better job sizing people up. He had been so enamored by her first impression that he had gotten tunnel vision, missed the important details; another thing he couldn't afford to do in his profession.

Ryan stood by the hostess podium feigning interest in the menu for another half a minute. He had no intention of eating there and even if he had he wouldn't need the menu to order. This chain restaurant served the exact same food for greater America as its six or seven nation-wide competitors. Ryan was positive he could name a dozen things that the eatery offered without the bother of a menu. He assumed it was why these types of places were so popular among the sheeple. It was all about sameness and consistency; people took comfort in those qualities.

What he did instead was make sure neither he nor the lady had been followed. He always checked for tails, even though he was usually the one doing the following. It was another of his rules: just because you were a predator, didn't mean you weren't someone else's prey.

In his line of work it always paid to be careful. Being sloppy could cost you your life. The job to protect this woman was an anomaly. Ryan didn't protect people, he killed them. Well, not people. Things. He killed things. Vampires, werewolves, faeries, trolls, demons, witches — it didn't matter, Ryan killed 'em all.

This was a special case. Ryan's oldest friend had asked him for a favor. Some vampires were after this woman, and Ryan had agreed to make sure they didn't get her, at least until she could reach the safety of Chicago. What happened to her after that, and why they were after her in the first place, Ryan didn't know and didn't care.

It didn't bother him that he was out of his element. He figured the bodyguard duty would be the same thing as hunting monsters, only easier. This time the monsters would be coming to him.

Though he doubted it would come to that. Ryan planned on depositing her in Chicago by breakfast the next morning. He figured the worst part of the job would be the line at airport security and the gropey TSA agents.

It had been years since Ryan had been to Chicago. The first thing he planned to do after delivering this woman safe and sound was to catch a White Sox game at Cellular Field. Assuming everything went as scheduled, he'd be eating a hotdog, drinking a beer, and watching the Sox take on Detroit this time tomorrow night.

Ryan didn't know why Bill wanted the woman protected. Maybe she was a relative that he had never mentioned before, maybe she knew some secret that Bill wanted, or maybe he was doing it just to piss the vampires off. Whatever the reason, it was none of Ryan's business. He trusted the man asking the favor implicitly. If Bill wanted it done, that was good enough reason for Ryan.

Ryan didn't have many friends for the same reason he didn't get emotionally involved with women. He didn't want them to get hurt, or risk the chance that they would be used against him. Bill was the exception to his rule, one of the handful of people Ryan would call a friend. So when Bill asked him to make sure this lady made it to

Chicago, Ryan agreed immediately. He abandoned the break he was taking after chasing that werewolf all over the Sierras, loaded up the car, and made a beeline for the San Francisco Bay Area.

A long time ago Bill had saved Ryan's life from the very things he now hunted. Since then he became Ryan's closest friend, almost a father to him. Not that they saw each other much; they lived in different states and both had careers. Ryan's was hunting monsters; Bill's was running an import business. Antiques and artwork out of Europe.

On the rare occasions they did get together, they spent the night reminiscing or talking about current affairs. Sometimes they just sat and had a few drinks, quietly wasting away the time on Ryan's back patio.

Periodically Bill would contact Ryan about a job. Bill traveled a lot and knew what to look for and when he found something he'd call Ryan. It was a good fit; Bill had a knack for finding things that needed killing and Ryan had a knack for killing them.

Ryan hoped this job would involve none of that. He placed the menu back in the holder on the side of the hostess podium, satisfied that no one else in the room was interested in the lady—or at least unusually interested. With her looks, every straight guy in the place had already noticed her. But it was a restaurant bar, and most of the guys were either with dates or their families. Their loss.

Ryan sat down next to her, got the bartender's attention and, like the woman beside him, ordered an archaic drink. A CC7. It would be his last drink until they got to Chicago. He didn't drink on duty. Everything he hunted was stronger and faster than he was, and he couldn't afford the slightest handicap. He shouldn't be having this one, but Bill had warned him that the lady was a handful. Ryan wasn't a patient man, so he figured he might need it.

The bartender doubled his tip by not only knowing what it was that he ordered, but having the Canadian Club on hand. They didn't have 7-Up of course, so Ryan had to settle for one of the poor substitutes, but he didn't ding the man for the restaurant's questionable stocking decisions.

Ryan took a sip of his drink as the lady turned to him with an expression of practiced patience. She assumed he was about to drop a line on her and was clearly ready to give him the preemptive brush off. She had done it so often that it was automatic.

Ryan set his drink down and faced her. Damn, she was even more beautiful up close. Something in his chest jumped, but he quickly beat it into submission and headed the woman off before she could tell him to take a hike.

"Ryan. I'm your escort to Chicago," he said, extending his hand.

"*You're* Ryan?"

The woman gave him the once-over, not bothering to hide her displeasure or take the proffered hand.

# # #

Carmen appraised the man opposite her. It was something she was good at, sizing people up. He was somewhere between twenty-five and thirty. Tall, well built, not overweight. It was hard to say exactly how fit he was; he wore a heavyweight dark green shirt tucked into loose-fitting black pants covered in pockets, and over it all he had thrown a baggy tan canvas jacket. None of it was fashionable, no matter how many decades you went back.

The rest of him was clean cut: chiseled features with short-cropped brown hair. He was definitely more ruggedly handsome than pretty boy. A thin white scar started below his right eye and ran a few inches down the side of his cheek. Another more obvious one crossed his chin. But most telling was his demeanor. The way he carried himself had a cool, hard edge that she recognized well. The man was a killer.

When Charles said he was sending protection, Carmen had assumed the person she was to meet would be the head of a security detail, not a single man. She assumed he would be a professional, not a thug. She was used to security wearing suits. They blended in to the types of places she frequented. It was why she had dismissed him when she saw him at the podium earlier. She decided that the only place this man would blend into would be a homeless shelter or, more optimistically, a blue collar dive bar full of unemployed construction workers.

But Charles had been confident, almost too confident, and in all the years Carmen had known Charles, he had never let her down.

Even so, she was beginning to feel she had made a mistake going to him. Carmen had been a little shaken when she heard the news. Three more attacks. One more of their own had been killed. Peter and Elizabeth had only narrowly escaped with their lives. That's what prompted Carmen to ask for help in the first place.

But a full day had passed since then. Carmen had calmed down, began to make peace with Henry's death, and now was quite sure she could handle matters herself. But first she had to figure out what to do with the "protection" that Charles sent.

# # #

"I wouldn't lie to you, you're too pretty," Ryan said in response to her skepticism.

"I've always found the opposite to be true. Men lie to the pretty ones the most."

"Only men that can't get what they want by playing it straight." Ryan noted that she had no accent. It was a thing he listened for automatically. It helped in his line of work, especially identifying vampires. They had certain tells: under thirty, attractive, slightly elongated and sharp canine teeth, pale skin, faint accents leftover from wherever and whenever they were from. Many tended to hold on to little bits of their past: a piece of fashion, an affectation, outdated turns of phrase.

She cocked an eyebrow, looking into his cold gray eyes. "And I take it you play it straight, and have no problems getting what you want?"

When their eyes met Ryan's heart did that thing again. He wasn't sure what it was about her, but whatever it was, it worked. "I do when I get the chance, but my vocation doesn't exactly lend itself to a whole lot of opportunity, if you know what I'm saying."

"Are you telling me you don't encounter pretty girls in your line of work?"

"Not that don't end up dead."

It was true. Hunters tended to be predominantly men, and not necessarily attractive ones. The women he encountered while hunting were either monsters or were so damaged by monsters as to be off limits.

Even when he found a woman he liked he never allowed a relationship to move forward, at least not anything long-term. Getting close to someone was just leverage for the other side, something that could be used against you. One of the things that gave him an edge was that he had nothing left in the world he cared about losing, nothing of consequence that anyone could take away from him.

A long time ago that had been different, but not anymore. Now he did the taking, and he planned on keeping it that way.

# # #

Carmen watched his expression change. It was like reading an open book. First cocky, then thoughtful, then angry. Probably at being such a failure at what he did. What the hell kind of bodyguard had Charles sent her? Not only was he bad at it, he freely admitted it.

"Well, at least you aren't overconfident in your abilities. So, you've been doing this long?" Carmen asked, taking a sip from her layered, multi-colored drink.

"Awhile," Ryan answered.

"And people still hire you?" Her trust in Charles was being shaken like a martini. Carmen wondered if Charles owed the guy a favor and was giving him a pity job. She made a mental note to, next time she saw Charles, to thank him *properly* for sending this guy.

"Most of the time I do it for free, why?"

"That makes more sense. I can't see too many people lining up for a bodyguard with your track record."

"What are you talking about?" Ryan frowned.

The guy was slow, Carmen thought. Maybe he was some distant cousin to Charles. She knew they used to inbreed a lot on that island Charles came from. "I thought that, since most of your clients ended up dead, you probably couldn't be charging too much of a premium."

Ryan's look had gone blank with confusion at her last statement. She waited for him to drool, but a light bulb flickered to life behind his eyes. The revelation was plain as day. The man smiled and let out a chuckle. "Oh! No, see, I don't normally do this type of work. I'm more offense than defense. In fact this protection thing is a first for me."

It was becoming obvious to her that Charles was trying to do two favors at once: hook Carmen up with a bodyguard, and supply this lug with a job. It would have been a noble gesture if it wasn't going to cost Carmen her life. She couldn't believe Charles would do this to her.

"Wonderful." Carmen speared the cherry in her drink with a quick jab of her narrow red straw. She pretended it was Charles while she wiped the offending fruit onto her napkin.

The man adjusted slightly in his stool. "Don't worry, I got you covered. This will be just like killing, but in reverse. Hey, you're not going to eat that?" Without waiting for an answer, Ryan took the cherry from her napkin and popped it in his mouth and washed it down with a swig of Canadian Club and 7-Up substitute. He held up the stem. "I met a girl once who could tie one of these things in a knot with her tongue. I guess everybody's got a talent, right?"

When she frowned rather than answering, Ryan gave a shrug, and then reached into his glass with his fingers to try to pluck out his own maraschino cherry. A CC7 shouldn't have had a cherry, but Ryan liked them so he forgave the bartender for the faux pas. "These little guys are the best part."

Carmen's frown deepened. "You're not even a—" She stopped herself and closed her eyes for a moment, reining in her mounting anger. Once it was under control she continued.

"Look, no offense, but I thought this was a bad idea when Charles first suggested it, and I'm thinking it's an even worse one now."

After the cherry fell to the bottom of his glass, Ryan gave up using his fingers and picked up Carmen's discarded straw. "No idea who Charles is, but I wouldn't worry yourself about it. By tomorrow morning you'll be safe and sound in Chicago, and I'll be out of your hair forever. We'll both be happier." Ryan's brow creased as the cherry managed to adeptly dodge the straw. He tilted the glass as much as he could without spilling and redoubled his efforts to skewer the uncooperative red orb.

"By tomorrow? And how exactly do you propose we do that?" Carmen cocked her head and crossed her arms waiting for the answer.

# # #

There it was. Ryan knew she had been too perfect. Not only was she in fact bitchy, which he had assumed, but she was obviously a little slow to boot. She had the looks to get away with it. Most men would forgive her because of that, but not Ryan. He liked his women to have at least a modicum of intelligence.

He tried not to let his disappointment in her cognitive ability show as he set his glass down on the bar, cherry resting happily at the bottom. "The same way most people get from California to Chicago: by airplane. We'll be catching the 11:45 out of SFO. I already checked, and there are still open seats. If we leave now we'll make it to the airport in plenty of time. It's even a non-stop flight; the trip should take less than five hours. With the time difference, you'll be in Chicago at dawn. We'll grab a cab to wherever it is you want to go, and voila—we're done. Easiest gig I've had all year."

"Are you crazy?"

"Excuse me?"

"I couldn't take that flight even if I wanted to. Which I don't."

"Why not? Oh, don't tell me you're on the no-fly list."

*Christ*, Ryan thought, *who was this woman?* If she was a fugitive from justice it was going to seriously up the difficulty of getting her to Chicago. Ryan knew Bill had been hiding something about her. He had sensed it. He'd hoped it was something less inconvenient like uncontrollable body odor, or Tourette's syndrome.

Carmen shook her head. This guy was some combination of dense and mathematically challenged. It would be daylight before they got out of the airport. "No, I'm not a terrorist, I simply don't do airplanes. Flying is unnatural. And even if I did fly, that time doesn't work for me."

*Just peachy*, thought Ryan. This complicated things. It meant a road trip. It meant spending the better part of a week with this woman. So much for his ballgame. His hotdog. His beer. They would still make it to Chicago by Friday, of course, but it would be too late. The Sox would have left the city for their game against Cleveland.

He thought back to last night when Bill called. Bill had asked for Ryan's help finding someone to handle an impossible job. He desperately needed to find the best bodyguard there was, one who could not only handle vampires, but a high-maintenance and thoroughly difficult client.

Ryan immediately offered, but Bill had declined, saying this client was important and he needed someone with experience. When Ryan persisted Bill stressed that the client would be exceptionally difficult to work with, and he wasn't sure Ryan could handle it.

Bill had baited him perfectly, and they both knew it. It was a game they played. But Ryan was still going to punch Bill in the jaw next time he saw the man. He owed him that much for thrusting this piece of work on him.

"Fine. We'll drive," Ryan said, wondering if maybe buying the lady a nail file and some bubble gum would keep her quiet until Chicago.

"I think I'll pass."

"Relax. Babysitting you is not my idea of a good time, either, but a lady in your predicament can't be too careful *or* too picky. Going to Chicago alone when you've got someone trying to kill you is stupid, and just because I don't usually do this type of work doesn't mean I'm not good at it."

"No, that's usually *exactly* what it means." Carmen reflected that not only was this man rude, he was also as dumb as a post. The only thing he could possibly protect would be attendance figures in a remedial class.

"Look, I gave a guy my word that I would get you safely to Chicago, and that's what I'm going to do. What *you're* going to do is listen to everything I say, and do everything I ask. Do that and you'll make it to Chicago alive. After that," Ryan shrugged, "you won't be my problem."

Carmen was losing patience. She had come all the way up to the Bay Area from L.A. for this? She could have been in Las Vegas by now, safe with her friend Sylvia.

If Charles hadn't personally vouched for this man, Carmen would have hauled him into the parking lot and had him for dinner. She was hungry. She hadn't eaten in two days and it made her crankier than usual, which is why she was particularly proud of her self-control when she smiled and said, "While I appreciate your misplaced optimism, I'm better off without you."

"No offense, honey, but if bloodsuckers are after you, you don't have a prayer without me."

"Bloodsuckers?" Both of Carmen's brows raised up this time.

"Yeah, you know, vampires? You *do* know that's what's after you, right?"

Ryan sincerely hoped she did. It would make things even harder if she were in denial about them. Most people were. Vampires were fiction as far as they were concerned. But Ryan wanted to assume, seeing as they were trying to kill her and all, she would at least know they existed. He let out a sigh. This job was going from bad to worse.

"Yes, I'm quite aware of that," Carmen said, using three fingers to rub one temple. By the man's tone it was becoming obvious that he had no idea who she was, or simply didn't care.

"Okay, good, that helps. Now don't worry, I specialize in bloodsuckers." Ryan tried an encouraging smile, which Carmen thought made him look even slower.

"Charming. Again, thank you for the offer, but I'll take my chances on my own."

"You don't understand. I'm here to help you," Ryan said.

Carmen could sense his mounting frustration, probably exacerbated by her use of words larger than one syllable. But she decided to give him one last break for Charles' sake. Maybe this guy really needed the money and was seeing his payday slip away.

"Don't worry — I'm aware you're being paid for this job. I'll make sure you get your money, okay? I'll see to it that Charles pays you, right after I slap him in the face for sending a goon to look after me."

Goon? Ryan had been called worse, but he still had some pride. He thought he at least rated "thug" or even "muscle." Goon was kind of low down on the minion totem pole.

His patience was gone. It was time to set things straight with her.

"Okay, let's try this again. It wasn't an offer. A good friend of mine asked me, as a personal favor, to haul your ungrateful ass across the country and make sure that you reach the other side alive. Don't ask me why. After meeting you I can't come up with a good reason for it myself. But I gave him my word, and I never go back on my word."

It was clear the goon was going to continue with his tirade, but Carmen didn't care. She was done. She removed her fingers form her temple and used them to make a stop sign, extending her palm out toward his face. "Spare me the 'I have to do this out of honor' speech. Now if you'll please excuse me, I have to go."

Carmen rose to leave, but Ryan snaked out a hand to catch her wrist. She tried to pull away and found, though his grip was gentle, it was unyielding.

Ryan gave the woman the stare he normally reserved for creatures he was about to snuff out. He had honed the menacing scowl over the years, and was particularly proud of it. "Look lady, either you come willingly and we can enjoy the beautiful countryside this great country has to offer while we roll down the highway playing the license plate game and singing songs, or I can knock you out, tie you up, and toss you in the trunk. Either way I'm personally delivering you to Chicago."

# # #

Even though the man was strong, Carmen knew she could break the grip, along with his arm. But his move had already garnered unwanted attention from the bartender. If she damaged him here she would have a mess to sort out.

Carmen's brow furrowed, her eyes traveling from his hand on her wrist to his face. It had been a long time since anyone had talked to her like this. Decades, in fact. Even longer since anyone had dared grab her. The last person who did experienced a sudden, forcible separation of his head from his body.

But she couldn't stop a smile from playing at her lips. It had been a while since she encountered anyone quite so bullheaded. As dumb as this guy was, and as useless as he probably would be as a bodyguard, he might be amusing for a couple of days at least. He could serve as a distraction, and with everything going on maybe it would help get her mind off things.

And once she became bored with him, she could have a nice meal and then discard the dullard somewhere along that beautiful countryside he'd mentioned.

"Fine," she said, sitting back down. He released her wrist and she extended her hand to him. "I'm Carmen."

# # #

Ryan looked at the proffered hand, thought about stiffing her like she had done him when he tried to shake earlier, but took it anyway. He didn't shake a lot of women's hands, and the ones he did were usually limp. Ryan didn't care for limp handshakes. Every time he encountered one he felt himself having to retract his grip lest he crush them. Hers wasn't limp; it was firm and confident. Pleasant, if cool.

Ryan was a little unsettled by the predatory grin that had crept its way into the lady's features. Something about it troubled him. But he shrugged it off. There was no way she could be worse that the monsters he normally tangled with.

# Chapter 2

They finished their drinks in silence, each one wondering what they had done to deserve the other. Finally Ryan's straw stuttered. With the liquid gone, he was finally able to fish the cherry out of the bottom of the glass.

He ate it, and then asked, "Have you eaten?"

"No."

"Do you want to grab a bite before we leave? It's a long drive to Chicago and I want to make some progress before we have to stop."

"No, thank you. I'm fine." Carmen set her own empty glass down.

"Are you sure?" Ryan asked.

Carmen nodded.

At first Ryan was content with her answer, until another thought pushed the satisfaction aside. "You're not one of those girls who has to stop every hour to use the bathroom, are you? I'm not saying you have to pee in a jar, but I'd like to stop only when we need to get gas or sleep. I have four days to get you to Chicago, and I'm aiming to make it with a few days to spare."

"You'll find I have excellent bladder control."

"A woman after my own heart. Now, are you sure you don't want grab a snack to go? Maybe something to take along with us? Last chance."

Carmen's eyebrow was back up. This guy was harder to figure then she thought. She scanned the establishment again. There were practically no single people in the restaurant. It was all families or couples. "It would be more trouble than it's worth."

Ryan shrugged. "Your call, but no complaining that you're hungry later. Deal?"

Carmen nodded assent then slipped off the stool. The action gave Ryan a good view of her legs, and he decided that if he could convince her not to talk, this wouldn't be such a bad trip after all.

Once they were both standing, Carmen gazed up at the man. Even though she was wearing four inch heels she found that he had a good half foot on her. She put him about six feet two, broad shoulders, trim, lousy sense of style. She liked his looks and could work with his poor taste in clothing. It was just too bad he was an idiot; there was no fixing that.

Ryan threw down a twenty to cover their drinks and a decent tip. "Did you drive?" he asked as they walked out of the restaurant. It was a brisk evening and Ryan's breath emitted a slight vapor as he scanned the full parking lot.

"I took a taxi," Carmen said.

"No bags?"

"I had to leave L.A. in a hurry."

"L.A.? What are you doing all the way up here?"

"Meeting you."

"Huh. Well, that explains the getup you're wearing— not exactly traveling clothes. Not a problem, though. We'll stop somewhere on the way and grab you something decent to wear. My car's over there." Ryan nodded toward a row of cars at the far end of the dimly lit parking lot.

Carmen prickled at Ryan's comment. *She* was wearing a six hundred dollar dress from a respected designer. He on the other hand looked as if he had raided a thrift shop. One of them was sorely in need of something decent to wear, and it wasn't her. She scanned the lot for his car. "The Porsche?"

"No, two over," Ryan said, starting to walk toward his car.

"The Civic?"

"Other way."

"You drive a station wagon?" Carmen eyed the Cadillac CTS-V. Every time Carmen built up a mental image of the man, he did something to tear it down.

"Yup. It has as much room as an SUV, but better handling and it's faster." The last bit was an understatement. Not only was the car a limited edition model built by the factory for speed, Ryan had it further modified to suit his, or any Formula 1 driver's, needs.

Carmen stopped to stare at the back of the squat car. "You do realize there's no way you could have thrown me in the trunk."

Seriously? She was going to go there? Ryan thought as he stopped and turned toward her. He wished he had charged Bill money for this job after all. "You want to try me?"

Carmen folded her arms and cocked her head, continuing to stare at the angular back of the car appraisingly. "You'll lose."

"Oh yeah?" Ryan glanced around for witnesses.

"Yes. Your car has no trunk to throw me into."

Ryan looked down shaking his head, chuckling despite himself. She was a regular comedian, though he had to admit she had a point. He was going to say as much, but his comment was cut short when he caught movement in his peripheral vision. Not the regular movement of a family heading to or from their vehicle, or even a rat or raccoon scurrying across the black top scrounging for food. This had not only been low and fast, but large. The figure darted out of sight between a pair of SUVs.

Ryan moved, placing himself between Carmen and where he had last seen the shadowy form. His hand went inside his jacket, but he waited to draw his weapon. He wanted to make absolutely sure before he pulled out a gun in a parking lot.

Another blur, this time on the other side. That meant two of them. Ryan drew his gun with one hand, while he fished the square key fob out of his pocket with the other.

"Move!" he said, unlocking the doors to his car.

He tried to give Carmen a shove toward the wagon for emphasis, but his hand met air. Carmen was already in motion, her reactions lightning quick as she raced forward. Ryan dashed after her.

As soon as they broke into a run the first assailant leapt from cover. It bounded over the hood of a minivan, crossing the twenty yards between them at inhuman speed.

Ryan expected the move. His arm snapped to the side, tracking the approaching creature as his gun spat angrily in the night. Bullets won't kill a vampire, but they slow them down a lot depending where you hit them. Ryan shot this one in the head three times with his .45 semiautomatic.

The vampire instinctively veered off to avoid any more punishment, its hand going to its ruined face as it stumbled sideways.

Carmen had the door open when the second one struck. It had circled around and dropped below the nose of the Caddy. It launched over the car at her, but she was quicker, ducking under the door as it flew over, its nails tearing at the empty space where her head had been.

Ryan whirled and snapped off two rounds at the second attacker. They buried themselves in its side ineffectually, but served to get the thing's attention. Having now registered Ryan as a threat, the creature dropped into a martial arts stance in front of him.

God-damned wonderful, Ryan cursed silently. Not only was the vampire probably not a new one, it was trained in combat. Ryan hated that. It was bad enough that monsters tended to be quicker and stronger than humans. When they started doing martial arts and using guns it just pissed him off.

Ryan reached under his coat and grabbed a wooden stake as the two of them assessed each other. Stakes wouldn't kill a vampire either, but striking one through the heart it would incapacitate it, putting the creature in sort of a coma. Then you could kill it at leisure. Tradition held that either beheading or fire worked. Over the years Ryan found that blowing one into enough pieces did the trick as well.

The vampire dropped into a crouch, arms out, feet in a ready stance. Its teeth were bad, but the nails were worse. They were preternaturally strong, and razor sharp. You had to avoid those at all costs, because they were likely to sever something you needed.

Behind him he heard the sound of a car closing in, probably their attacker's backup. Ryan had to finish this one fast. As long as the vampire in front of him was mobile, he couldn't afford to take his eyes off it to see what was coming.

Ryan made a decision: he purposely opened himself up, giving the thing an invitation. He waited for it to take the bait, but this one was smart. It left Ryan no choice but to make the first move before either the car got there, or the one he shot in the face earlier made a second appearance.

Just as Ryan was about to lunge he saw the lady he was supposed to protect walk up behind the vampire in front of him. *Shit.* This time Ryan's curse was audible. He had told her to get in the car. How stupid could she be? She wasn't even armed. She would have been better off running straight out into the darkness screaming her head off, tripping in those stupid high heels like they did in the movies.

Ryan thought frantically. He had to act. He couldn't shoot it, lest he get unlucky and blow right through the vampire and into Carmen, who was now almost up on it. What the hell did she think she was doing? If she got herself killed on Ryan's watch Charles would never forgive him.

Ryan made his move. The vampire tensed, ready for him, but they never got a chance to see who would come out on top. Before Ryan reached the thing Carmen had punched it square in the back with a vicious jab.

Ryan couldn't believe it. The lady was an idiot. Sure, she was in good shape and, heck, maybe she even had some training, but all a punch like that was going to do was announce her presence to the undead monster. Who, he realized with horror, might actually be fast enough to whip around and tear Carmen's head off her shoulders and still turn back in time to deal with Ryan.

But it didn't. Instead, the vampire arched its back, threw its head skyward, and screamed in agony before crumpling to the pavement.

When it was no longer blocking Ryan's view of Carmen he saw why. She was holding its bloody heart in her hand. Ryan had forgotten that one. That was a fourth way to kill a vampire: rip out its heart with your bare hands. Carmen looked at the beating organ with distaste before throwing it to the ground.

*Oh crap*, Ryan thought. Then he did something he never did, not as long as he remembered. He stood absolutely frozen, unable to move. His brain glitched while it tried to process the new information.

He was saved from his mind's own Blue Screen of Death by the training the military had drummed into him years before. Instincts took over as the car roared up on them. Ryan spun to see a black BMW sedan closing in fast. He snapped off his remaining three rounds at the driver's side windshield. All three hit their target, right where the driver's head should be. But the car didn't swerve. It remained on a collision course with them. The car was going to win.

Ryan prepared to dive for Carmen. It had to be at the last second, so the driver couldn't compensate for the move. He hoped he could knock her far enough out of the way in time. It was fifty-fifty. He was about to lunge when the car veered at the last moment. At first Ryan thought he must have hit the driver after all, but then he saw the side windows of the car were all the way down, and he knew what was coming next.

Ryan launched himself at Carmen, who had been crouched low, too busy readying her next action to react to the car's unexpected maneuver. Ryan realized that she had been preparing to leap over the charging BMW.

Ryan tackled Carmen, pushing her down and shielding her with his body as the car fired its broadside. He prepared for the roar of gunfire, the impact of bullets, hopefully against his Kevlar vest.

Instead there was relative silence followed by a blazing pain in his right shoulder and another lesser hot pinch in his lower left side. He knew that the second hit had been a graze, but the first one hadn't. The concealable type of Kevlar body armor he wore was good against small caliber bullets, but not against the slower moving sharp point of a crossbow bolt.

Ryan rolled off of Carmen as the BMW M5 screeched to a halt down the aisle. "Get in the damn car!" He roared, ejecting the empty magazine from his gun and slamming home a new one.

The black sedan stopped fifty meters away. It shifted into reverse, then the rear tires spun and smoke obscured the back of the car as it headed their way. Ryan took aim at a point low down at the car, in the general direction of the tires.

Carmen was up before he finished yelling. She hadn't seen Ryan coming, and was startled to be knocked aside. She had been even more startled at what the car had done. Like Ryan, she had assumed it was going to try to ram her, not veer to the side and shoot at her. She had been too intent on timing her jump to react to the unexpected maneuver. Now, despite her better judgment, she reflected that he'd just been hit by two crossbow bolts meant for her, and so she followed his order and headed for the open door of the wagon.

That's when she saw the vampire, the one that Ryan had shot in the face. It glided noiselessly down the row of cars opposite theirs, hunkering in the shadows between the vehicles.

Carmen called for Ryan to watch out, but he must have already seen it. He turned and sent the rounds originally intended for the BMW's tires at the crouched figure. His gun spat eight shots in two seconds. All hit within a two-inch radius, destroying the vampire's left knee cap and pitching it forward in a tumble of screaming agony.

The BMW was blocking the rear of his car by the time Ryan shut the door and pushed the ignition button. The engine rumbled to life, its power reverberating through him. The BMW prevented him from backing out, but there was no car in front of the Caddy. Ryan threw the car into drive, trying to remember if there was a concrete curb in front as he hit the gas.

The back window of the wagon blew inward as the car's sudden acceleration snapped the occupants' heads back against their seats. The wagon shot forward under a hail of bullets, fishtailing as it turned down the aisle toward the exit.

The BMW driver put his car into drive and swung out onto the mostly deserted four-lane road not far behind the Caddy. Both cars went to wide-open throttle, but as the 800 horses of the wagon's modified LS6 engine ran free, the BMW vanished behind them.

# Chapter 3

"You're a fucking vampire," Ryan snarled, easing up on the gas pedal as he took an off ramp. He switched freeways, heading south through Gilroy and over the Pacheco Pass. It would add miles to the trip, but might throw off their pursuers. At some point soon he would have to do something about the car's shattered back window and the bullet holes in the tailgate or they would draw unwanted attention.

"No shit, Sherlock," Carmen said. At Ryan's look she added, "What? If we're going to start swearing and stating the obvious." She opened the window and flung out the bloody crossbow bolt she had pulled from Ryan's shoulder moment ago. She tried to ignore the smell and the rumbling of her stomach, forcing away thoughts of the hunger that tugged at her primal instincts. If she gave it any attention it was liable to consume her—and the man next to her.

Ryan spared a quick glance at his passenger for the tenth time in the last minute. Instinct and adrenaline were slowly giving way to rational thought, and rational thought was not liking where it found itself.

Carmen rolled the window up, rested her elbow against the door and let her head drop into her palm. She finally spoke. "What the hell did you think I was?"

"Not a vampire. You can't be."

"Oh, why not?" Genuine interest made Carmen raise her head.

"Because Bill gave me this job," was Ryan's unhelpful reply.

Carmen figured out that Ryan hadn't known *who* she was by his lack of respect, but now, as the full picture of his ignorance came into view, she wondered again about Charles' judgment in sending her to him. "Are you saying you didn't know what I was when you took the job?"

"Of course not! Are you crazy? Do you think I would have agreed to this if I knew you were a monster? The hell I would! I don't understand this at all. Bill should have asked me to kill you, not protect you."

"Sorry to be such a disappointment. Your friend sounds like a great guy, by the way."

In his mind, Ryan ran through the encounter in the restaurant to see how he could have possibly missed the indications. She never gave him enough of a smile, or any smile, to get a good look at her teeth, but he supposed her canines could have been sharp. She didn't eat, but then again they were sitting at the bar. It was night, but again, not an unusual time for a meeting. Her hand was cold, but she was a woman…

"Besides, you're too old," Ryan mused, aloud.

"*Excuse* me?" Carmen suddenly wished she hadn't tossed that bolt out of the window. She had the urge to stick it right back where she had found it.

Ryan realized he probably shouldn't have verbalized the last comment. He recognized that some women were vain about their age, a trait apparently maintained even after death. There was no need to antagonize the monster. Sitting there bleeding next to it was more than enough provocation to send her lunging across the car at him. There was no way he could defend himself against a vampire in these close quarters without coming to grief.

Ryan weighed the odds of surviving a head-on collision. If he turned the wheel at the last moment with his left hand, and at the same time used his right to pop her seat belt before either the impact (or she) killed him, he might pull it off. She would be sent hurtling through the windshield, while in theory between the seatbelt and the airbags he might be okay. Of course then he'd be in the middle of nowhere, at night, with a wounded angry vampire and a wrecked car. But he'd have the element of surprise. And he was armed.

Carmen turned to him, her glare demanding an answer to her last question. Ryan was careful to keep his eyes on the road, avoiding hers. Vampires could make the weak-willed do their bidding if they could lock eyes with them. It was a potent form of hypnosis.

Ryan wasn't weak willed, but he also wasn't going to take a chance. The stronger the vampire, the harder it was to resist. And given what she'd done in the parking lot, Ryan wasn't about to take any chances with this one.

She wasn't giving up. "Well?"

"I mean, most vampires are younger. You know, they're turned in their early twenties or even teens. You must have been, what, twenty-five or something?" She was clearly in her thirties when she died, but the diplomacy came out of its own accord. Ryan reasoned that it was instinctual, having to do with self-preservation.

"Thank you for that failed recovery, but I was thirty-six when I was turned." Carmen paused, slightly puzzled. "You know, you're the first person I've ever told that to. I guess my secret will die with you."

Ryan chewed on the implications behind that statement as they sat in silence for the next few miles.

"Besides," Carmen finally said, "Many vampires are turned when they're older."

That was a stretch, Ryan thought. He had run across his fair share of vampires, and they were all good looking, and almost exclusively young. Still, there had been a few older ones, men who could maybe be called distinguished. "Some *guys* are, sure. But not women. Let's face it: you lot only turn the people you find attractive."

# # #

When his words were met by a low growl, Ryan decided to stop speaking. His thoughts snapped back to the problem at hand. Bill couldn't have known what she was, could he? It was impossible. Why would Bill have asked him to drop everything to deliver a vampire, safely, anywhere? Let alone all the way to Chicago. It made no sense.

But Bill had asked him to do it, and if Bill had asked him there must be a good reason. Maybe the creature was going to give up a large nest of her brethren, or even someone important like an ancient master vampire.

That made sense. Her life in trade for something more important. Ryan imagined it was the location of a member of the Council, the elusive group of vampires that reigned over the undead monsters. If he could bag himself a Council member he'd be a legend. To his knowledge no hunter had ever come close to locating a member of the Council, let alone killing one. They were practically myths.

Information like that might be worth letting her live. Or was it? She was a vampire. Depending on how old she was, she could have murdered dozens, if not hundreds of people. Did she deserve to live? Was any trade worth letting her go? It made more sense for him to kill her as soon as he got the chance, or simply abandon her and let whoever was after her do the job for him. The thought of abandoning her made him happy. That wasn't so much of a blatant breaking of his word, it was more like ignoring it.

Even as the idea crossed his mind, he knew he wouldn't do it. He had promised to deliver her safely to Chicago, and he never failed to complete a job he was given. It was one more of his rules—apparently one that needed revising.

Of course, he had made no promises about what happened to the monster *after* he delivered her safely to Chicago.

### # # #

Carmen had been watching the Ryan's expression for the last fifteen minutes. Assuming she made it to Chicago alive, which was doubtful given her present company, she was going to throttle Charles. What had he been thinking putting her in this man's protection?

She struggled to find a motive for her friend's actions when a dark thought crept up and wedged itself in her mind. She wanted to discount it, but couldn't. The pattern was now undeniable. Someone was taking them out. Two dead in as many weeks. Four attempts in total. It was only by sheer luck that Elizabeth and Peter had survived. This could no longer be considered a coincidence. Even more troubling was that it had to be someone on the inside. Someone who knew not only *who* they were, but *where* they lived. No one else could have found them.

Other than her best friend Sylvia, Charles was the only person in the world that Carmen trusted implicitly. She had called him right after she heard about Henry's murder to ask for advice. They discussed skipping Chicago. Could they even hold the Convocation after what happened? But Charles insisted that their annual meeting must go forward. They couldn't afford to appear weak, not with Europe watching them hungrily.

Charles assured her that he would find the ones responsible for the murders. Until then, he said he would send her protection. He said he trusted them completely and would guarantee her safety. All Carmen had to do was get to the Bay Area and this savior Charles provided would do the rest.

And then she met the guy. Not only was he human, and of limited intelligence, but he seemed to have an intense dislike of vampires. The implications of these three facts hit her the same time she saw the malicious smile creep into Ryan's expression. Someone should tell the guy he didn't do devious very well.

# # #

"You said your employer would normally hire you to kill me?" Carmen asked aloud.

The sudden question cut into Ryan's thoughts. He had been wondering exactly how far into Chicago he would have to bring her before his promise was technically fulfilled, leaving him clear to kill her. The city limit? Or would it have to be the city center? Or was there a specific destination he was supposed to take her? Bill hadn't mentioned one. If there was a drop-off point, then killing her would definitely have to wait until then.

"Not hire. I do it for free, as a public service," he said.

"You're a vampire hunter," Carmen stated.

The wedge in her mind grew, its pain demanding attention. Charles had created her. She had known him for centuries. But the facts were impossible to ignore. Charles might be trying to kill her. Charles could be the one responsible for the recent murders.

Ryan nodded. "Though I prefer just *hunter*, no modifier. I don't like to narrow my career options. I'm an equal opportunity kind of guy. I also kill werewolves, trolls, demons, whatever. A monster's a monster."

"Oh, this couldn't possibly get any better." Carmen's laughter was hollow and she placed her fingers on her temples to massage away a budding headache. "Pull over at the bathroom up ahead."

"I thought you said you had excellent bladder control."

"I do. According to the sign we just passed, Los Banos is the name of next town. Pull over there. You go your way, I'll go mine. We'll both be happier in the long run."

*There it was!* Ryan thought. Only in those two words. The first sign of an accent. Almost undetectable. Out loud he said, "No."

She turned to look at him. "No? What do you mean *no*? Do you really want to try to kill me? Do you know what your chances are? In this car, with that shoulder?"

What troubled Carmen was that she saw that the man had already considered his chances, and seemed to have concluded that they weren't zero.

Ryan had momentarily forgotten about his shoulder, having mentally compartmentalized the pain into a small box as he had been trained to do. The bolt that struck him in the side had only gazed him. It ended up lodged between his ribs and his vest. He yanked that one out as soon as he sat in the car, tossing it in the back seat as he lost the BMW. The one in the shoulder had been worse. Though not life threatening, it was a handicap. He remembered being unable to lean back in his seat. So he leaned forward, ordering Carmen to take it out.

She had done so immediately, with no tiresome hesitation he would have expected from a typical person. Her strength easily forced it out the front of his vest in one quick motion. He was grateful that she had been smart enough to push it forward. The bolt had been a broad head tipped with large triangular blades designed for hunting large game. Pulling it backwards would have caused a lot of damage.

The pain was a continuous throbbing ache, but Ryan was used to pain. But bleeding next to a live vampire he was not used to. He shifted uncomfortably, changing his grip on the wheel. He hoped his shoulder had stopped leaking, though he doubted that mattered. Like sharks, vampires could smell blood from a good distance away, and he was covered in it. This was not good.

"I mean no," Ryan said at last. "We part ways after I deliver you to Chicago and not before." A promise is a promise, and he owed Bill, so he would fulfill it. But this was it, whatever the man's reasons were, Bill had violated Ryan's trust. Ryan could no longer work with the man. This was the last time. The end of their friendship.

"Are you an idiot? You're a hunter. I'm a vampire. Don't you think we'd both be a lot happier if we ended this relationship now, before it takes its natural course?"

"I gave a man my word."

"Oh, great. The one guy left in this century who believes chivalry is not dead, and I'm stuck with him. Look, I don't know how else to say this, but I would rather not have you for a traveling companion. Please go away. Now that you know what I am, you know I am quite capable of taking care of myself."

"Vampires are not immortal; I kill them all the time. You would have died in that parking lot without me."

He stated it as fact. It gave Carmen pause. Would she have? She hadn't had time to think about it in the moment, and in the hours since, she had been too focused on being mad at Charles to worry about her narrow escape.

She replayed the events in the parking lot. There were at least five of them. All vampires. They weren't newly made. She thought about the car coming for her and her decision to try to leap it. The two bolts that hit Ryan could have very easily struck her. If one had gotten lucky, hit her in the heart...

Carmen pushed the thoughts away. "I'm asking you nicely. It's not something I usually do more than once. As it is, I might have lost one of my only true friends. Let's not make this night any worse."

"Wow. Less than an hour and you already call me a true friend? Honey, even I'm not that hard up for people that like me."

"What?"

"I'm just saying you might want to rethink your life choices. If you consider some guy you just met in a bar to be a friend, then you have some serious issues. I mean other than being dead," Ryan added.

"Of course you're not a friend! I was referring to Charles, the man that I turned to for help. The one responsible for sending you to look after me." She pointed back and forth between them. "We—you and I— are not friends. I would rather not spend what are potentially my last days on earth with someone who wants me dead."

She saw his grin and realized he had been playing with her. He might not be as entirely stupid as she first thought. But then again, he had the audacity to tease her, so maybe he was.

Ryan's smile had already faded as he mulled over the important part of what she said. "So you think it was a set up. Your friend hooked us up, figuring I would kill you?"

Carmen folded her arms across her chest, more out of protection from the idea than anger at the man who voiced it. "Figuring you might *try* to kill me. Yes. Maybe. I don't know. God I hope not."

She stared back at the window in misery, the emotions of the past two days all coming to a head at once. The death of her friends. The attempt on her own life. The possible betrayal of a man she had known forever and loved like a father. She refused to let the tears flow. She never gave into emotional displays. It was what gave her the name that everyone called her behind her back. And she was not about to start now. Certainly not in front of this guy.

*Oh, God, please don't cry.* Ryan thoughts echoed Carmen's. *Vampires can't cry, can they?* Ryan pondered the possibility. He hoped not. Ryan never knew what to do when girls cried, and he was pretty sure it would be worse with a vampire.

"I don't buy it. That means he duped my contact. Not sure I can believe that. Bill's usually pretty thorough, and he sees straight through bullshit," Ryan said, hoping to pull her thoughts to something less tear-inducing.

"If Charles wanted to 'dupe your contact' as you put it, he would," Carmen stated.

"I guess anything's possible. So what's your move if it *is* your friend that's trying to kill you? Kill him first?" Ryan asked, before realizing his mistake.

"I have no idea." Carmen went back to studying the barren hills.

*Don't cry, don't cry, don't cry.* Ryan chanted in his mind as he said, "Hey, I really doubt it's him. So, who else might be after you?"

"I don't know," Carmen told the window.

"Well, think. Who have you made mad recently? Besides me. There must be someone. You seem like you'd be good at it."

When he didn't get an answer he continued, "Under normal circumstances I'd guess you overdid it with a meal and killed a person, left a trail, and ended up with hunters on your tail. But those guys back there weren't hunters, they were vampires. So think." When she remained quiet he tried prompting her, "Start with the last ten vampires you pissed off lately."

Ryan wanted to get her mind off of her likely betrayal. Stop her from crying. If she started crying the only way Ryan could think of to get her to stop was to stake her. It wouldn't kill her, but it would render her immobile. Quiet. Suitable for transportation….

Carmen cast a glance back at Ryan, saw his malign expression and went back to the window.

When Carmen continued to remain silent, Ryan sighed. "I understand you don't trust me. I don't trust you, either. But it might help to talk about your situation."

"How can I trust you when you're plotting out the best way to kill me?" Carmen asked.

"I'm not thinking of killing you," Ryan said, with his conscience clear and a stake tucked inside his jacket. He wondered if, while she was busy looking out the window, he would be fast enough to pull it out and stab her with it.

"I don't believe you," she said.

"Believe what you like. The truth is that I promised to bring you to Chicago alive, and that's what I'll do. But we're going to have a better chance of living through this if I know what I'm up against. So, who could it be? Did you steal any money from the vampire mob? Sleep with someone's husband? Adopt a werewolf? See something you shouldn't have? Pissed off a member of that mysterious Council you guys have?"

In a rare betrayal of surprise, Carmen started at Ryan's last question. The man knew about the Council. This was a bad development. Even as most humans were clueless about the existence of vampires, most hunters were clueless about the Council. Its existence was a closely guarded secret.

Most hunters didn't know that vampires were divided into two very different classes: Street and Society. Hunters went after Street, because that's all they knew about. Those were the ones that didn't have the support to prevent them from getting caught. The ones that fended for themselves. Hunted for their food. They existed by themselves or in small groups.

Then there was the Society. Organized, sophisticated. They had supplies of food. Most of it was skimmed from hospitals or blood banks, the rest from willing donors. They almost never hunted. They lived normal lives, or at least most had above-ground personas. They even had a formal government—the Council—a group of vampires that set and enforced the laws.

Only a very few hunters ever stumbled upon the Society's existence, and almost none knew about the Council. Those that did were dealt with quickly. Seeing as Ryan might have saved her life in the parking lot, Carmen almost regretted that he would have to die.

"Well? Anyone? Or is the list so long you don't know where to start?" Ryan asked, figuring it was the latter.

Carmen gave a slight shrug on one shoulder. "I mean it. I don't know. Someone has been killing vampires and, yes, I realize another vampire is responsible. But I don't know who it is. If I did I would tell you, so you could go do what you do."

"So, we know it's not hunters. It's not a vampiric serial killer, because serial killers work alone and don't send hit squads. And it can't be random, because you and this Charles guy suspected that they were after you, or I wouldn't be here. That suggests that even though you don't know who it is, you know the motive, or at least a pattern to the attacks. There are a lot of vampires in this country. Why are they so hot to kill you specifically?"

Carmen gave another half shrug. He wasn't as dumb as she first thought. She dialed up his IQ to a hair above average.

"So, what's the pattern? What do all the dead vampires have in common?" He prodded.

Carmen was keeping that to herself. There was such a thing as too much information. Ryan was already beyond that point, and she wasn't about to feed him any more. Both Ryan and this Bill knew about the Council. They might know more people who did as well. She would have a lot of loose ends to tie up once this business was finished.

"I have no idea. And you do realize we're going the wrong way," Carmen said, finally clearing her thoughts enough to process where they were.

"We're heading south to 15. It's longer than the Northern route, but hopefully it will throw off whoever is after you. I'm assuming they have limited resources and can't cover every road in the U.S."

Ryan paused before continuing. "And I know you're lying about who's after you. Considering you can't just get on an airplane, for all I know you really are a terrorist and it's some secret vampire branch of the Federal government that's hunting you. And if it's a three letter agency, then they in fact *can* monitor every road in the U.S."

"I *can* fly, I simply choose not to. If we were meant to fly we'd be able to turn into bats."

"You mean you can't?" Ryan asked.

"Of course not. Vampires don't turn into bats."

"Yes, they can."

"No, we can't. It's a myth. Like not having any reflection, and being adverse to holy symbols. I assume the latter two are about our not being able to face what we've become, or feeling abandoned by God."

"It's not a myth. I've seen it. You simply aren't a very good vampire. Maybe one day you'll run across someone more competent who can show you the ropes." Ryan paused. "I can't believe you're scared of flying."

She had no idea if he was teasing her, or he was simply ignorant. She looked up at the ceiling trying to draw divine patience before answering. "Why not? It's a perfectly rational fear. And even if I did fly, that airplane you wanted to put me on got in after dawn, which presents obvious problems, and—" Carmen's voice trailed off.

The car had no sunroof. Instead of the glass rectangle she had expected to see, there were strange symbols drawn into the headliner of the car. They wove in and out of four identical circles, each directly over one of the car's seats, including one that hovered directly over her head. The symbols seemed to move and crawl when she tried to focus on them.

"Stop! We need to get out of this car!" Carmen said.

"Why?" Ryan checked the review mirror. He had been on the lookout for tails. He was pretty good at it, and as far as he could tell no one was following them.

"Someone has spelled us."

"What?" He followed her gaze up to the ceiling. "Oh, that. That's just a protection circle to ward off scrying. You know, magical eavesdropping? It also makes sure no one can use magic to track this car and whoever is in it."

"I thought you were a hunter. You had a witch spell your car?" Carmen accused.

"A witch is only a human with certain skills. Besides, he was a Shaman, not a witch."

"And a vampire is only a human with an aversion to the sun and dietary restrictions," retorted Carmen. She studied the circles a bit longer. She wasn't an expert on magic, but she was pretty certain the symbols above her were not made by any shaman.

"There's a difference," Ryan said, but he knew Carmen was right. Ryan had only grudgingly allowed the Shaman to spell his house and his cars. Bill had personally vouched for the man, swearing that he could be trusted. In fact, it was the Shaman that had gotten Ryan into saving animals, providing Ryan a purpose beyond killing monsters, and giving him something to do with all of the money he inherited from his parents. Ryan had even hired David, the Shaman's son, to work at the Sanctuary. David was a budding shaman himself, despite Ryan's constant warning about power and its inevitable corruption.

"Oh really? Tell me about this difference, I'd love to hear it," Carmen said.

Faced with Ryan's silent indignation, Carmen changed the subject. "I need to stop in town. Your blood is getting hard to resist."

"I thought you said before we left you weren't hungry." Ryan thought about his suggestion of grabbing food "to go" back at the restaurant, and its implications. He was liking traveling with a vampire less and less.

"I said eating would be more trouble than it was worth. I didn't think you'd be bleeding all over me. I guess we could just pull over. It would be quicker and more efficient to use you, anyway."

"Oh, hell no. You keep your fangs away from me."

"Fine, but I have to eat."

Ryan couldn't exactly argue the point. He didn't like it, but he was going to have to compromise with the creature. "Okay, we'll find someone for you to…feed off of when we get to town, but no killing. I mean it."

"Wow, I'm impressed. You're going to stand by and let me eat? Drain some poor innocent person of their precious bodily fluids?" She was teasing. She knew it was mean, but she couldn't resist. It wasn't often she had the chance to make a hunter squirm. She didn't encounter many and when she did she normally killed them. Occasionally she might Push them into talking first to give up their compatriots. But it was a one-sided conversation devoid of any humor. Playing with Ryan was almost fun, and it got her mind off things.

"No killing. And no children," Ryan insisted.

"Of course not! What do you think I am? I never touch children, and killing anyone only causes problems. We haven't killed our prey in decades."

"Bullshit. You're a monster. Your kind kills innocent people all of the time! I've seen it." Ryan's voice had risen to a shout.

Carmen was taken aback by the outburst. It was the first time Ryan had lost even an iota of control. She guessed that his rage was related to why he was a hunter in the first place. She kept her tone neutral, so as not to provoke an attack. She had no doubt she could kill him, but if he wrecked the car in the struggle she would be reduced to hitchhiking. "For the most part we don't kill. The unfortunate exceptions are due to outlaws and eccentrics."

"Street vampires," Ryan said.

"Exactly."

"So you're Society?"

His insinuation that she could be anything but made her hackles rise, but she forced herself to not react. "Of course. Anyway, I was kidding. I don't need to eat, but I do have to use the lady's room."

"Fine, but if you think I believe that the Society blood suckers don't kill, you're delusional." Ryan was silent for the rest of the drive, stoically ignoring Carmen's subsequent attempts to get under his skin.

They stopped at an all-night diner in Los Banos. While Carmen used the facilities Ryan turned on the dome light over his seat and examined his shoulder. It wasn't as bad as he thought, wouldn't even leave much of a scar. Still, it was going to be a long time before he was going to be throwing any balls with that arm.

Ryan climbed in back and got the first aid kit. He stripped out of his ruined shirt and his vest, tossing the vest into the back. He cleaned the wound as best he could, then used superglue to seal it. He covered it with a bandage and pulled on a fresh shirt, barely staying conscious as the pain from raising his arm tore through his entire side.

Carmen still hadn't come out of the restaurant by the time Ryan was finished, so he entered the brightly lit eatery, throwing his ruined shirt in the garbage can that stood by the door on the way in. He ordered a cup of coffee to go from a middle aged lady who called him "Honey" and was tactful enough not to comment on Ryan's sorry state. He thanked her for the coffee and walked back out to his car hoping he had removed all of the blood from his face, and the waitress wasn't now dialing 911.

While he continued to wait, Ryan filled the time fixing the back window with some clear heavy plastic sheeting and duct tape he kept for just such an occasion. In his line of work, windows got busted more often than one would think. He slapped some magnetic bumper stickers touting bass fishing and Army veterans over the worst of the bullet holes and called it good.

When everything was more or less secure and Carmen still wasn't back, Ryan figured the bloodsucker had bailed on him. Maybe she'd slipped out the back of the restaurant and into the bustling metropolis of Los Banos, California.

Ryan popped the back of the wagon, sifted through one of his duffel bags until he found a small hand crossbow he could use with one arm, and was ready to start searching the streets for the vampire when he saw her exit the restaurant and walk over to the car.

"You ready?" Carmen asked, standing in front of the passenger side door. She gave him a funny look as he quickly shoved the weapon back into the duffel bag and zipped it closed.

"I'm not even going to ask what took you so long," Ryan said, but he knew now what it was. Despite her denial she must have been hungry and thought it would go over better if she pretended she needed to pee rather than eat someone.

"A lady's secret," Carmen said getting in the car. "Nice window, by the way."

"It's redneck chic. Bullet holes and bumper stickers."

The next thirty minutes were spent fighting over the radio. Ryan decided he had wasted enough time talking to the creature and had put on classic rock in preparation for the long drive ahead. It was good driving music and would take his mind off of the crappy day he was having.

Carmen immediately switched it to top forty.

Ryan had a pretty eclectic taste in music, and he liked top forty. What he didn't like was someone taking over the radio when he was driving. It was another of his rules: the driver got to pick the music.

Ryan switched it back.

Carmen leaned forward, turned the tuning dial until top forty played once again, then held her finger on the touch screen display to make the station a satellite preset.

Ryan switched it back. "It's my car. I get to pick the stations."

"Wow. Your car? Isn't that a bit childish?"

"No. And besides, even if it wasn't my car the driver *always* gets to listen to what he wants. It's the rule."

"Says who?" Carmen hit the top forty preset.

"It's the rule," Ryan repeated, changing it back to classic rock.

They took turns flipping stations for several minutes before Carmen said, "I've got centuries, how about you?"

Ryan harrumphed, but stopped changing the station. *The trip couldn't end fast enough*, he thought, trying to clear his mind. He breathed slowly and deeply, pushing the jumble of emotions and questions away and letting the music and the road take over. It was another technique he had learned in the Military. Useful for long tense waits.

Carmen broke the silence of the last several hours. "We need to stop."

"Again? For crying out loud, I stopped for gas less than an hour ago."

"That was three hours ago, and I thought you were going to bring me to Chicago alive, no matter what. Or have you changed your mind and decided that delivering a pile of ashes would be good enough?"

Ryan looked at the clock and realized she was right. It was five thirty. The sun would be up soon. They had just driven through Barstow and he was getting ready to turn around and head back to the city when he spotted an exit sign advertising a couple of fast food restaurants and a hotel two miles ahead.

The guy behind the counter of the Sleazy-Eight leered at Carmen a little too openly for Ryan's liking. She either didn't notice or didn't care, but the man's blatant disrespect annoyed Ryan. It prompted him to stress that he and his *wife* needed a room. For good measure he stared the dude down, letting him know in no uncertain terms what the results would be if he kept eye-humping his lady.

Once the guy pushed the plastic keys across the counter, which Carmen snatched up before Ryan could extend his hand, Ryan shot the man one last glare for good measure and then hefted up his duffel bags. Ryan's shoulder was throbbing and he was forced to carry both bags with his good arm as he followed Carmen up the stone outdoor stairway on the outside of the building and down the hall to their room.

Ryan marveled at her backside as she walked. Given his recent exchange with the hotel manager the hypocrisy was not lost on him, but he justified his own leer by telling himself that she was a vampire, so he couldn't actually be interested in her in that way.

But man…. He shook his head as he followed her. She must be used to the type of looks the hotel guy had given her, because with an ass like that he was sure she got a lot of them.

Carmen swiped the key and opened the door, momentarily pausing to assess the amenities. Ryan was so lost in thought, he almost crashed into her. At the last moment he pulled up, managing to only nudge her with the bags, though even that caused her to lurch forward into the room.

She looked back and glared. "Ease up back there!"

It took Ryan a few moments to register the problem. It was a typical cheap hotel room: a rickety dresser sat against the wall, topped by an old CRT television that tipped slightly. Near the window was a small round table, bookended by a pair of uncomfortable-looking faux leather chairs, neither of which looked like they would support the weight of a real person. On the wall hung a large mirror that may or may not have been hiding a camera linked to creepy-hotel-guy's computer. And taking up the majority of the room was one king-sized bed, covered with a horrible orange bedspread whose faded floral pattern was obscured by countless stains.

"Hadn't thought of that," Ryan said, his attention focused now on the lone bed. "Wait here. I'll go ask for a different room."

"Do you really want that letch thinking we had a fight? Besides, wouldn't it draw attention to ourselves? Is that really smart?" Carmen suppressed the smile that wanted to leak out. Teasing this guy was too easy.

Any humor was lost on Ryan as he said, in all seriousness, "You're right. I'll take a chair." He placed his duffel bags on the circular table and pulled out one of the chairs, noting the wobble with resignation.

"No you won't, darling. We'll share the bed. We're married, after all. But I get the inside, farthest from the window. And don't go opening up the curtains when you wake up. Oh, and I don't go for the modern approach: if we're going to be husband and wife, I expect a ring on this finger!" She wiggled up her naked left hand to showcase her point.

"I don't think that's a good idea," Ryan said. "More accurately, I think it's a terrible one." He noted that she wore a delicate gold watch around her slender wrist. Most people had abandoned watches in favor of their phones. Ryan hadn't. Time was important, and the more options you carried around to tell it the better. His watch was analog, matte black metal, and sported a dial for three different time zones, plus a stop watch.

"I don't care what you *think*. It's been the standard for centuries. Also, despite the current trend, I prefer my gold to look like gold. You can keep the platinum and white gold. Make mine yellow. A solitaire is acceptable, but nothing over one carat. That's simply tacky."

"That's not what I meant," Ryan said.

Carmen walked up to him. "Of course not, dear. Now let's take a look at your shoulder."

"I already took care of it," Ryan said, backing up as she advanced.

"I'm sure you did. Now take your shirt off." If she had to deal with this guy one more day, at least she would get to see what was under all those layers of clothes he insisted on wearing.

Ryan was not happy. Was she trying to disarm him so she could take him out? Maybe. Probably. But he wasn't about to show weakness in front of this monster. They were like dogs. You had to maintain the upper hand. Show them who was boss. He had to let her know she didn't scare him, that he could handle her in any circumstance.

He stopped his retreat around the table, strategically stopping within reach of his duffel bags. He took off his jacket and threw it over the chair. Next he removed his shoulder holster, making sure it also was within reach if she threw down. Finally, he pulled off his shirt. It took everything he had to fight back the grimace as the pain threatened to make him swoon.

Carmen blinked at the combination of muscles and scars. To say Ryan was toned was an understatement. There was simply no fat. His body was perfectly sculpted, with the muscles of a professional athlete rather than a body builder. But that body had seen more wear, tear, and abuse than she thought possible for a man his age.

He was wrapped in scars. Some were identifiable: teeth marks made by werewolves, vampires, and other things less obvious. Claws. Bullets. Burns. Other defacements of his flesh were a faded mystery, just blurry reminders of past damage he had suffered.

The latest scar-in-training concerned Carmen the most. She peeled off the crooked bandage Ryan had hastily applied to reveal an ugly wound with some type of red tinged plastic smeared over it. She ran her finger gently across the scab, ignoring Ryan's almost undetectable flinch at her touch. She went around to his back and found the same result.

"Is this glue?" she asked finally, her nose an inch away from Ryan's shoulder.

"Yeah, I didn't have time to sew it shut. Besides it's hard to sew your own shoulder in a dark car."

"Seriously, you used glue?"

She obviously wasn't up on emergency field dressing techniques. "What? It works fine."

"Where is your first aid kit?"

Ryan nodded toward one of the two bags, the prospect of a vampire administering first aid both foreign and unsettling.

Carmen unzipped the duffel and rifled through its contents, which consisted of a whole lot of weaponry. "Wow, it's like a redneck treasure chest." She picked up the hand crossbow she saw him toss in when she came out of the restaurant and examined it.

"Different tools for different creatures," Ryan said.

"Creatures, huh? Careful what you call the lady who is about to work on you," she said, tossing the crossbow back into the bag.

"You're not a lady," Ryan said.

"Really? I could have sworn you were looking at me like I was when we were walking up the stairs a moment ago. Ah, here it is!" Carmen said when she finally found the first aid kit. "This had better contain more than glue and a stapler." She searched through the well-stocked interior until she spied what she was looking for.

"Nah, it has duct tape too," Ryan said, embarrassed that she had noticed him noticing her.

"I hope you're not scared of needles." Carmen licked the tip of the white thread, and then squinted out of needless habit as she pushed it straight through the center of the needle's eye on the first try.

Ryan watched her uncertainly as she threaded the needle. "All depends on who's using them," he said.

"You can't possibly be scared of little old me. Why—" Carmen kicked off her heels, sinking down four inches. "I'm like half your size."

"I thought size didn't matter?" He tried to track her, but she had circled out of sight behind him. He was half naked and unarmed in a hotel room with his back to a vampire. He was a dead man.

"That's just what we tell guys to make them feel better about themselves. Now stand still. Okay, taking off my shoes was a bad idea." Carmen stood on her tippy toes so she had a better view of the wound, briefly placing one hand on Ryan's good shoulder for balance.

She noticed he wore a heavy metal chain around his neck, like members of the military wore to hold their dog tags. It was a bit outdated for her taste. She remembered seeing something hanging from it when he had first removed his shirt, but she had been too distracted by the rest of him to pay attention to what it was.

She peeled off the glue in one quick yank. To her surprise, Ryan didn't move or even comment at what must have hurt like heck. Nor did he react when she swabbed the wound with alcohol-soaked gauze. She was impressed despite herself.

Ryan used the mirror that hung beside them to watch her work. The vampire's brow was furrowed in concentration as she cleaned the wound.

Now that the glue had been removed, taking the scab with it, a small trickle of blood began to flow. Carmen felt Ryan tense as his blood ran, but pushed aside her own nagging urges and dapped away the liquid with a hand towel before she started work with the needle. She worked quickly, cleaning the wound thoroughly before beginning to suture it closed.

After finishing the wound on his back, she moved around to the front. Ryan thought it would be easier having her in front of him. But she had to get close to work, and when he looked down at her, the little black dress she was wearing gave him more view than he was comfortable with. He stared over her head at the closed door of the hotel room.

As Carmen worked she took a look at what hung from his chain. It wasn't dog tags, but a series of wedding rings. One man's ring along with an engagement and wedding ring set of a woman. *Well, that answered the question of why he had become a hunter*, she thought.

After she stitched up the wound and applied a clean bandage, she kissed her finger and touched it to the bandage. "There, all better." She looked up at him and smiled.

"Thanks," Ryan said, not sure whether to be more surprised by the motherly kiss and smile, or that the vampire hadn't lost control at the sight of his blood.

Ryan stepped back from her, and grabbed his toiletry bag and a pair of sweats out of the other duffel bag. It was then he realized they had never stopped to buy anything for Carmen to wear. He offered to run back into town and take care of it.

"And let you pick out my clothes? I'll pass."

"What?" Ryan asked frowning.

"Have you seen yourself? I think I'll avoid the army surplus look, thank you very much."

Ryan looked down at himself, then over at his duffel bag where several duplicates of the same outfit that he had worn that day were neatly folded. "It's functional."

"I prefer to have some form thrown in with my function."

"Oh, don't worry, I would have taken care of your form. That's what the lingerie department is for."

Carmen gave him a sly look. "Sure is, it's why I have a frequent shopper card."

Ryan was going to reply, but stopped himself when he remembered he was flirting with a vampire. Instead he said, "Okay, we'll stop and grab you some things in the morning. Er— evening. I'm going to get changed."

When Ryan came out of the bathroom Carmen was sitting on the bed flipping through blurry stations on the old square TV. She pressed Power on the remote and set it down on the bedside table. "My turn," she said, grabbing her clutch purse.

While the vampire was in the bathroom Ryan double checked the curtains, closing both the inner and outer ones tightly. To make sure he didn't open them out of habit, he grabbed the roll of duct tape out of his duffel and ran a line of the gray sticky stuff down the center, securing the two drapes together.

Then, because he typically overdid things, Ryan taped the bottom and sides to the walls as well. He wasn't going to fail at his job because he accidentally vaporized his charge in a fit of sleepy forgetfulness.

Next, he checked behind the mirror. He wasn't paranoid, but the manager had been a little too creepy. Ryan shrugged when he found that it was fixed to the wall, figuring it didn't matter. Even if there was a camera, there sure as hell wasn't going to be any sort of show for the guy to watch unless it was Ryan's murder.

Ryan noticed the vampire's phone resting where she had left it on the nightstand next to the TV remote. He picked it up and swiped the screen. It flickered to life and he was happy to see it wasn't locked. He pulled up the phone's number and wrote it down on the hotel room notepad, along with several promising looking entries in her address book. If he was lucky, he now had the line on half a dozen vampires. Pleased with himself he turned the phone off and set it down where he found it.

Finally he performed his routine bedbug check. He did it in every hotel room he stayed in, seedy or not. He examined the sheets, mattress, and headboard for signs of the little vermin. It was only when he finished his check that the irony hit him.

# # #

Carmen wrapped a towel around herself, and hung up her wet underwear. She had wrung them out as best she could, hoping they would dry by morning. She wished she had time to collect at least some of her personal effects before she ran, but there had been no time. All she had was her phone and small clutch purse with some money, credit cards, and ID, lipstick in a color she decided she wasn't fond of after she bought it, and her keys.

She had been out for the night when the call came. A neighbor had noticed some strange men around her house and gave her a ring. The house alarm hadn't been tripped, but when she called the human that served as the live-in security guard and caretaker for the house, there was no answer.

She had been down in her San Diego house and hadn't brought any retainers. She had far fewer than most of her kind, and there was so much work for them to do back at her main home in Santa Carla that most of the time she traveled alone. Until recently it had never been a concern.

After what had happened to Henry, Carmen didn't risk checking it out in person. She had immediately called Charles and heeded his instructions to head north to meet Ryan. She grabbed a dingy hotel room along the way to wait out the daylight hours, and only barely arrived at the restaurant in time. She had been wearing the same outfit for forty-eight hours and it made her skin crawl.

She noted when she entered the room that Ryan had taped the curtains shut, which was curiously thoughtful considering she was pretty sure he planned on killing her at some point.

Ryan was in bed, and leaning against the headboard as far to the edge of the bed as possible without falling off.

"Turn out the lights," she told him, having no intention of providing a show.

Ryan hesitated, obviously not liking the idea of being in a dark room with her, but he reached over to hit the button on the base of the bedside lamp. The room went dark, her eyes instantly adjusting.

A moment later the bed jostled as she climbed in. Ryan waited for a minute before finally scooting down. Then he lay on his back with his eyes open, left hand gripping a wooden stake. He lay in the exact same position, stock still, for fifteen minutes. Ryan had been special forces in the military, but he hadn't been sniper. He was great with guns, just as long as his targets were close. But he pretended he was a sniper now. Deadly quiet, focusing all his attention on his senses. Waiting for his prey to make a move. Ten more minutes passed. He hadn't detected the slightest movement, but he knew she was next to him. So close he could reach out and touch her, but try as he might he couldn't even hear her breathe. Not that she had to, but most of them did, either out of habit, to pass for human, or so they had air ready in case they wanted to speak.

Ryan never had a problem getting to sleep before. Though he was a notoriously light sleeper, with the slightest sound or disturbance liable to wake him, getting there was never an issue. In fact, he could fall sleep almost instantly, anywhere, in any condition — another gift from the military. But tonight was an exception. He was wide awake and showing no signs of dozing off.

His mind was having trouble coming to grips with the fact that he was not just sharing a room with a vampire, but the same bed. It was dark and he knew that, realistically, if she attacked him now he had very little chance of surviving. If she attacked him while he slept, he had none.

He cleared his thoughts and took slow deep breaths, trying some more of the breathing exercises a friend in the service had taught him. It was the standard weapon in his arsenal he used to calm his nerves and make himself relax in stressful situations. Slowly he pushed all thoughts of the monster next to him out of his consciousness and focused instead on breathing.

"Are you going to lie there all night staring at the ceiling?" Carmen asked after the heavy breathing started. She had been unable to sleep herself. She had spent the past half hour lying there watching Ryan watch the ceiling.

"Don't you mean lay here all day?" Ryan asked. Great, he thought, not only could she see in the dark, she was watching him.

"Either way, you're going to be tired if you don't sleep, and how can you protect little old me if you're tired? Besides, all that heavy breathing is a little creepy."

Ryan thought about her words. Did he need the sleep to protect her, or protect himself from her? That was the question. "I'm having trouble sleeping. And how can *you* call *me* creepy?"

"Would you prefer it if I slept under the bed? I understand that's the custom for us monsters."

"It wouldn't help."

"Closet?"

"Um…no."

"Well, guess what? It isn't easy for me to relax around you either," she said, turning over to lie on her back.

"You want *me* to sleep under the bed?" Ryan asked, finally seeing that the dilemma cut both ways. It never crossed his mind that maybe she was having similar worries about their sleeping arrangement.

She turned back toward him. "No, but let's make a deal. You're obviously a man of your word, and I never go back on mine. How about if I promise not to bite you, and you promise not to stake me. Deal?"

Ryan thought for a second before deciding it was the best he was going to get. "Yeah, okay. Shake on it?" He reached over and encountered something smooth and soft, and most definitely not a hand. He recoiled in horrified shock. "You're not wearing any clothes!"

"You thought I was going to sleep in that dress?"

"Well no, but…"

"Looking for my underwear? I've been wearing them for two days. I washed them out; they're hanging over the shower rod. They wouldn't fit you anyway."

Ryan stumbled in vain, trying to formulate a response until he felt a cool hand take his and give a firm shake. "There. Now go to sleep."

Ryan knew vampires needed eye contact in order to persuade humans to do their bidding; it didn't work in the dark. Even so, minutes after Carmen's command, Ryan drifted off into sleep. Carmen was in his dreams, only to his surprise they were not nightmares.

# Chapter 4

It had been too long since Ryan woke up with a woman. Sure, he had gone to bed with his fair share, but sleep rarely entered into it. And there was never breakfast. No attachments. It was one of his rules.

But he questioned it now. He forgot how nice it felt having the soft curves of a woman's body tucked close up against him. He brought his arm out and around her, so he could run his hand down her smooth back and over the curve of her—

Ryan's eyes snapped open. He felt Carmen snuggle closer now that his arm was no longer between them. Without turning his head he glanced to the side. It was still dark, but a faint gray light crept in to the room from the top of the curtains. Enough light to inform Ryan that the last day had not been a bad dream. He was indeed laying face up in bed, his arm around a naked vampire that was draped over his right side.

It took willpower, but he resisted the urge to squeeze before slowly removing his hand from her rear. She murmured something unintelligible and repositioned. Her leg slid forward so that it was now bent and resting on top of his. One of her arms lay across his chest. Her head was, fortunately, on his unwounded shoulder. Ryan was pinned.

Vampires were notoriously sound sleepers. Ryan had killed many without them ever knowing he was there.

Ryan was positive if he moved slowly he could slip out from under this one undetected.

Carmen smiled. It had been a good dream. She didn't want to open her eyes. The night had been warm and comfortable; she hadn't slept like this in ages. She moved further into the warmth, reveling in its embrace as it encircled her. Then it moved, shifting beneath her, trying to get away. It shouldn't be doing that. That's when Carmen remembered where she was, and her eyes opened wide as Ryan slid out beneath her.

By his expression Ryan had learned that sneaking up to stake a sleeping vampire was different than moving under one. He looked like a trapped rabbit, and Carmen's face mirrored his as she sprang back out of bed, scrambling to pull the top sheet up in front of her.

Ryan turned away to give her privacy, though not quite as quickly as he could have. Ryan told himself he waited because he had reservations about putting his back to a vampire, not so he could steal a glimpse of Carmen naked.

Carmen picked up her dress off of the table, and then backed towards the bathroom. Before she made it Ryan spoke. "There are spare razors in my bag."

"Excuse me?" Carmen asked, confused. Did he want her to slash her own wrists?

Damn. It had slipped out. Ryan felt the prickles when she put her leg on top of him answering a question he had never thought to ask: did a vampire's hair still grow? "Um…for your legs. You're stubbly."

Carmen flushed, thankful he couldn't see it in the dim light. She hadn't been able to shave for three days now; it was low down on her list of priorities. A true gentleman would not have brought it up. Of course a lady would not have flung herself over a guy in a way so he noticed.

Not that she did it on purpose: she hadn't! She couldn't help it. She had always taken over the bed, even before she was turned. And she liked nothing more that the feel of a man next to her. The hard muscles, the warmth, the smell. She forgot how much she liked the feeling.

Carmen refused to feel guilty for her unconscious actions. Besides, she hadn't missed the fact that Ryan had tried to get a good look at her before turning. It was dark, and the sheet more or less provided a shield, so he didn't get much, but it wasn't for his lack of trying!

She pushed the thoughts from her mind and rifled through his bag until she found the package of cheap disposable razors. She took one, and then went into the bathroom. She showered and dressed. Her panties were dry, but the thick padding of her bra was still damp. She would just have to go without.

She wiped the steam from the mirror and examined herself. She had no makeup except for that unpleasant-colored lipstick. She decided to skip even that. No one but Ryan would see her until Vegas, and she couldn't care less about him. She could take care of cleaning herself up once she got into town.

Her hair was a mess, however, and it couldn't be left to fend for itself. Her little clutch didn't even have room for a brush. She looked at the counter where Ryan's toiletries lay at attention, all perfectly arranged on a hand towel. Each faced the same way, set an equal distance apart, like they were marching into the sink. She grabbed Ryan's comb and ran it through the tangles until they were gone. Then, just because, she moved each one of his neatly arranged items slightly so their uniformity was shattered.

She wondered if he would even notice, or if he had OCD and would immediately put them all back.

# # #

When the bathroom door had shut Ryan turned to find Carmen gone. He was disconcerted to note that he was slightly disappointed by her absence.

He spent the next ten minutes checking his GPS to make sure he had alternate routes memorized in case things went pear shaped.

When that was done he cleaned his forty-five. He had only put a few rounds through it, but it was always good to do when he had the chance. And it kept his mind off things, like how nice waking up with her had been, and how much that bothered him.

Carmen came out of the bathroom holding something in her hand. She tossed it to Ryan who caught the black projectile without thinking.

"It's still damp; could you put it in your bag?"

Ryan looked at the black bra. It was padded. He hadn't realized vampires were so vain. For that matter, he never understood padding in the first place. Some women were large and some were small, he didn't particularly mind either way. He always thought the padding was more for themselves rather than guys. For the most part guys liked breasts without reservations. In fact, Ryan preferred smaller and perky over large.

"Planning on adopting it?" Carmen's question made him jump; Ryan realized he might have been holding the damp article longer than he should have, and sheepishly put it in his bag.

Carmen's unstyled wet hair fell to her shoulders, and she was devoid of any makeup. Even unadorned and in the dim hotel room light Ryan thought she was still the most beautiful woman he had ever seen. He blinked. That was not supposed to happen. Somehow she must have used her vampire mind tricks on him. He would have to be more careful about looking into those beautiful brown eyes…

"Hello? Wake up. What's going on with you? It's your turn. You do take showers, right? Please don't tell me I have to spend the next several days in a car with cat-piss guy," Carmen's voice almost whined.

"What? No, I take showers!"

"Seeing is believing." She nodded at the bathroom.

"So you want to watch huh? That happens to me a lot after I take my shirt off around women." He realized he was doing it again. Flirting with her. With *it*. He shook his head; he had started humanizing her. It would only make killing her more difficult.

Ryan grabbed an outfit out of his duffel bag that was indistinguishable from the one he wore the day before and headed for the bathroom. The first thing he had to do after getting to Chicago was find a date. With a real live woman. It had obviously been too long. His body was simply reacting naturally to what it *perceived* was a real woman.

Carmen ignored Ryan's last remark. Or tried to. She was halfway tempted to try the handle and see if it was locked, but instead forced herself to sit down on the bed and think about what was going on with her world.

Two of them murdered, two more had narrowly escaped with their lives. That was four attempts. No — five, she had been number five. That meant all of them were in danger. There was no denying it anymore, no matter how much she tried.

Carmen had called her best friend Sylvia as soon as she had the chance after she and Ryan were attacked in the parking lot. She had spent fifteen minutes on her phone in the bathroom of the diner in Los Banos going over what happened, and what their next steps should be.

Carmen didn't care anymore that Charles had told her not to tell anyone where she was. Not when he might be the one trying to kill her. She trusted Sylvia more than anyone now. In fact she was the only one Carmen trusted.

She looked at her phone sitting on the bedside table. She thought about calling Charles, asking him point blank if he was the assassin. At the last moment she stopped herself. What would it prove? If Charles was trying to kill her, he would simply lie and say he wasn't. He was a remarkable liar. Calling him would prove nothing.

And did that really make any sense? Charles sending Ryan to kill her? Charles was smart, cunning, and shrewd. If he had sent a hunter to kill her he would have chosen the best. Someone he knew wouldn't fail. Not the reject in the bathroom.

Carmen knew instantly that she wasn't being honest in her assessment of Ryan. He was skilled enough. She might have died in the parking lot if it hadn't been for him. But she hadn't. He had saved her.

Ryan clearly was under the same impression that she was, he had been sent to protect her. Surely if Charles wanted her dead he would have made sure the guy knew what and who she was. It was clear that Ryan hadn't known what she was, let alone *who* she was. Any hunter would have leapt at the chance to kill her. And they would have brought a team, especially with a prize such as herself. Hunters were by and large cowards. Like werewolves and their packs, hunters almost always worked in teams.

Perhaps Ryan was faking his ignorance? She thought about it, dismissing it almost immediately. No. Ryan was too bad of a liar for him to hide his true intentions from her. He wasn't the type of slick hunter that could feign being prey, allowing himself to be taken somewhere, and then turn the tables on the vampire. It was obvious that Ryan was more of a guns blazing, questions afterward — if he remembered to ask them — kind of guy.

She remembered the shock on Ryan's face when he saw her, realizing what she was. It was genuine surprise. Surprise mixed with horror. He certainly hadn't known. Yet despite that, he had stayed by her side. Ryan was nothing if not a gentleman. Well, as much of one as existed anymore. He could have easily attacked her when he found out what she was, or even left her on her own when they had come for her in the parking lot. But he didn't. He even threw himself in the way of danger, taking the wooden bolts that had been meant for her.

She brushed away the thought. She couldn't afford sympathies for the man. He knew too much already. He would have to be killed, along with his friend Bill, and anyone else who knew about the Council.

What about this Bill that Ryan knew? Maybe he was the one that betrayed Charles and her both. Charles had found Ryan through him, he could have set it. She needed to find out who Bill was, talk to him. But no. Again, And Bill had sent Ryan to protect her, not kill her. He made

Ryan promise, as a personal favor to him, to keep her safe. And Bill had obviously known that Ryan was a man who kept his promises.

But then why was she wasting time thinking about him? There was no denying that he was physically attractive, but so were a lot of men. Maybe, if she had been looking for a relationship — no, not a relationship, not with Ryan. A fling. If she had been looking for a fling, Ryan might be worth passing a week or two with.

Carmen shook her head. No more flings for her. Purely physical relationships had lost their appeal centuries ago. Sylvia kept trying to get Carmen to lose herself in carnal pleasures. Carmen had tried, but they didn't help. She craved something more than sexual encounters. She craved an emotional connection. The type of relationship she wanted was few and far between, and couldn't happen with a human, and certainly never with a vampire hunter!

She had more important things on her mind, like figuring out who was killing them and why. Carmen began to pace the room, formulating a list of suspects. It would be easier if she could talk to someone, bounce ideas off of them. She always worked problems better if she could talk them out.

It would have to wait until she was with Sylvia. She certainly couldn't tell Ryan what was going on!

Ryan. She wondered if Ryan was his real name, and how old he was, and where he was from, and if he was married. He must be. Or have been. He wore their rings. Did he have a family? Children?

Carmen couldn't stand it any longer. She went over to the table and snooped through his wallet. She told herself it was for self-protection. Find out as much as she could about the enemy.

There was slightly over a grand in cash. Four credit cards, each with a different name. A Montana driver's license and insurance card, both with the name Ron Frost. A concealed handgun permit issued in Montana, also under the name Ron Frost. A "buy nine get one free" card from a nation-wide sandwich shop that had six stamps. No pictures of a family; no pictures what so ever. It was all bogus. The only thing not fake was a yellow post-it note with blocky handwriting that had the time and location of where she had met him.

Next she rummaged through his duffel bag with the clothes in it. She found what she expected: Military style black cargo pants. T-shirts. Solid color button up shirts, in various shades of drab. Tighty-whiteys, but in colors instead of white. Paired-up gym socks, all black. Three dog-eared spy thrillers with their spines broken repeatedly. One handgun, even though she counted at least three other handguns when she had searched the other bag last night looking for the first aid kit, plus the gun she saw him sneak into the bathroom when he went in a few minutes ago. Her damp bra. And finally a single deck of worn playing cards with a red diamond patterned back. The man was hopeless.

# # #

Ryan exited the bathroom to find Carmen sitting on the bed with her hands in her lap looking entirely too innocent. She held up a deck of cards. "Do you play?"

"Obviously. Those are my cards. Hey, those are *my* cards! You went through my stuff!"

"Technically my clothes were in there too, so it's our stuff."

"I thought you didn't want to wear it because it was wet."

"Does it look like I'm wearing it?" She arched her back so he could be sure.

"Then why were you going through our stuff? And you look better without it by the way."

Carmen raised her eyebrows, and then looked down at her chest. "You think so?"

"Yes, the padding is silly. Yours are perfect as they are." He was doing it again. Not only had he

57

complimented her, but he had let her distract him from the fact that she had been going through his stuff!

He wondered if she had been sabotaging his equipment while he had taken a shower. No, she wouldn't do that, it would be self-defeating. He wouldn't be able to protect her.

He wondered what she was looking for. His name? Address? A way to track him down once this was over? She would find none of those in his belongings. Nothing he carried with him could lead anyone back to the Sanctuary.

"Hearts."

"What?"

"Do you know the game or not?" Carmen asked.

"Never played it. I'm more of a poker guy. And solitaire."

But he learned quickly. The two passed the next couple of hours at the small round table until the sun set. First Carmen taught Ryan Hearts, later they played card games more suitable for two.

Then it was back on the highway. Carmen declined the offer to stop at a large big box store in the next town to get clothes. She pressed the icon on the car's touch screen display, thankful for the consistency of satellite radio stations, and reclined back into the comfortable seat ready to listen to the same twenty songs recycle for the next however-many hours.

"Not this again," said Ryan, giving his car's display a disapproving look. "How about we take turns? You got to listen to what you wanted to yesterday, today it's my turn."

"Fine, but you have to rub my feet." Carmen suddenly turned sideways in the cramped compartment, managing somehow to plant her bare feet in Ryan's lap.

The car swerved before he regained control. Ryan resisted the urge to look sideways. With her feet up at this angle, and that very short dress, he could have quite a view. Instead he leaned over and changed the station. He decided to throw her for a loop and picked classical. Ryan liked classical, especially when he was very stressed.

Carmen leaned back against the door, rested her hands in her lap and closed her eyes.

Pachelbel's Canon played and Ryan and began slowly massaging the bottom of Carmen's foot with his thumb.

Carmen opened one eye at the musical choice. Then she closed it again and smiled. She took a deep breath, letting it out slowly, demonstrating for Ryan the proper way to relax. She allowed the music to wrap around her, forcing every bad thought out of her mind. The massage was wonderful. The best she had in quite some time. Ryan knew how to use his hands.

Before long her mind wandered freely to settle on pleasant thoughts. Eventually, thoughts of where else Ryan could use his hands slowly began to creep their way to the forefront. Carmen was too relaxed to do anything but welcome them.

Ryan kept his eyes firmly on the road while he massaged her foot. It was cool in his hand, but then in Ryan's experience all women had cold feet. Dead or alive, it didn't matter. This one was shapely, with perfectly manicured nails painted in dark red. He worked on the foot moving from the heel to the ball of her feet, then the tops. Finally he gave each of her toes attention earning an even larger smile of contentment from Carmen.

Ryan risked taking his eyes off of the highway for a moment during a straightaway. He studied her in the shadows of the car. He reaffirmed his statement earlier about the bra. He wouldn't change a thing. Her figure was mesmerizing. Her features warm and pleasant. Though shut now, her eyes were always full of life, even when things were going badly for her. He even liked the small mole, set to the left and slightly above her mouth. And, oh, that mouth — full lips without being overdone. The languid wry smile that always seemed to be at home on it.

Ryan's hand made its own way up her calf, which was smooth now. Toned. Carmen squirmed almost imperceptibly under his touch, but not in annoyance. Her lips parted and Ryan imagined what it would be like kissing them.

Ryan's survival instinct took over. In a last ditch effort to prevent himself from going where he didn't want to go, Ryan decided to discover if vampires were ticklish.

"Ahhh!" Carmen screeched, yanking her feet back as quick as a snake, her eyes snapping open wide with shock. Her chest heaved. "No tickling!"

"I guess so," Ryan chuckled as he answered his own question.

"Yes, I'm ticklish, thank you very much." Carmen rotated and propped her feet up on the dash, safely out of Ryan's reach. She reached to her right side and found the button that made the seat back recline. She leaned back and the hem of her dress went from dangerous to illegal.

Carmen found that she was annoyed. She wasn't sure if it was because Ryan had tickled her, or because the tickling had interrupted a fantasy that involved him doing something entirely different with her. It was obvious that the stress of the current predicament was making her behave foolishly and suffer impossible thoughts. She needed to get rid of this guy fast before she did something even more foolish.

Ryan made sure to keep his eyes on the road. "Where are you from?" Ryan asked. Straight ahead, he told himself. Look straight ahead.

"Spain, but don't you dare ask when," she replied.

"Fair enough."

"How about yourself?" she asked.

"Have you ever been married?" Ryan countered, declining to answer the question.

"Once, before I was turned. You?"

"Any kids?"

"Yes, I had two. Yourself?"

"Is Carmen your real name?"

"Yes, at least a shortened version of it, and this seems to be awfully one-sided."

"It's a pretty name. It suits you."

She smiled despite herself. "Thank you. Seriously, are you going to answer any of *my* questions?"

Ryan hadn't planned on it. As long as he kept it one sided then he could view this as an interrogation, rather than a conversation. He wasn't sure how he felt having a conversation with a vampire. Sure, he had talked to them before, but if it wasn't to trade one-liners before he killed them it was to extract information so he could kill more of them.

This was different. He didn't need the information to ascertain if she was a monster, since he already knew it. And the questions he was asking weren't so that he could locate her, as she was within arm's reach. He realized he asked the questions because he honestly was interested in her answers.

But he had no intention of providing his own. He kept his information private even from the hunters he worked with. Information, personal information, could be used against him. It could be used as leverage, or to find out where he or his associates lived. It was dangerous. No one got it. It was one of his rules.

Given that, he had absolutely no idea why he spoke. "I was born in Massachusetts, a small town called Milford. Spent most of my childhood there. Moved to Tennessee when I was twelve. Stayed there until I was eighteen when I went straight into the military. Got out after six years. Spent the next half dozen moving around. Following the jobs."

"Never married?" Carmen asked, thinking of the rings he wore on the chain around his neck.

"My profession is not exactly compatible with the institution or, honestly, long-term relationships in general."

"Are you saying you've never had a girlfriend?" she asked.

"Of course I have!"

Carmen knew he was lying. He was terrible at it, and she was good at reading even competent people. "What's the longest time you've ever been with someone?"

"Six weeks. My Junior year," Ryan said, remembering.

"Wow, epic. And why did you end it after all that time?"

"Things were getting too serious."

"Of course they were."

"Look, I can't afford to have a wife. How would that end? I'll tell you how, in one of two ways: Either I wouldn't come home one day, because something I was hunting had killed me. Or, I would come home to find her dead, because something I was hunting had killed her. Either way, it's not a happily-ever-after ending. So I don't do relationships. That's one of my rules. No breakfasts, if you know what I mean."

"That's bleak. Ever thought about retiring?" She asked the question even though she herself had all but sworn off relationships since the one giant, enormous, huge, epic failure of one that had ended almost a century before. It had left her financially and emotionally in tatters, and she had no desire to repeat that mistake.

"No." It was another fib. Ryan thought about retirement more and more lately. Most recently after he had tracked down that werewolf that tore up some campers up in the Northwest. He had taken some time off to test the waters, devoting himself to his Sanctuary. And then he had gotten the call from Bill, bringing Ryan all the way to California and the mess he was in now. "You?" he asked.

Carmen laughed, "Every once in a while I think about trading it all in, reveling in the sun again, becoming a beach bunny, or maybe a suntan lotion model."

"You certainly have the figure for it," Ryan said.

Carmen smiled, she threw her head back, arched her back and struck a dramatic pose that Ryan couldn't resist but gawking at. "You think so?"

"What do you do, anyway?" Ryan asked her tearing his eyes from her.

"You mean besides stalking my victims, draining them dry, and leaving their cold dead bodies in alleyways?"

"Yeah, besides that. Do you have a job?" Most vampires didn't. A rare few were old enough that their investments carried them. The rest simply pushed people into giving them what they needed. At least the Street ones were like that. He didn't know about Society, but he suspected they had an even easier time of it.

Others creatures had to work, though. Witches and werewolves were like humans in that respect, stuck pulling nine-to-fives to pay the rent.

"Not as such. I've never had a real job. Before I was turned I tended to my family and ran the household. That was a job of sorts, though we had servants who performed most of the actual labor. After I was turned, well, I've never had to work," Carmen said. The first part was the truth, the second a lie. These days she worked more than most brokers. Not only did Carmen run a territory and a moderately successful business, she kept an eye on numerous less-than-successful investments. It was enough work to keep her more than busy.

"So what do you do with your time?" Ryan asked.

"I knit."

"You what?"

"I knit. It's when you take two needles, some yarn, and you make things out of them. I prefer afghans. I used to do needlepoint, back then I preferred pillows, but I came to the conclusion over the last century that my patience has dwindled. I'm now more suited to knitting."

"You're serious?"

Carmen nodded. "You?"

He couldn't tell her. It was simply too much information. But he did anyway. "When I'm not killing monsters, I rescue animals."

"Like plucking cats out of trees?"

Ryan nodded. "Big cats. I have a small wildlife refuge. I take care of abandoned exotic animals. Ones that people get as pets because they think they're cute, then they grow up, start eating a few ponds of raw meat a day, and they aren't so cute anymore. Or sometimes when animal rescue finds them in deplorable conditions and removes them forcibly, they call me to provide permanent housing."

He didn't know why he told her. It was stupid. There were only so many exotic animal rescues in the nation. If she was smart she could find his. Find him. Of course, she was sitting right there next to him and it wasn't as if she made any promises to keep *him* safe until Chicago.

"Why animals?" she asked.

"I don't know. Maybe because they're like kids, innocent. They don't kill each other for fun or sport."

"So why do you kill us if it's not for fun or sport? What happened?"

Ryan clammed up. Carmen had pushed too far and he shut down. Carmen knew most hunters did what they did because someone had killed a loved one. They did it for revenge. Occasionally you got other types. Ones whose religion led them to believe what they hunted were abominations and had to die. Or adrenaline junkies that did it for the rush. But Carmen was pretty sure Ryan didn't fall into either of those categories.

She wondered if Ryan had been lying to her about being married and having a family. But she didn't think so — he was an awful liar. He had told her the truth. That only left so many options. The most obvious was that the rings belonged to his other family, the one that had raised him. Someone had killed his mother and father. She wondered if he had been forced to watch.

# # #

It was before nine when Carmen directed them to a large indoor mall in the suburbs of Las Vegas. She and Sylvia frequented the multi-storied structure every time she visited. If there was one thing her oldest, and probably last, true friend loved to do, it was shop.

Ryan was not at all happy with the revelation that they were going shopping in a mall. "This is a road trip. You don't need a mall. They're not only overpriced, they're inefficient. Target would have had everything you need, cost a lot less, and take half the time."

"Need, maybe. Want, not so much. Come on. I'll make it quick."

"That's impossible," Ryan said. By design, he had limited experience with women and shopping. The little experience he had wasn't good, and none of it was quick. He hurried after Carmen into the mall wondering which was worse: playing twenty questions with a vampire or taking one shopping.

First up was a high-end department store where Carmen focused in on several outfits with laser precision. She certainly knew what she wanted and was indeed fast. She had a definite style, and was able to eyeball her size, instead of relying on the completely useless numbers printed on the labels that existed only to make ladies feel good about their size.

Ryan admired Carmen's efficiency. He hated women who spent hours upon hours trying on clothes. What he didn't like was having to actively participate. Apparently Carmen was used to wearing tailored business suits, and though she was adept at picking her correct size off the rack, she not only insisted on trying everything on, but she actually made Ryan stand outside the dressing room and provide his opinion on each article of clothing. As if his opinions somehow mattered — she had made that clear this morning when she dismissed his offer to run and get clothes for her.

If Ryan had been honest he would have said everything looked good, because it did. She had excellent taste and knew what complimented her amazing figure well. Heck, who was he kidding? Despite what she was, he had to admit he would find her hot if she dressed in a paper bag. But he didn't have to be honest, not to her, and he hated clothes shopping. Plus, he was angry that she had gotten information out of him.

So as punishment when she came out to model form-fitting sweaters or fashionable skirts he randomly sprinkled in back-handed compliments and hesitations before actual ones. His feedback forced Carmen to do a second run into the store for more clothing, adding thirty minutes to the shopping process.

Ryan reminded himself that he was doing this to punish her, not because he simply enjoyed watching her model in front of him, allowing him to openly marvel at the way she made everything look good.

Carmen finally caught on when Ryan had been distracted by an unattended toddler running amok through the nearby shoe department. He watched as the mother absentmindedly chatted away on her cell phone, blissfully ignorant regarding the location of her child, who was sitting amidst a pile of shoes he had taken down from various displays and trying to swallow a shoelace.

Ryan was frowning at the mother, considering saying something to her when his peripheral vision caught Carmen coming out of the dressing room. "No, those make your ass look fat," he said absently.

Unfortunately for him, Carmen had been trying on a different top with a pair of leggings that they had already agreed looked good. Carmen crossed her arms and glowered at Ryan. Then she frowned, looking less certain, and glanced back at the offending piece of anatomy.

Ryan realized his mistake, and quickly qualified his statement, "Relax, I was joking, it's not too fat. For your age."

Carmen spun around, furious.

"So, you all set?" asked Ryan, smiling.

Carmen aggressively grabbed the handful of clothes she had previously decided on buying, then went back to her dressing room with a couple of additional items that had been tossed on the discard pile due to Ryan's comments. Then she made him pay for everything, because "they might be tracing her cards." He didn't have to know she always carried five grand in cash with her for emergencies.

Carmen made sure to deliver a few more looks that promised grim retribution for Ryan's offense before heading next door to the shoe department. She tsked disapprovingly at the toddler, now busy making snow angels on the carpet, and worked around him to pick out two pairs of shoes, one brown and one black, that together could accommodate every outfit she purchased.

Before leaving the store she added makeup, a brush, her favorite scented lotion, and a few other personal products. After each department she thrust the bags out to Ryan without giving him any opportunity to refuse becoming her pack mule.

Ryan was satisfied even as he stumbled under the burden of the last bag that was tossed his way. The vampire had been blissfully silent since his ass comment, and with the acquisition of the shoes he was sure they were finally finished. Carmen had purchased more than enough clothes for the next several days and, down to one good arm, he had run out of ability to carry anything more.

He had been reduced to carrying his credit card between his teeth, it having become too burdensome to drop all of the bags to get to his wallet and then pick them back up every time they stopped to make a purchase. He had halted his mental tally when the total reached a thousand dollars. Carmen had spent more in one evening than he spent on clothes for an entire year.

He stopped and readjusted his grip on the three bags in his left hand when Carmen took a right instead of a left upon exiting the store.

"Where are you going? The car's that way," Ryan said, trotting to catch up.

When Carmen's destination became apparent, Ryan stopped and said, "Oh, no way."

"You can't expect me to wear the same underwear every day, can you?"

"Well, no."

"Or would you prefer that I don't wear any? I can do that." She shrugged, heading back out of the store.

"No, no, by all means, get some! But you don't need me to do it."

"Are you certain you don't feel the need to be there to tell me how fat my ass looks, or how flat my chest is?" she asked.

In answer, Ryan did an about-face and walked to the Game Shack across the way.

Carmen found Ryan there fifteen minutes later playing Death Karts 2 on the store's demo X-Box, her department store bags piled up around him.

"Dinner time. You pick," said Carmen, adding two small pink sacks to the pile and handing Ryan back his depleted pre-paid debit card.

"Okay. Chinese." They had passed a food court with one of those nation-wide joints he liked. He knew the food they served wasn't authentic, but it tasted good to him.

"That's racist, but if we happened upon someone who's Chinese I won't object."

"What are you talking about?"

"My dinner, of course. I know how much my having to eat pains you, so I thought I'd ease your burden by letting you select my prey. I mean meal." She smiled at him.

Ryan paled. "I'm not going to pick out someone for you to snack on!" He had known this was coming. There was no way she could fast each night during their trip. Well, maybe she could, depending on how old she was. The older vampires could go longer without feeding. But he didn't know how much of a meal she got back in Los Banos, and he had no intention of traveling with a starving vampire to find out just how old she was.

"Why not? It's not as if I'm going to kill them. They'll be perfectly fine when I'm finished," Carmen said.

"I'm not doing it."

"I have to eat. I thought letting you choose who would help."

"Let me get this straight. You're trying to get my buy-in by letting me contribute to the decision making?"

Carmen looked up at the sky. "From what I understand, it will make the whole thing easier for you."

Ryan shook his head. "I don't know what management books you've been reading, or why, but I give you my permission to pick who you want to bite without me."

"Oh, I have your permission do I?" Carmen's glance returned to focus on someone back on Earth.

"Yes, but remember, no killing and no kids."

"Any more restrictions you would like to put on my diet?" she asked.

Ryan opened his mouth to say something, and then wisely shut it again. He realized he had been heading down a path that was likely to end in Carmen eating a pack of girl scouts out of spite.

"Let's go. I'm hungry and I need to change out of this dress," Carmen said, then began a brisk walk to the car. Ryan struggled to not drop any of the bags as he scrambled after her.

Less than a half-hour later, Carmen had pushed the man at the check-in counter of the Arabian Nights Casino into comping them a room for the night. A few minutes after that, Ryan sat on the bed to read the room service menu while Carmen changed clothes in the bathroom.

Carmen held the black garment in front of her. Ironically the dress would have served her well in the glitz of the casino floor, but three days in it was long enough! She wadded it up and tossed it in the bathroom trash can.

She selected her outfit, then frowned at herself in the mirror, plucking at her chest and moving from side to side for different angles. She don't know why she had bought the bras she had. Padded bras were one of the few technological innovations in the modern age that she truly embraced, and here she was back to sheer lace ones.

She checked the time on her phone after applying her makeup. She was supposed to meet Sylvia in her Casino in an hour. That gave her time to eat, and then lose Ryan. She could lose him first of course; it's not like she actually enjoyed his company. But where was the fun in that? After the stunt he pulled in the store she had every intention of making him suffer through picking out her donor.

She exited the bathroom to find Ryan still sitting on the bed, now reading the card with the TV channel listings. When he looked up and smiled, she couldn't help herself; she smiled back.

Carmen was wearing the same outfit that Ryan had said made her ass look fat. It didn't. The skin-tight black leggings clung to her shapely rear nicely, the burgundy button-up shirt was a happy compromise between dressy and casual, and he had a thing for boots. He also noted her chest was smaller and a more naturally contoured than when he first met her. He leaned forward to get a better look. Either she wasn't wearing a bra, or it wasn't padded.

"Stop staring," Carmen said, turning to leave the room.

"Can't help it. You look good," Ryan said from behind her.

She almost stopped at the compliment, but instead managed a casual sounding, "I know."

They stood in silence in the elevator. Carmen tried to not let the pleasure she gained from Ryan's words show, and Ryan chewed over what she was about to make him do.

They exited through the lobby and headed out onto the Casino floor, weaving their way through the lights and sounds until they came to one of the many bars that littered the giant den of sin. They sat at a table that bordered the floor, which offered an ideal vantage point for people watching.

A waitress came up and took their orders: A Mai-Tai for Carmen and a 7-up for Ryan. He gave the waitress a grudging *I guess* when she asked him if Sprite was okay.

"What happened to the Canadian Club part of the equation?" Carmen asked.

"I don't drink on duty."

"What about back in that restaurant where we met?"

"I hadn't officially started the job until we left the restaurant."

"You think we're going to have trouble here in the casino?"

"I don't know. But what I do know is that what's out there already has enough advantages over us; no need to give them any more."

"Us?" she asked.

He covered up his absent minded mistake quickly. "Us humans."

"Right. We certainly wouldn't want to lump the two of *us* together." Carmen took a sip of her drink. She was hungry. She had been in the process of cornering her prey when her neighbor had called about the lights in her windows. As soon as she hung up her phone, Carmen had abandoned the man she had gone to all that trouble of picking up. She made a run for it without even taking a drop of blood from him and now she was paying the consequences. It had been centuries since she had gone this long without eating.

When the waitress brought them a second round of drinks, Carmen broke the silence. "So it's been fifteen minutes. Pick someone already. I need to eat, and we need to get back on the road so you can get me to Chicago and we can part ways."

"You're awfully cranky. Didn't you just eat less than twenty four hours ago?"

"What gave you that idea? When was I supposed to have eaten? I've been with you the whole time. And I saw you checking yourself for bite marks in the hotel room after we got up, so you know I didn't sample you."

Ryan hoped she had missed that. "I thought that's what you did when you went in to that diner. Remember? In Los Banos? When you disappeared for twenty minutes?"

Carmen shook her head as she scanned the casino floor. Then she speared the cherry in her drink with her straw without bothering to look at the glass, and absentmindedly held it out to Ryan.

Ryan frowned, took it off of the straw and ate it. "If you weren't feeding, what exactly were doing in there?"

"Do you really expect me to provide you with details of my bathroom exploits?" Carmen glanced at him, eyebrows raised.

Ryan shut up. It only lasted a second. "So when was the last time you ate?"

"Three days ago."

Ryan paled. That was an awful long time for anything to go without food, let alone a vampire. It was an impossible amount of time for a new one, maybe even for one a hundred years old. Invariably they went feral, instinct taking control from their minds. When that happened vampires became unreasoning killers, only looking to fulfill their basic needs any way they could.

Carmen was older than Ryan had assumed. Much older. "How old are you?" he asked.

"I'm going to pretend you didn't ask me that."

"You're really going to make me do this?" Ryan asked, trying in vain to spear the cherry at the bottom of his glass while he digested the new information.

"Yup."

"Fine. Her." Ryan nodded to a very pretty, overdone girl who was either preparing for an audition in a tawdry reality show or was a high-class call girl.

"Her, huh? You wouldn't prefer that guy over there?" She indicated a tall, dark and handsome gentleman at a craps table.

Ryan shrugged. "If you want."

"No, no, I said you could pick. The prostitute is fine. But if I catch something, it's on you." She cast a sideways glance his way. "You want to watch? You know, to make sure I don't go too far?"

"I'll pass."

Ryan did watch as Carmen talked to the girl who was obviously waiting for her John. The two of them had a brief conversation before heading off in a direction that was not to the nearest restrooms.

"Shit." Ryan got up and hurriedly followed. Carmen was leading the girl to the elevators. Ryan made it to them just in time to jump in with the two girls, causing the doors to jerk open just before they closed on him.

"Well, hello there. Changed your mind?" asked Carmen.

"You're going up to the room?"

"What did you expect? In a casino, there are only so many options that don't have cameras," she said.

The girl looked confused, but Carmen gave her a wink then locked eyes with her. "We don't want what we're about to do to end up all over the internet, now, do we? You don't mind if my boyfriend watches, do you?"

The girl giggled and shook her head.

Ryan followed them into the room, and then watched as Carmen smiled at the girl and began stroking her head, leaning over to whisper into her ear. Ryan was about to leave when Carmen pulled the girl into a deep embrace. Their mouths locked.

Ryan paused, watching as the two women kissed. The blonde girl's hands moved down the length of Carmen's body, and one hand reversed its motion to come back up to caress a breast.

Ryan stood in awe of the spectacle, betting the girl was happy Carmen wasn't wearing a padded bra.

The blonde's dress hit the floor and Carmen explored the girl's body, her hand running down to her hip and sneaking under the strap of her thong. She started to slide it down, then stopped. Carmen turned to Ryan and said, "Are you going to just stand their gawking? Wouldn't you prefer to join in?"

Ryan started, shook his head, and hurriedly backed out of the room. He closed the door behind him and decided some of his deep breathing exercises were in order.

As soon as the door clicked shut, Carmen pulled back from the girl. Not that she didn't enjoy it; Ryan had excellent taste in women. But the whole spectacle had been a joke. She had been messing with Ryan because she thought it would be fun. She knew most men would have jumped at the opportunity to be with two women, even if one of them was destined to be the main course. Most guys thought with their libido and rarely strayed beyond the moment.

Not Ryan, though — he had declined her offer. Declined the prospect of two women at once, and Carmen knew why. It wasn't because he was gay; she hadn't missed his desire or the impressive bulge that developed as he watched them. Yet still he walked out of the room. The reality was that he hated vampires. Carmen found the revelation disappointing and lost all the appetites she might have had. She had her meal, but it didn't provide her much satisfaction outside of satiating her hunger.

Carmen exited the room a short while later to find Ryan leaning against the wall of the hallway breathing heavily. "Time to go," she said, handing Ryan the key card.

"What's this for?" Ryan looked down at the card then up at Carmen. She looked flushed, refreshed, and depressed. It was an odd combination.

"So you can check to make sure I left her alive."

"I trust you," Ryan said already turning towards the elevators. As he said it, he realized a funny thing: he did trust her, at least about the girl.

Carmen walked beside Ryan, her thoughts conflicted. Ryan actually seemed surprised she had given him the key, like he had never intended to make sure she hadn't killed the girl. Like he trusted her. She almost had second thoughts about what she was about to do. Almost.

When they exited onto the Casino floor, Carmen waited for a distraction to make her move. She didn't have to wait long. An elderly lady won a jackpot on a nickel slot. She shrieked, jumping up and pumping her hands in the air.

Ryan turned at the sound of the bells and shouts of joy. When he turned back to Carmen to comment on the lady's luck, the vampire was gone.

# Chapter 5

"Shit!" Ryan said for the second time in an hour as he did a 360 on the red carpet. There was no sign of Carmen, but the Casino was packed. At first he thought Carmen had seen something shiny and walked off, but after searching the floor in vain for five minutes he realized that she had given him the slip.

He grabbed a seat at the nearest bar, pulled out his cell phone and dialed a number. It went through to voice mail, but Ryan expected it would. The guy he was calling was paranoid and screened all his calls.

Ryan left a message, and then waited until the callback came. It took less than a minute.

Ryan clicked Talk. "Hello, Jacob."

"Gun? Is that you?" Jacob asked, using Ryan's nickname. Ryan exclusively went by a nickname when he worked jobs. A lot of hunters did. It helped keep them anonymous. The less people knew about you, the less they could tell to the ones that might wish you harm.

"Yup. Need you to trace a phone for me," Ryan told him.

"Please tell me you have the number," Jacob said in a weary tone.

"Of course I do." Ryan relayed it to him.

"You want to know who owns it?"

"No, I know that. More or less. The name will be bogus, I'm sure. I want to know where it is."

"You're in luck: Kevin's here. He can do it right now, but it will take a few minutes."

"No problem. I'll wait. How close can you get me to the phone?"

"Few hundred yards."

"That should be enough."

"So, back on the job, huh? I heard you were taking a breather after that last one. Some werewolf almost tore off your shoulder?" Jacob's tone conveyed little doubt that Ryan would stay retired, missing an arm or not.

"Forget my shoulder; you should have seen what he did to my Jeep. And, yeah, I was on an extended vacation until a friend gave me a call. He had something he wanted me to handle."

"Oh? Which friend?" Jacob asked, an ear out for the competition. Jacob wasn't just in the business of information, he also provided jobs. And occasionally, when the jobs paid, Jacob took a cut. A lot of hunters used Jacob because he had a knack for tracking down monsters. His intel was the best in the business. Jacob was the one that had told Ryan about the vampire Council and their secret government. Ryan still only half believed it.

"Bill," Ryan said.

"Bill, huh? Near as I can tell, he only uses you."

"He normally doesn't even have jobs; he's really more of a friend than a handler. But he ran into something that he thought was up my alley."

"Don't get me wrong, Gun, I'm not blaming him! You're the best there is. Everybody knows that. Not like the amateurs I usually work with. You get in, get the job done, and get out. You understand how this whole thing is supposed to work. You know, *killing* monsters? Unlike some other folks I know."

It was a strange statement, and hit a little too close to home for Ryan. Was that an insinuation? It made him wonder just how good Jacob's information was. Could he possibly know what Ryan was doing? No, that was impossible, because no one knew that except for Bill.

Ryan chalked the comment up to Jacob's being an odd duck and let it slide.

"Marie, stop that — it's distracting." Jacob's voice had become distant. He was talking to someone else in the room with him.

"Who's Marie, and exactly what is she doing?" Ryan couldn't believe the old man was getting himself some action.

"A burr in my side is what she is, and she's playing with my infrared cameras again. I just had them installed in the new place."

From far away came, "Aw, a burr? I thought I was more like a hickey." Then louder as she neared the phone, "Hello, there, I'm Marie! Jacob's new business partner." Ryan could almost hear her hand waving.

"Now don't you go trying to get your hooks into him, too. Leave us be for a minute. Shoo."

"But I like the way he sounds. And I don't want to put my hooks into him. I was thinking more about his putting something into me."

"Will you please go away, woman! I agreed to work with you, not house you, and certainly not pimp you out. Sorry about that, Gun. We almost got that trace."

"This is my building, how could *you* be housing *me*?" Marie's voice floated in from the background again.

"You might own it, but I lease this floor, and that makes it legally mine!" Jacob said.

"What happened to the store?" asked Ryan. The last Ryan remembered Jacob had operated out of some sort of appliance repair shop.

"Vampires burnt it down back in September. Had to relocate." Jacob's voice said to him. Then to someone away from the phone, he added, "But I'm having serious doubts about my choice of new locations."

Ryan smiled at the thought of old Jacob finally getting some, wondering if she was a crazy as he was. "She sounds like quite a handful."

"Ryan, you have no idea. Oh, you're in Vegas! You working that job with Beau?"

"What job?" Ryan had met Beau once and didn't care for the guy. He knew what he was doing, but he took too much pleasure in it for Ryan's liking. Ryan killed monsters because of what they were, and what they did to people — more specifically, what they had done to him and his family. At least that's how it started. Now, all these years later, he did it more as a public service like he had told Carmen. So others wouldn't have to suffer like he had. But he never once remembered liking it. Beau was different. Beau did it because he enjoyed killing. To Beau it was a rush.

"There's a line on a couple of vamps in Vegas," Jacob said. "Two girls... Hold on a second. Marie, you get out of my nephew's lap this instant! Kevin, what do you think you're doing? I told you not to let her do that! I don't care if there is only one chair! I have my eye on both of you!

"Sorry about that. Anyway there are two vamps out there. Supposed to be really tearing up the town if you know what I mean. It's a money job. Big bucks, biggest I've seen in a while. Half a million if you can deliver proof that you've bagged both of them."

"Half a million? What the hell did they do?" That was a heck of a lot of money, Ryan thought, especially for a job. Most jobs didn't pay much, or even at all. If you were lucky some relative would clean out a savings account and offer you a few thousand. Half a million sounded like a hit ordered from the Vatican.

"I don't know; probably delivered food to the homeless. Christ, Ryan, they did what they always do! Killed people. In this case it looks like they must have gone and killed some rich people. I got the info if you want to horn in on it. Beau might cut you in if you call him and ask to join his merry band of cut-throats. Or you can take it out from under him for all I care. Guy makes my skin crawl," Jacob said.

"Nah, thanks. I've got enough problems to worry about. I have my own vampire that managed to give me the slip, and I need to track her down before something happens." Ryan almost finished with "to her" and managed to bite it off at the last moment.

"*You* let one get away? That's a first! Well, your secret's safe with me. And you're in luck: we got a location on that phone. That's funny… puts your vamp within a hundred yards of the Midnight Casino. That's where Beau was headed. Looks like we got ourselves a nest. You and Beau might have to split that bounty after all."

"Thanks, Jacob."

"No problem, Gun."

"Happy hunting!" Marie's voice chirped from a distance.

# Chapter 6

Ryan handed the valet his ticket. The kid came back a moment later with a nervous smile. "Sorry sir, but your wife already collected your car."

"My what? Oh, you have got to be kidding me." Not only had Carmen ditched him, but she stole his car and all of his gear along with it. Ryan was furious. Never ever mess with a man's car.

Ryan wasn't a gambler; he had only been to Vegas on a couple of occasions, and he had never been to Midnight. As it turned out the newish casino wasn't too far away, maybe halfway down the strip from the Arabian Nights. He hopped in one of the waiting taxis camped in front of the Arabian Nights parking lot entrance, and was let out in front of Midnight less than five minutes later. He figured he was no more than twenty minutes behind Carmen.

He paid the driver then surveyed the facade of the side entrance to the casino. Nearly all the casinos themed, and this one was no exception. The theme here obviously was midnight. Dark blue neon, tricks of light casting ominous shadows on the circular driveway packed with cars, hidden speakers playing the hooting of owls, artificial wind through artificial trees.... It was like the set of an old horror movie.

The main entrance for foot traffic was on the strip; this one was designed for guests arriving by car. Carmen had taken his car, so Ryan reasoned she would have entered the Casino here.

There was the typical row of taxis as well as dozens of private vehicles in states of loading, unloading, or waiting for passengers. He saw his blue station wagon parked off to the side with several other cars waiting to be moved by the valets into the attached garage.

He knew Beau's team would wait until their mark was out of the Casino before they made their move. Casino security was simply too good to try a job inside of one. As Carmen had noted before, there was no way to escape from being caught on camera in a Casino, and they each employed an army of armed security guards.

Ryan was torn between checking his car to make sure his gear was still there, and heading into the Casino to look for Carmen. He had finally decided on the casino when he saw her. She was walking out of the hotel, but she wasn't alone. She was with another lady and a pair of bruisers in suits.

At first he thought they had gotten to her. Either Beau's team or the vampires that were after her had somehow caught her in the casino, and now were taking her out to, well, take her out. But as Ryan observed Carmen and her escorts he could see her smiling. Both of the girls were chatting and laughing as they walked up to a pair of black stretch limos waiting at the curb flanked by the large goons.

One of the guys hurried forward to yank open one of the doors before the girls reached the car. As soon as they got in, the door was shut and both cars sped off, passing through the parking garage before they emerged half a minute later out on the street.

Ryan hurried over to his wagon trying to keep an eye on the cars. He lost them when they entered the garage. He adjusted his vantage point so he could see the garage exit. He watched as both cars emerged onto the feeder road. Each turned in a different direction when they reached the Las Vegas strip.

Clever. They split the cars in case anyone was watching the casino. Any pursuers would have to either take a guess as to which car to follow, or divide their resources.

Ryan grabbed the magnetic hide-a-key from under the rear bumper of his Caddy and took out the metal valet key. If he hurried he could catch up to one of them. Of course the problem with Vegas, at least if you were fleeing Vegas, was the limited number of options you had. There were only so many highways out of town.

Ryan popped off the plastic plug that hid the keyhole in the door and was about to insert the key when something caught his attention. A couple of valets had wheeled out a cartful of designer luggage and were loading it into the back of a gray Chrysler 300 with severely tinted windows. Behind the guy loading the luggage was a second bellhop, his arms full of familiar shopping bags, two of them small and pink.

Ryan slid the key into the keyhole and popped the lock of his Caddy as the 300 drove toward the parking garage. Ryan was even more impressed. *Both* of the limos had been a diversion.

He started to get in his wagon when he heard, "Hey, sir, what are you doing? That's not your car!"

"The hell it isn't." Ryan slammed the door and started up the Cadillac. He pulled out of the parking lot, a couple of hotel personnel running in pursuit. Fantastic. He was going to be arrested for stealing his own car.

Ryan took the direct route to the strip, bypassing the garage. He pulled to the side and then waited, despite the angry honk from a cab that had pulled up to his rear bumper. Seconds later the 300 exited the garage. Ryan gave it some time, and then pulled in a couple car lengths behind the Chrysler, ignoring the finger from the cabbie who sped by on his right.

Ryan stayed well in back of the car he was tailing, which was making its way toward highway 15. He wasn't in any hurry to confront Carmen and what he suspected were her multiple vampire companions. As long as they were headed in the right direction he was content to follow them.

Ryan would deal with Carmen and her new friends when they next pulled over. He checked the clock; it was a few minutes after midnight. Chances are they would be forced to stop for gas long before dawn. At least he hoped so. He had filled up when they entered Vegas, but he doubted he was getting the same mileage as the Chrysler, and he couldn't afford to stop for gas before they did and risk losing them.

Ryan dialed up some classic rock, settled back in his seat, and trailed the Chrysler to the sound of Warren Zevon reciting the virtues of "Lawyers, Guns, and Money."

# # #

Carmen sat beside her friend, relaxed for the first time in days. A limo would have been more comfortable for the long trip, but she was pleased with herself for coming up with the plan to switch the cars.

Carmen knew that if the killers were after her, then they were after Sylvia as well, and the two of them couldn't afford to be too careful. She knew they would be watching the casino; it's not as if Sylvia ever hid the fact that she spent most of her time there since building it five years ago. Carmen didn't shy away from the spotlight, but Sylvia positively thrived in it. She relished her role as Hotel Maven and Las Vegas VIP.

Carmen looked over at her old friend. Sylvia had always lived in the moment. It was a wonder she had made it this far, but she seemed to have a guardian angel. Things tended to go her way. It's one of the things that drew Carmen to her: Sylvia's eternal optimism and propensity for having fun even in the worst of times.

Sylvia winked, then took a pair of bottles out of the small ice chest between them and began to prepare two samples of her take on a bloody Mary. She called it a "Bloody Joseph."

"Only two hours old, and you should have seen the donor! Or better yet sampled *everything* he had to offer. It's a pity we couldn't have taken all of him with us," Sylvia said as she stirred the plasma and vodka cocktail and handed it to Carmen.

"So tell me all about what happened the past couple days," Sylvia said, sipping on her drink. "And I want the slow version, not the 'I'm in a bathroom hiding from my babysitter and only have a few minutes' one that you gave me before."

Carmen tasted the concoction in her glass, finding the combination of blood, vodka, and spices to be mediocre. She preferred rum, her taste running towards sweeter things. She shrugged, took another drink and sat against the far corner of the seat so she could face her friend as she recounted the last several days.

Sylvia had already heard about the murders, of course. They all had. Johannes was killed first. Everyone assumed it was hunters that had somehow gotten lucky. He was coming home one night with a companion when they were attacked on the steps of his New York condo. Johannes was powerful — almost a thousand years old — and his companion over five hundred. There were no witnesses, but the entire first floor of the high rise was left in ruins. That's why everyone had assumed it was hunters at first; they had used explosives.

Then the next three attempts came almost two weeks later, one right after the other. All at the victims' homes.

Fortunately two of the attacks failed. Both Elizabeth and Peter had escaped by the skin of their teeth. Henry hadn't been so lucky. They trapped him in his Maine estate during the day and burnt it to the ground.

They had tried the same thing with Elizabeth in Florida, but she managed to escape her burning home through a secret tunnel that the attackers hadn't known about. Peter was attacked as well, but at night. He managed to not only escape, but kill several of his human attackers, though he also lost his beautiful house to the flames.

They would have never known vampires were involved if it wasn't for two witnesses. The first was a human security guard of Elizabeth's. His job was to monitor the security cameras on her estate. When the attack came he was able to copy the video and email it to the Council before he was killed.

One of the cameras caught the vehicles they had been using: two full-sized vans and a sedan. The sedan had tinted windows, and several times during the assault one of the humans had gone to the car for instructions. That wasn't enough evidence of vampire involvement on its own, and most of the Council dismissed it until the second witness came forward.

The second witness had been better. One of Henry's human groundskeepers had been tending to his estate when the attack came. The man heard the commotion and rushed to the house. He hid in the woods, using a pair of binoculars to watch.

This attack had started closer to dusk, the killers probably having misjudged the time it took to reach the remote estate. The groundskeeper relayed that as soon as the sun went down a vampire had gotten out of a car and walked the rubble of the estate. He knew it was a vampire because he recognized the man from parties Henry had held at the house.

The Council had prepared a mug shot book like the ones the human police used. It comprised all of the Society vampires. There was great risk putting together such a tome, but they had to be sure. Someone had suggested a power point presentation, but the idea was quickly dismissed. An electronic file could be too easily copied, whereas a paper book could be destroyed once the identification was made.

It never happened.

Before they had a chance to have the man look through the photos and pick out the vampire he had seen at Henry's, the witness had been killed. They found his body in the secure room at the New York Hall with his throat torn out. Someone had gotten to him while under the Council's protection, in one of the Council's own buildings. It was indisputable proof that they had a traitor amongst them.

And then they tried to kill Carmen. First at her primary residence in California, and then again at the restaurant. She wondered how they had tracked her to the meeting with Ryan. She had been careful to not be followed.

She wondered if Ryan was in on it, but quickly dismissed the idea. Not only had he been shot saving her, he was an incredibly bad liar and she would have known instantly if he had betrayed her. But someone surely had. This led her thoughts back to Charles....

"I know all that!" Sylvia said, exasperated by her friend's long-winded recounting of the past weeks followed by a minute-long silence as she stared in thought at her half-finished cocktail. "What I want to know about is this vampire hunter Charles hooked you up with. Was he as bad as you thought?" She leaned forward, eager for the gory details.

"Worse." Unable to help it, Carmen leaned forward too. "Stubborn, barely sentient, and rude."

"Uh huh, but was he hot?" Sylvia prodded.

Carmen nodded, unable to hide her smile. "Very."

"So, how was he?"

Carmen shrugged, leaning back. "I didn't get the chance to find out."

"What? Are you telling me you didn't sample the other side before you killed him?" Sylvia feigned astonishment that such a thing could happen. It wouldn't have with her, of course. She would have drained the man dry in more ways than one. But ever since Carmen had suffered through a bad breakup almost a century ago the girl had avoided relationships like the plague.

In answer, Carmen took a sip of her drink and gave a small shrug.

Sylvia knew her friend, and she was dodging the question. Surprise and excitement welled up in Sylvia as she pressed on. "You didn't kill him! Carmen — you let him live! He knows what you look like, who you are! What were you thinking?"

"Of course I killed him. Do you think I'm stupid?" Carmen said dismissively before trying desperately to change the subject. "Now tell me what you've heard about the murders. What's going on?"

Sylvia eyes narrowed. Carmen was lying. That meant she liked the guy! Sylvia hadn't seen her friend interested in someone since Hector. God, was that a mistake; the man was as exciting as a brick wall. She decided to let the subject rest for now. She'd get Carmen drunk first, then pry the information out of her.

In the meantime, Sylvia told Carmen everything she had heard. Sylvia was always awash in the latest gossip. A constant stream flowed through her penthouse apartment in the Casino. She was untouchable there. Her security was amazing. She would have kept herself holed up in safety until this entire thing blew over but, like Carmen, she had to attend the Convocation. Sylvia consoled herself with being able to travel there with her friend rather than alone.

Carmen listened as Sylvia expounded upon the current theories of the murderer's identity. They ranged from old secret societies, to the European Council, to vampire anarchists, to the United States Government, to a member of their very own Council!

To Sylvia's knowledge no one besides Carmen had been attacked since the last three incidents, but then again everyone was in hiding. The only people who hadn't disappeared were herself, high up in her impregnable Casino, and Anne and Hugo in their massive Chicago estate. But even Anne and Hugo had doubled their security, particularly the armed human guards that were used during the day. Sylvia had even heard they hired a pair of trolls, the near un-killable thugs of the supernatural underworld.

A dull humming sound interrupted their conversation. "Mine or yours?" asked Sylvia, searching for her phone.

"Mine." Carmen took her phone out of her clutch. The caller I.D. read "Ron Frost," the same fake name Ryan had on his license and most of his credit cards.

It was Ryan. How had he gotten her number? She distinctly remembered not giving it to him. She found herself smiling anyway and was about to press the 'answer' button when Sylvia snatched the device from her hand.

"I wonder who this is?" Sylvia asked, studying the unfamiliar number on the phone's display.

"Sylvia, give it back."

"Why? This wouldn't be that vampire hunter you killed, would it? Making a collect call from the other side perhaps?"

Carmen was fuming. "I didn't have a chance to kill him, okay? Besides, he doesn't know who I am. He thinks I'm some nobody with a burning need to get to Chicago, running from a couple of vampires who want her dead. Don't worry about him. I lost him back in the Casino. There's no way he can find us."

"It seems like he's not in as much of a hurry to lose you, as you were to lose him. Though you did give him your number, so you weren't all that anxious to lose him after all, were you?" Sylvia asked, her brows raising playfully.

"No! I mean yes! I don't know how he got my number," Carmen finally said.

Sylvia laughed, "Of course you don't. It just slipped onto a napkin that wound up in his pocket. Or was it accidentally typed right into his phone?"

"I didn't give him my number!" Carmen protested as her phone began to vibrate again.

Sylvia glanced down at the phone. "Persistent though, isn't he? You must have really left an impression on the poor man. Tell me all about it."

"Sylvia, nothing happened. I already told you. Yes, he helped me out of a tight spot at the restaurant, but if it weren't for having to meet him there, I wouldn't have been in trouble in the first place. This wasn't my choice. Charles thrust him on me!"

"What I want to know is, once he was on you, did he keep thrusting?" Sylvia prompted.

"Sylvia! Please, there was no thrusting involved. As soon as I realized he was taking us through Vegas I was counting the hours until I could lose him and meet you."

"By my calculations you must have spent a whole day in a hotel room with the guy. And he was — what were the words you used? Very attractive? And nothing happened. Not even a snack?"

"Not even a snack," Carmen said as her phone began to ring once again.

"Liar." Sylvia smiled at her friend, and then answered the phone.

# Chapter 7

They were thirty minutes east of Las Vegas when Ryan spotted the tail. A black Yukon with tinted windows passed him before slowing down to settle in a few cars behind the Chrysler 300. He wouldn't have noticed it at all if it weren't for an identical second Yukon that passed him and planted itself behind the first one.

Ryan wasn't much on coincidences, and two identical SUVs that had been going twenty over the speed limit and now were content to follow along just under it were too much for him to buy. He had no idea how they found Carmen; the switch at the Casino parking garage had been pretty slick. The only reason Ryan caught on was because he recognized the shopping bags. There's no way they would have known about those.

Then it hit him. They had even done it before, at the restaurant where Ryan had first met her. They hadn't followed Carmen there, as he had assumed. She proved back at the Casino that she was smart enough to avoid being followed. They had found Carmen the same way he had found her at Midnight: they were almost definitely tracking her phone.

Most vampires weren't big embracers of technology. They were like your grandparents, the ones that could barely turn on their computer or program their DVR. But not all of them. A few welcomed the computer age, others were made while it was already underway, and some were clever enough to use computer-savvy humans. Things were changing.

Vampires using technology annoyed Ryan. It's like when they used guns, or martial arts. It upset the playing field.

A new thought occurred to Ryan. Jacob had said he had a line on two vampires. Both women. Both in Vegas. Both at the Midnight casino. No way was that a coincidence. Not only did someone know Carmen was headed through Vegas, but they knew that she would be meeting this second vampire shortly after she got there.

This had inside job all over it. It was someone who was either intimately familiar with Carmen and not only knew she had a friend in Vegas, but where that vampire would be. Or maybe someone was monitoring her communications and overheard Carmen setting up the meet with her friend on a phone call. Either way they were using hunters to do their dirty work.

Ryan activated the voice command in his car and impatiently recited Carmen's phone number, area code first, at the request of the pleasant lady's voice.

It rang four times before going through to voicemail. He left a message asking Carmen to call him. He didn't know if the call was being monitored, and didn't want to give himself away by leaving a voice message about the tail if it was.

Ryan called three more times in the next five minutes. All dumped straight to voicemail. It looked like he was going to have to wait for Beau's team to make a move, and then improvise.

He was reaching for the 'hang up' button on the car's display, when on the third ring of his fifth attempt someone picked up.

Sounds of commotion came through the Cadillac's speakers. "Sylvia, don't... I'll handle this... No! Give it to me!... Why don't you want me to talk to him if you're so innocent?...I don't care if you talk to him, I told you nothing happened. Now, let me have it... Obviously you *do* care, and something *did* happen or you wouldn't be so nervous… I'm not nervous, I'm annoyed. Sylvia, give me my phone!"

Finally a woman's voice answered. The sound was light and playful, and not Carmen. "Hello, Maria del Carmen de Luna's phone. May I help you?"

"What? Who is this? Put Carmen on," Ryan said. More sounds of scuffling came over the car's speakers.

"Whom may I say is calling?" asked the voice.

"It's Ryan."

"Last name?"

"Just Ryan."

"Well, Ryan Just Ryan, would you happen to be the unfortunate soul who was assigned to look after Carmen?"

"Yes."

"How sweet. Miss her already? Frankly it's a bit odd, though. Most people find her irritating."

"Could you please put her on?" Ryan was proud of how nice he asked, despite his growing frustration with the lady.

"You know, if she wanted to talk to you she would have picked up the first four times you called. Or maybe not ditched you in the first place. Calling this many times makes you either desperate or a stalker. Either way, it's not attractive."

"Look, I'm serious—" began Ryan.

"So am I. No one likes a guy that tries too hard."

Ryan took a deep breath and let it out slowly in an attempt to remain calm, momentarily forgetting about a vampire's keen sense of hearing.

"What's with the heavy breathing? Do you do this on a lot of calls?" The voice faded as she spoke away from the phone's microphone. "Wow, Carmen, no wonder you wanted to put miles between yourself and this guy."

"Yeah, he does that," came Carmen's voice. It was muffled, indicating she was farther away from her phone than the other lady. More rustling came over the wagon's speakers and then Carmen's voice became louder as she regained control of the phone. "Ryan, give it a rest. I'm fine. I'm with friends now. Go home."

Ryan was about to warn her, but there was more commotion as Sylvia wrested back the phone. "Tell me, vampire hunter, what was it like having to spend a night alone with a vampire? Did you get much sleep?"

Ryan wished he could have a night alone with this vampire. He suspected the results would be very different. "It was great. Now could you put Carmen back on, please?"

"You didn't have any urges to stake her? Because, you know, it's been awhile since she's had a good shaft thrust into her."

Even Ryan's human ears picked up the gasp and ensuing ruckus. There were more sounds that might have been blows.

"Sorry to disappoint you," Ryan said, "but there was only one bed, and while I really wanted to put my stake into her, I didn't want to have to sleep in the wet spot afterwards." Ryan could do corny innuendo too. But he was losing patience. If the delays went on much longer he was going to have to tell this bimbo about the tail in plain English and let the chips fall where they may. Ryan's hope that he would be able to convey the message to Carmen with more subtlety was rapidly dwindling.

"Wait!" said the voice. "There was only one bed? And you both slept in it?" Her voice faded again. "You didn't say anything about one bed!"

"That's because it wasn't important. Now would you grow up and give me back my phone?" The phone was now being held away from both of them.

"Wow, *that's* why you're so cranky." The voice got louder as she spoke back into the phone. "Did you know she's an absolute bitch when she hasn't had any? And she hasn't had any for a long, long time. Did you know her cold-fish attitude even earned her a nickname? You must have done something to really rev Carmen up and remind her how much she loves— Ow! Hey!"

That was it. Ryan gave up on being sly. He was going to have to tip his hand to anyone who might be listening and hope for the best.

Ryan shouted in his car, knowing the vampire's keen ears would hear him through the distant phone's speaker, despite their spat. "Carmen! You've got hunters on your tail. The two black SUVs a few cars back. Probably more waiting somewhere down the road. This phone might be compromised."

The sounds of scuffle ceased. Carmen's voice came though his car speaker loud and clear. "Wait, what are you talking about?"

"Isn't it obvious?" said the distant voice of the other vampire. "Your bodyguard changed his mind about not staking you, and called some of his friends to come and help him. Now he's having second thoughts."

"No," Ryan said. "If I wanted to kill her I would have done it already. There's a contract out on the two of you for half a million. A team followed you from the Midnight Casino. You're heading for a trap. You need to turn around and get back to Vegas before it's too late."

But it already was. Ryan didn't know if they were listening to the call, or if it was coincidence, but the semi-truck the 300 was passing suddenly swerved. It struck the Chrysler, sending it crashing off the highway and onto the broken ground of the dessert.

The Chrysler had accelerated to eighty to pass the truck when it was hit. The car's driver braked hard as his car rumbled over the desert, but before he could slow down any significant amount the vehicle's right front end hit a boulder.

The car flipped on its side and began careening across the desert, trailing massive plumes of sand before finally falling onto its roof. It plowed along for another dozen yards before its forward momentum stopped, and it spun slowly in place amidst a giant cloud of dust and smoke.

Ryan's car handled a lot better on the road than the pair of SUVs, but all that changed as soon as they got off of it. Ryan killed the Caddy's lights and brought his car to a sliding halt as the two Yukons pursued the out-of-control Chrysler.

Ryan hoped the hunters had been too intent on their prey to notice the station wagon slowing down one hundred yards behind them. The SUVs split up, each coming to a stop on opposite sides of the ruined 300.

Ryan flipped the auto-on switch of his dome light to off, then jumped out of his car and ran around to the back of the wagon. He had already committed to his next course of action. The job required it. If he was lucky, maybe he would find some way to live with the consequences.

He popped the hatch, unzipping the duffel bag and grabbing out an FN FAL rifle. It was an accurate gun, already set up with a night scope. He sprinted toward the still-spinning lights of the Chrysler 300, stumbling over the uneven ground of the dark desert as he searched for a good vantage point.

Before the 300 had even stopped rotating, the fire from automatic weapons lit up the night. Ryan went prone, turning on his rifle's scope and flipping open its front and rear dust covers. He sighted in on the scene almost a football field away.

Men had exited each of the SUVs and were using their vehicles as cover. They had stopped just past the Chrysler so they could catch the occupants in a crossfire without the risk of hitting each other.

Two men had taken up positions behind the SUV on the right, covering the passenger side of the 300. Three figures had exited the SUV to the left. Two of them covered the driver's side of the Chrysler, while the third crouched low behind the Yukon and began working on some type of a weapon.

The driver of the Chrysler was immediately cut down by bullets as he climbed out of the window. He rolled, still moving despite the shots slamming into him. It was obvious to both the hunters shooting him and to Ryan that he was a vampire, and a tough one.

The bullet-riddled driver managed to come up in a crouch, pull out a sidearm, and return fire. He was not only a heck of a shot but, as a vampire, he could see in the dark.

Ryan watched through his scope as one of the vampire's shots hit a hunter. The man's head snapped back and he dropped.

Another figure exited the passenger side of the 300. He dove out, rolled, and fired at the two men on his side. He was also trained but, unfortunately for him, was not a vampire. He was killed within seconds during the exchange of gunfire. The vampire hunters' assault rifles relentlessly riddled the man's body with bullets in case he hadn't been human.

The rear window of the Chrysler burst out. A high-heeled foot followed, and kept on kicking until the shattered sheet of glass fell to the sandy ground.

Ryan prepared to give the two girls cover fire when he saw the figure that had been working on the weapon behind the car to the right stand and ready his toy. It was a rocket-propelled grenade launcher.

Ryan was a natural shooter, rather than a sniper. He was deadly at close range with iron sights. In the heat of combat he could make impossible shots, instinctively hitting targets, even ones that were moving fast.

Ryan was much less impressive at long range using a scope. Even at only one hundred yards, an easy shot for a trained marksman, Ryan had problems. As soon as he had time to think about a shot, his accuracy decreased dramatically, to the point where he tried to avoid it. He left the long range stuff to more competent people.

Because of this Ryan didn't even attempt to do something clever like go for a wounding shot in the leg, or shoot the RPG out of the man's hands. Instead Ryan sighted the crosshairs over the man's center of mass, the largest target possible. One that would likely kill the victim. Ryan fired at the hunter holding the RPG, wondering as he pulled the trigger if he knew the man.

Ryan wasn't sure if his first bullet hit the target and threw the man off his aim, or if the guy was a really bad shot and managed to miss all on his own. Whatever the reason, an instant after Ryan fired the RPG went off, sending its rocket streaking forward to strike the front of the car, rather than the passenger compartment.

The vampire driver disappeared in the ensuing explosion, which momentarily lit up Ryan's night vision optics. As soon as it cleared Ryan fired his second shot. There was no doubt that the second bullet struck true. There was a spray of blood from the target. The spent RPG fell to the ground, followed by the man who had dropped it.

Carmen and Sylvia sprang out of the rear of the burning Chrysler to find themselves instantly caught in a hail of gunfire. The two vampires made a break for the open desert at impossible speed while bullets tore into them. It looked like they both might make it until one of them was struck by the large wooden shaft of an arbalest, a giant crossbow favored in the vampire hunting business.

It missed her heart, instead piercing her kidney. She kept running until the line went taut. The thin, but extremely strong, cable held her slender frame in check for a heartbeat before it hauled her backwards off her feet.

After killing the man with the RPG, Ryan switched his focus to the hunter next to him. He wanted to clear all of the hostiles from one side, giving Carmen a clean escape route.

Ryan fired several rounds before one finally struck home. The man jerked a bit and stood upright for a second or two, taking his time before slowly sliding down the side of the Yukon. As he slid he dropped his weapon, his hands moving to clutch his wounded side.

Ryan moved his scope to the right to sight in on the second set of shooters. He stopped, and then backtracked to where he had scanned past the outline of a woman against the flames. She was being dragged backwards along the desert.

Ryan heard Carmen scream the name "Sylvia!" as he moved his aim back to the remaining hunters. He couldn't get a clear shot at either of the two men. They must have realized that Ryan was out there shooting at them, because both of them had ducked behind their vehicle.

Ryan rose from his cover, running sideways and forward across the desert until the two men came into view around the SUV.

Ryan realized the pair had spotted him when a bullet whizzed by his head an instant before the crack of gunfire.

That wasn't right, Ryan thought. There shouldn't have been a delay like that. A bullet beating the sound by that much meant the shot had come from a lot farther off than the two remaining hunters Ryan was running toward.

That's when Ryan saw the semi parked off in the distance, the one that had ran the Chrysler off of the road. The truck was stopped alongside the highway over four hundred yards away. Blinking yellow hazard lights outlined its rectangular shape. There was a flash from the window.

Another whiz followed by a bang signaled a second near miss. Sniper. And he was targeting Ryan.

Ryan increased his speed and began to zigzag.

Now that the winch on the front of the SUV was reeling in the vampire, the hunter dropped the giant crossbow in favor of a shotgun. He began scanning the darkness for whoever had been shooting at them while his compatriot covered his back in case the second vampire hadn't fled and was instead circling around to have a go at them.

Ryan fired at the pair of hunters. His shots got their attention, and both of them were looking his way now. They brought their guns to bear. The three men exchanged fire as Ryan ran toward them at an angle, trying to make himself a harder target for not only them, but also the sniper.

Ryan hit the first one, dropping the man as he felt hard strikes against his own body armor. The hunter Ryan had just killed used an M4 rifle, and the smaller 5.56 millimeter rounds failed to penetrate Ryan's Kevlar vest. Instead the bullets flattened, turning into jarring impacts. Ryan felt like he was being rabbit punched in the chest by a welterweight boxer, or hit with a hammer.

The second hunter was using a 12 gauge shotgun. The buckshot the man fired was also stopped by the vest, but Ryan saw the man quickly eject the remaining shells and load new ones into the bottom of the shotgun. Ryan guessed the hunter figured he was a vampire and was busy correcting his choice of ammo.

Sylvia kept running despite hearing Carmen scream out her name. She ran until the bullets stopped coming for her. Then she altered course, circling through the darkness to come back at their attackers.

She had been hit several times, and the wounds in her leg were slowing her down. Even so, she was fast. She ignored the agony that wracked her body. Bullets might not kill, but they still hurt like hell.

As she drew nearer to the cars she moved low, pausing for an instant to tear off her high-heeled shoes and fling them to the side. Barefoot she was not only faster, but completely silent.

A gun battle raged behind the far SUV. The man hired to protect Carmen must have been following them as well. Sylvia watched as he traded bullets with two hunters while Carmen was thrashing on the ground, being steadily pulled toward the front of the Yukon.

Sylvia came up to the nearest Yukon and found two hunters. The first one was dead. The second lay slumped against the SUV, hand pressed against his side. He was talking into an earpiece. The man saw her at the last instant, and almost had time to draw the handgun from its holster before she tore his head off. She discarded the head and moved on to circle their burning wreckage of a car, making her way toward the second SUV that shielded the two remaining hunters.

Ryan was less than ten yards away now. He had thrown down his empty rifle and pulled out a handgun. Combat was different than practice. Men who could nail the bull's-eye on a target range all day long, even trained soldiers and law enforcement officers, lost their aim when real combat started. Especially when it was close, and death became a distinct possibility. Ryan had no such issues. He thrived in combat. He entered a different state, like a professional ball player entering the Zone.

As Sylvia got within a few dozen yards behind the two hunters, the man to her left dropped as a bullet blew through the back of his skull. Further off Sylvia saw the man who killed him, and assumed it must be Ryan. He was already firing his handgun at the remaining hunter.

The second hunter, Beau, raised his shotgun as his colleague fell dead at his side. The vampire he had shot with the grappling hook, the one with a half-million dollar bounty on her head, was now at the SUV pinned to the winch, shrieking in agony. The vampire's bodyguard was shifting his aim toward Beau. The guy was good and Beau had to make a split second decision.

Beau made his choice. He hoped the sniper in the truck would take care of the bodyguard as he went for the winched vamp. He turned to fire his shotgun at point-blank range into her head. The shotgun was now loaded with dragon's breath rounds. They were specially designed to spew thirty feet of flame. From this range it would almost certainly finish the vampire.

The sniper was too slow.

# # #

Carmen couldn't help screaming as the winch continued pulling the grappling hook inward. Now that she was snug against the SUV and had no more room to move, the hook began tearing through her.

She reached behind her back, struggling to find the clip that held the cable to the bolt. Out of the corner of her eye she caught the hunter aim his gun at her head. She closed her eyes. It had been a long life.

She heard three shots, but none of them hit her. Then came the sound of something heavy and metal falling to the ground.

Beau was struck three times before he could pull the trigger. His Kevlar vest took the first two rounds that hit him, but the third shattered his ulna. He dropped the shotgun. Reflex and training sent his good hand moving instinctively to his waist. His pistol cleared the holster and rose upward to focus on his attacker.

"Gun?" Beau said with a frown, before a pair of simultaneous booms. In the same instant Ryan's bullet struck Beau's forehead, the sniper finally fired, blowing a hole through Ryan's chest.

The sounds of the next two shots were so close together they could have been one. But still she didn't die. Carmen opened her eyes and turned. The hunter was down. Ten feet in front of him so was Ryan.

Several more booming shots came from far away, accompanied by a man's scream that was prematurely cut short.

The winch continued to pull, the splayed out bars of the grappling hook making their way through her. Carmen hurt so bad it was almost impossible to focus. Finally, she released the clip. Freed, she staggered forward, grabbing the front of the hook and pulling as hard and fast as she could. She screamed, dropping to her knees as it came out, pulling parts of her with it.

Carmen crawled over to Ryan. The agonizing journey felt like an eternity and when she finally made it she half fell on top of him. He had been shot several times in the chest, but one large hole gushed blood. Carmen placed her hand on his throat. She could feel his pulse, but instead of crashing through her like it should have, it was a faint reverberation, like a far off drum preparing for its last beat.

Carmen touched her wrist to his mouth and prepared to bring the nail of her other hand down across it in a slashing motion, but before she could open herself up a hand grabbed hers and yanked it back.

"Are you crazy? Do you seriously expect me to lug around both of you? Go drink that guy there before he coagulates. I'll save your hero." Sylvia pushed Carmen toward where Beau lay, then bent over Ryan. She performed the same gesture Carmen had been about to, though she let her blood fall a few inches into his mouth, rather than touch him. Hunters weren't the cleanest of men, and there was no telling where this one had been.

When Sylvia had given Ryan enough of her blood to guarantee that he would pull through, she helped Carmen drain the hunter. The man's blood helped her body heal its own wounds.

Once Sylvia was sated, she went for the only car that wasn't bullet-ridden or on fire. She pulled the station wagon up to the carnage and helped Carmen put Ryan into the back seat. She grabbed the weapons Ryan had dropped and tossed them into the back of the wagon. Sylvia then kicked the trunk of the Chrysler several times until it vomited its contents onto the ground. Amazingly, their luggage hadn't had a chance to burn, though she noted with a scowl that it hadn't had as much luck resisting the gunfire.

Sylvia watched Carmen crawl in the back seat next to Ryan and shut the door behind her. Sylvia sighed, and then transferred their luggage into the wagon. She briefly scanned the area to make sure she hadn't forgotten anything, then got into the car and fired up the engine. She pulled onto the highway and mashed the gas pedal. The Cadillac roared to life, putting distance between them and the red and blue lights that now converged on the burning wreckage.

# Chapter 8

"Get rid of your phones." They were the first words Ryan had spoken since being shot four hours before.

"Why, it was our pleasure for saving your ass. You're very welcome," was Sylvia's even reply.

Ryan knew the lady behind the voice was annoyed, but not seriously so. What bothered him was how he knew it. Ryan's gray eyes opened a crack to meet a pair of concerned brown ones. "Get rid of the phones. Now. It's how they're tracking you."

"Seriously, not even a thank you for saving your life?" said Sylvia over her shoulder.

"Thank you," Ryan said. Then he frowned, but not because he thanked her, it was because he had *wanted* to thank her, to make her feel appreciated. It might make her less annoyed.

Oh god, Ryan thought — the vampire had gotten to him. Somehow, when he had been knocked unconscious, this vampire must have used her mind control powers on him.

Carmen extended her hand between the front seats and wiggled her fingers until Sylvia hushed and put her smartphone into Carmen's palm. A cool rush of air entered the cabin as the rear window went down.

Carmen was going to toss the phones out the window when she saw Ryan. What she saw alarmed her: Ryan had gone so pale she wondered if he had internal bleeding.

Maybe Sylvia hadn't given him enough of her blood. "Are you okay?" Carmen asked, staring down at him.

Why the sympathy? Ryan didn't understand, but nodded grimly. "I'm fine. Take your sim cards out first, before you toss the phones." Ryan willed his hand to move down to a cargo pocket on his pants. It wouldn't reach. He tried to bend, but the pain almost knocked him out.

His vision clouded. A soft swirl of burgundy and purple washed across his face, the scent of iron and perfume filled his nostrils. Fingers tickled his thigh as a hand reached into his pocket. Then the strange vision was gone and he could see again.

Carmen now held three phones in her hand. She took the first and turned it around, staring at it.

Ryan explained to Carmen what a sim card was, and then talked her through how to locate and remove it. As a testament to how sad a state he was in, it wasn't until Carmen removed the third card, almost two minutes later, that Ryan realized his head was resting in her lap, and that it was damp with either his or her blood.

Once Carmen finally managed to get the last card out of its slot, all three phones went out the window somewhere along Highway 15 in the Rocky Mountains.

"And what if we need to call somebody? It's not as if there are a lot of payphones around these days," Sylvia complained.

She was annoyed again and Ryan was annoyed with her. "My advice is, don't," he said. "But if you really feel like alerting someone to our location so you can get shot at some more, there are a couple of burners in my bag. You can use those."

"Burners? Is that some type of drug I haven't heard of? I didn't think that was possible," Sylvia asked.

"Not drugs. Pre-paid phones. Disposables. No GPS. Use 'em if you have to, but please don't tell anyone where we are. I doubt there's enough left of my vest to stop any more bullets."

"Seeing as it didn't stop the last one, I'd say you were right. I don't suppose your vest came with a warranty?" Carmen teased. The small smile that played at her lips was her way of trying to make the best out of a bad situation that kept getting worse.

"What do you mean?" Ryan tried to concentrate on areas of pain. To his surprise there weren't many. He remembered being grazed in the leg, but he barely registered that one anymore. He knew he had been hit several times in the chest when he was running at the last two hunters, but none of those bullets had gone through his vest. Even his shoulder that had been hit by the crossbow two days ago felt okay. In fact the only real pain was smack dab in the middle of his chest. That guy still hurt. A lot. Ryan tried to remember being hit there, and couldn't.

He remembered Beau's confused look as he recognized Ryan. He heard Beau say his name as he tried to raise his weapon. He remembered killing Beau.

Beau had been the last hunter standing. So who had shot him? No. Not the last. Ryan remembered that there had been a sniper in the truck, one with the high-powered rifle. That must be who had hit him. But there was no way the lightweight vest Ryan was wearing could have stopped that rifle.

Simple answer: it hadn't, of course. A new chill eclipsed the last one. The vampires hadn't mind-controlled him. They had turned him. *That's* why he could feel Sylvia! He was a vampire.

Oh crap, oh crap, oh crap, oh crap. Ryan's mind whirled at the revelation.

"Are you *sure* you're okay?" asked Carmen. Ryan had gone even paler, if that were possible. "I'm giving you a little more."

Ryan's eyes widened in horror as Carmen placed her slender wrist up to his mouth. "Here, drink this, you'll be fine." She moved to cut her own wrist, but stopped as Ryan turned his head away. For a second she thought he might shatter his image as a tough guy and start whining, but he didn't.

He regained his composure quickly and turned back to stare directly into her eyes for the first time since they met at the restaurant. Since Ryan had realized what she was. Carmen remembered how those gray eyes struck her then. Intense, piercing, incredibly sexy. The pain she saw in them now was terrible.

"Kill me," he said.

"What?" Carmen didn't know what was going on with Ryan. Maybe he had gone into shock, or was having some type of post traumatic episode. Then it hit her. He had killed several humans to save her life. Maybe he couldn't live with himself, with the realization of what he had done. Ryan had decided he was a murderer of innocents and couldn't live with it.

"Are you fucking kidding me?" Sylvia said.

Oh no, thought Ryan, Sylvia was angry. He had upset her again. While Ryan struggled with his dismay over Sylvia's displeasure she continued, "We go to all that trouble saving you, and now you want us to kill you? I'm sorry, but if you want to die you're going to have to do it your own damn self."

Carmen felt her own regret surface at Ryan's grief. She knew what it was like to make decisions that would haunt you forever. She stroked his cheek trying to lend him comfort. "Thank you for coming for me. I owe you my life."

Ryan's bitter laughter shocked her. "If you were really thankful, you would have let me die."

"Okaaay," Carmen said pulling her hand away. None of Ryan's reactions in the past minute were what she had expected.

"Why did you do it? Some sort of sick joke?" Ryan asked.

"Why did we save you?" Carmen was so confused.

"I'd rather be dead than one of you."

Oh. Now she understood. Ryan thought they turned him. She winced. He would rather die than become what she was. Did he truly hate vampires that much? She imagined he did; after all, he killed her kind for a living.

"Carmen can you please stick a sock in Mister Melodrama back there?" asked Sylvia.

Sylvia wasn't angry any more. Now she was back to being merely annoyed. Ryan breathed an involuntary sigh of relief at the improvement. "Why did you turn me?" Ryan pressed Carmen.

"Why the hell would I want to turn you?" Sylvia answered before Carmen could speak. "Seriously. Who'd want to spend all eternity with GI Joe? I told Carmen it was a mistake to have me save you."

"Wait, *she* did it?" Ryan exclaimed, his tone accusatory. He was in shock. Now it made sense. Why it was Sylvia who Ryan felt, and not Carmen. For some reason the idea that Carmen let someone else turn him hurt. Why hadn't she done it herself? Was he that repulsive to her, or simply that inconsequential, that she asked another to do it?

Carmen opened her mouth to explain, but again Sylvia beat her to it. "Your girlfriend there was about to, but I stopped her before she became a martyr and bled out on top of you. Then I would have had to haul both of your asses into the car. As it was, she almost didn't make it. I think she was worse off than you were."

Ryan chewed on the idea that Carmen had tried to save him before saving herself. The idea that a vampire could do anything like that was foreign to him. The implications were troubling, almost more troubling than Sylvia's annoyance. Almost more trouble than where his head was resting as he lay there defenseless.

Ryan focused his attention on Carmen. She was staring out the window, a strange expression on her face. It was sadness, he thought. "You let her turn me?"

Carmen glanced down at him. "Of course not. No one turned you."

"Is he an idiot? I just told him that," said Sylvia.

"Then why can I feel her?" asked Ryan.

"Because she gave you her blood. Sometimes, especially when a vampire is old, a person that receives their blood develops a bond with them. Feels their emotions. If blood is shared the bond can go both ways," Carmen explained.

Ryan's eyes went wide again and Carmen jumped in to head off another of Ryan's assisted suicide pleas. "Relax. It only lasts until the blood is out of your system. You won't be forever stuck having to endure Sylvia's rampant lust."

"Better my lust than your calculated frigidness," Sylvia called back. "Maybe we can do an experiment: Ryan can try your blood next time and see whose emotions he likes better."

Lust? Ryan thought. So far all he got from Sylvia was various degrees of annoyance. Though it was fading now. It was being replaced by something different. Something warmer. Something primal. Ryan felt a stirring in his groin as Sylvia did something in the front seat.

"Stop that!" Ryan croaked. Sylvia giggled.

In a state of panic Ryan thought about baseball. Baseball. It was American. Nothing erotic about pitching a ball. He controlled his breathing. Letting out slow controlled breaths, focusing on what it was like to pitch a baseball. Breathe in. Breathe out.

Carmen glared at the front seat. "Sylvia, stop teasing Ryan. If any more blood leaves his main system he's going to pass out."

"He's doing the heavy breathing thing again," noted Sylvia.

Ryan peered up at Carmen, who was busy giving the back of Sylvia's head a dirty look. Ryan decided that if he was going to lust after anyone it would be Carmen. As the idea began to take hold Ryan felt a renewed sense of panic. He balked at the notion, forcing his mind to shift its focus back to baseball. When it wouldn't cooperate, he tried thinking about the task at hand. "We need to ditch this car."

"Why? I never thought I'd say this about a station wagon, but I kind of like it," said Sylvia.

"Because it might have been reported stolen," Ryan explained. "There was a little misunderstanding back at the casino when I picked it up. Apparently the valet got some crazy notion that it belonged to someone else." He stared pointedly at Carmen, who suddenly found something outside the window that caught her interest.

"Plus, the back window is missing and it's riddled with bullet holes. We're going to get pulled over," Ryan said.

"Fine, I'll take care of it," Sylvia said. They drove a few more minutes in silence before Sylvia pulled into the parking lot of a large truck stop. She parked the car in the shadows of an empty section of parking lot far away from the main building. Ryan continued to rest in Carmen's lap as Sylvia changed into something less bloody in the front seat. Once dressed, she headed out onto the asphalt in search of a replacement vehicle.

Ryan must have dozed off, because the next thing he remembered was starting awake when Sylvia opened the door to his car and smiled down at him. She was twirling a key ring around her finger. Attached to the ring was a bright green rabbit's foot.

Ryan insisted he could walk on his own, but Carmen supported him anyway. She knew he was too stubborn for his own good and, sure enough, as soon as they started walking Ryan almost collapsed. Carmen propped him up, but she could tell Ryan was trying not to put any weight on her, despite the fact that he could barely remain upright. She tightened her grip around his waist, forcing him to lean on her.

Together they followed Sylvia to a shiny apple-green tractor trailer.

"Who's going to drive that thing?" Carmen asked, staring up at the behemoth in disbelief.

"Me! I always wanted to try," said Sylvia, opening the door to the semi and tossing the bags she had removed from the wagon into the sleeper cab.

"I thought your license was suspended." Carmen said.

"It was, so I got a new one under a different name." Sylvia licked her lips as she tried to figure out where to put the key.

Carmen climbed up into the cab and took a look around. "Ew. This guy was not big on hygiene. Remind me to stop and get some disinfectant wipes on the way."

"How long before the owner misses it?" asked Ryan. He ignored Carmen's proffered hand, and struggled to get himself up into the truck.

Sylvia beamed. "He was so happy to give it to me, I'd wager we'll be in Chicago before he changes his mind, or even remembers it's gone."

Sylvia finally got the truck started, and after they pulled up to Ryan's car and transferred the rest of the luggage, Sylvia managed to get the rig rolling towards the highway, serenading them with a chorus of grinding gears.

They didn't have much time before dawn, and only managed another fifty miles before pulling over at a La Quinta hotel outside of Grand Junction.

After pushing the clerk into giving them a room, Sylvia let Ryan and Carmen into the hotel via a side entrance. Unless they could have convinced people they were extras in a zombie apocalypse movie, their sorry state would have raised too many questions had they hobbled through the lobby. As luck would have it no early risers came out of their room to witness the bloody duo shamble down the corridor.

Ryan was unhappy that they only got one room, but overjoyed to find that the room they did get came with two beds. The alternative was unthinkable.

The first thing he tried to do once he was in the room was remove his shirt. He failed. Despite the vampire blood working its healing magic in his system, it was too painful to move his arms up high enough. He gave up on the shirt, deciding it could wait until morning, or night, or whatever vampires called it when they got up. Ryan eyed the bed closest to the window with longing and shuffled towards it.

"Oh no, you don't. Not in that state," said Carmen, walking up to Ryan.

Ryan grunted and continued to shuffle. Why did it matter? It wasn't as if he would be sharing the bed with anyone. It was his blood and grime, and he could wallow in it if he wanted to.

Carmen stepped in front of him, cutting off his path to the warm inviting bed. It was clear Carmen wasn't going to give in, and Ryan was too tired to argue or shuffle around her. He tried to raise his arms again. And again he failed. He looked like some sort of sad bird that had been hit by a car and was futilely trying to flap away.

"Don't bother," Carmen said, taking Ryan's shirt in her two hands and pulling it apart. The cotton ripped. Sylvia stepped up and helped Carmen remove the shirt. Next came the vest. Once it was off, Sylvia held it in front of Ryan, wiggling her finger through the holes to demonstrate that the bullet had, in fact, gone clean through him.

The undershirt was the worst. Dried blood had adhered every inch of the cotton fabric to Ryan's skin. Carmen worked to peel off the front, while Sylvia did the back. Ryan was becoming increasingly uncomfortable with two vampires surrounding his bloody body.

His discomfort must have shown, because Sylvia asked, "What? Don't you enjoy having two women rip your clothes off in a hotel room? I was pretty sure that was every guy's fantasy."

Once the final tatters of the shirt were removed Sylvia admired what was underneath. "Oh my. Now I understand why you wanted to save him." She circled Ryan appraisingly, running a hand over his bare chest, letting her fingers trail across his shoulder and back as she slowly walked around him.

Ryan flinched at her touch, though it was as gentle as a feather.

When Sylvia's hand brushed over the oozing wound in his back, Ryan whirled on her, almost falling over as he did so.

Sylvia smiled at him innocently as she raised her finger to her lips and took a step back. "I was only looking."

Too woozy to remember to avert his gaze Ryan got his first eyeful of Sylvia, and had to admit it was not unpleasant. She was a vampire's vampire. Predatory, hungry, a sleek body punctuated by pouting lips, large breasts, curved hips, gorgeous legs....

*Wait, no!* Ryan purged the thoughts from his mind. The brief time he spent with Carmen had ruined him. Ryan was humanizing all of them now, not just Carmen. Never humanize your prey; it makes it difficult to kill them afterward. It's why you don't name your cattle if you're a rancher, or watch Bambi before you go deer hunting.

Once Ryan regained his senses he took a second look at Sylvia, trying to be subjective this time. She had died in her early twenties. She was a couple of inches taller than Carmen. Her hair was longer, and a much lighter shade of brown. Her eyes were a striking crystal blue. As with most vampires, she was beautiful. Her only imperfection, if you could call it that, was a slight dusting of freckles across her nose and cheeks. She was the farmer's daughter who had every hayseed for miles around falling over himself.

As Ryan teetered Carmen voice came from behind him, "I don't think he's saved yet."

Sylvia cocked an eyebrow. "Fine. But you do the honors this time, since you've obviously been dying to."

Carmen circled around to take Ryan's hands in hers. She found his grip warm and firm despite his sorry state. She led him to the foot of the bed he had been trying to get to earlier. He followed her complacently, mostly because he didn't have enough energy left to do much else.

"Sit down," she told him. Ryan sat in front of her. His posture was perfect, but he swayed dangerously back and forth. His eyes tracked Sylvia as she plucked some things out of her suitcase.

"You need to drink." Carmen held out her wrist to Ryan, who recoiled in horror and almost fell backwards onto the bed. "Look, you're hurt. It could be bad," she said, her patience waning.

Sylvia spoke up. "Maybe it's the wrist that's the problem. Why don't you try offering him a more tempting body part and see if he's receptive?"

"Why don't you take your shower?" Carmen suggested.

Sylvia shrugged. "I'm only saying there are much more interesting alternatives you could use than a wrist. If you want any ideas, let me know. I have a pair of them."

Carmen looked for something to throw at Sylvia, but her friend closed the bathroom door before she could find a suitable projectile.

"She's impossible! Anyway, you're in bad shape. You need this." Carmen thrust her wrist at him. Between Ryan's bull-headed stubbornness and her own pain pulsing through her body, her patience was wearing thin.

"I'm fine," Ryan said. He was loopy from blood loss, and his brain was involuntarily thinking of other parts of Carmen's anatomy she could be offering to him.

"You're not," Carmen frowned as Ryan developed a lazy smile. "What are you thinking about? And how are you supposed to protect Sylvia and me if you can barely stand?"

"I'm not here to protect her; I'm here to protect *you*."

Despite herself, Carmen smiled at the emphasis Ryan had put on the word you. "And can you honestly do that in your state?" she asked him. "Sure, now that you have Sylvia's blood in you, you won't die. You'll eventually get better on your own. And maybe in two or three weeks you could be raring to go. But by then it won't matter, because I'll be dead and you along with me."

She held out her wrist. Still he resisted, his head moving away from the offending appendage.

"I won't turn you, I promise," Carmen said softly.

Ryan's head dropped an inch and Carmen watched the internal struggle boil within him.

Carmen decided another strategy was in order. She took a half step forward, moving her hand away from

Ryan's face to run it through his hair. She enjoyed the feeling of his short cut. It was like running her hands the wrong way through a cat's fur.

Ryan started at her touch, but then remained still as she continued to rub his scalp. She brought her other hand up, using both hands to massage his head. After a minute his eyes closed.

The shower began to run as Carmen took another half step forward and guided Ryan toward her until his forehead rested between her breasts. She continued to massage his scalp.

His shoulders tensed as he realized what she had done, though he didn't pull away. She moved one hand down to his shoulder and began to knead the tight muscles, slowly working them until he gradually relaxed beneath her hand. Then she moved the other hand down to work on the other side, and before long the tension began to melt out of him.

Carmen slowly pulled herself away, keeping Ryan in place with her hands. He sat there relaxed, his head hanging. She kept kneading his shoulders as she moved around him to climb up on the bed.

Her chest brushed his arm as she circled behind him. She felt the hard bare muscles through her thin silk shirt.

She ran a hand down each of his arms, fingers gliding over muscles, admiring their every contour. She brought her hands up to his biceps and pulled him slowly against her. There was no resistance this time as the heat of his back pressed against her.

She continued rubbing the kinks out of his arms and shoulders before moving her hands around to his chest, then along his sides. Gently caressing his abdomen, Carmen smiled as the rippled muscles caused her fingers to jump as they moved up and down.

She brought her head forward and rested her chin on Ryan's shoulder, her cheek against his. The stubble was rough, like sandpaper, but she didn't mind. She explored his chest for a while longer, noting how slow and relaxed Ryan's breathing had become. She couldn't resist the urge to kiss his cheek, just a brush of her lips against him. He moved, almost imperceptibly. So subtlely that maybe she had imagined it.

She kissed him on the cheek again, and this time she was sure he had moved. But it hadn't been away; it had been ever so slightly toward her mouth. She nicked her wrist with a nail quickly, so the one hand could resume massaging his rock-hard chest.

She brought her wrist to his mouth while her lips kissed his ear. She whispered, "Please." Then kissed him again, lingering on his earlobe.

She felt Ryan's mouth unsteadily find her arm. Then his hand grasped her wrist, but it didn't pull her away. It held her steady as his tongue sampled her.

Her mouth moved down the back of his neck, spending time there before moving down to his shoulders as Ryan began to drink. Carmen brought her free hand around his side, scooting back enough to allow her access to his back. She was tracing a particularly long scar when she saw the trickle of blood wander down from the exit wound.

Carmen thought that Ryan must have opened the wound when he leaned back against her. The trickle was slowing rapidly as both her blood and Sylvia's kicked Ryan's natural healing process into hyperdrive. The coagulation was almost instantaneous.

Carmen moved her mouth down along his shoulder blade to meet the crimson line. She wanted only a taste. A single kiss. She smiled as the warm liquid entered her mouth. Her saliva would keep the blood from clotting and she didn't want that, so she moved away from the wound. But there was more that could be freely had. Carmen scooted back a little so she could bend down farther, tracing her tongue up Ryan's back where the blood had run. She paused every inch to kiss him. She had made it almost all the way back up to the wound when Ryan froze.

Ryan sat stock still for a second before he jerked his mouth away from Carmen's wrist. What was he doing? Oh my god, Ryan thought, he had let Carmen seduce him.

He had allowed her to use her hypnotic powers to force him into drinking her blood, coerce him into letting her kiss him!

Ryan got up, rapidly disentangling himself from the vampire. He half expected Carmen to resist, to attack him. But she didn't. As soon as he began to retreat from her, she pulled back as well.

Ryan stood shakily and turned to her, his eyes accusing. He saw the smear of blood on her chin. His blood. She looked away.

"You said I'd be okay! You drank from me! I'm going to turn!"

Ryan hadn't heard Sylvia coming. He would never admit it to himself, but Ryan had been so caught up in Carmen that he hadn't even heard the shower shut off minutes before, hadn't felt Sylvia's satisfaction at having been clean. So when the sharp sting of her slap hit him on the back of his neck, it caught him completely unaware.

"Give it a rest, moron. You're not going to turn. For a vampire hunter you're pretty ignorant. It's a one-way deal: you turn by ingesting our blood. Yours has nothing to do with it. Well, mostly."

"Mostly?" Ryan echoed, turning toward Sylvia as he rubbed the back of his neck with his good hand.

"You are such a baby," she said.

Carmen spoke, her voice distant. "Our ingesting your blood doesn't in any way impact your turning. You know how you can feel Sylvia's emotions? She meant that it can happen in reverse. If we ingest a person's blood when they have ours in their system, then the link can go both ways. We can feel their emotions."

It was then that Ryan realized if he concentrated he could separate the emotions washing over him. The anger he felt was genuinely his, the annoyance was certainly Sylvia's, and then there was something from Carmen. Disappointment — not hunger, not anger — just *disappointment* with a touch of something else. Hurt?

He knew he had caused it, and he didn't know how to react. So he went for his duffel bag, surprised that he was already feeling more steady. He unzipped the bag and grabbed a pair of sweats and some clean underwear out of it.

Ryan walked toward the bathroom, then stopped suddenly. "Wait. You said a person is turned by drinking a vampire's blood!"

"Yeah, so?" Sylvia said.

"I've had both of yours tonight!"

Sylvia shrugged. "So stop getting shot."

Sylvia ended her advice there, but at Ryan's horrified look Carmen added, "Relax, you haven't ingested enough to turn. You'd know it if you had. Your body would be overwhelmed, you'd develop a major fever, and then you'd die. But in all seriousness, Sylvia is correct. Don't get shot again, because if you need our blood to survive, one more dose in the next day or two and it's better than fifty-fifty that you *will* turn. Or, if the bullet actually kills you outright, you already have enough of our blood in your system for you to turn anyway. Though changing that way is much riskier."

"How?" Ryan asked, trying to figure out how that would be possible.

"Because," Sylvia said, "if you die of an overdose then, by definition, you should have plenty of blood to successfully complete the transition. If you die of something else, you might not have enough. And you know what happens then, right? You either end up as a feral vampire or a zombie. Both of those options kind of suck."

Sylvia smiled and a less-than-placated Ryan walked into the bathroom without saying another word. Ryan turned on the shower and tried to ignore the smell of scented soaps and lotions that permeated the air. He tried even harder to ignore the fact that he was two-thirds along the way to becoming a member of the undead.

He looked in the mirror, opened his mouth, and checked his canines first by eye, then with the tip of a finger to see if there was any unnatural elongation. Not finding any, he shut his mouth and surveyed his wounds.

Once Ryan confirmed that both the entry and exit wounds were already scabbed over, he took full advantage of their advanced healing and stood under the warm water and tried to collect his thoughts.

How had he let himself get to this point? Why hadn't he walked away from the job the instant he found out what Carmen was? Why hadn't he killed her? She had no problem using her powers to feed from him, to force him to drink her blood.

But she hadn't used any powers.

In fact, Ryan realized that Carmen had made a point to not once enter into eye contact with him. She even went so far as to move behind him, making it impossible. The choice of what had happened on the bed had been entirely his own, and that's what troubled him the most.

# Chapter 9

Ryan awoke to find that he was once again sleeping with a woman. This time was almost stranger than last, considering that this time he remembered going to bed alone. Sylvia and Carmen shared the bed farthest from the window while he had taken the other.

Neither woman had spoken to him after his shower. Well, Carmen hadn't spoken to him; Sylvia talked incessantly, but hadn't said anything worth remembering.

Ryan had wanted to say something to Carmen, to acknowledge her help. He had spent the twenty minutes while it was Carmen's turn to shower tuning out Sylvia's nonsense and trying to come up with the right thing to say. But he had failed, and in the end they had gone to bed in silence.

But now here she was, lying against him. He was pretty sure she was naked. He knew she hadn't gone to bed that way. He would have remembered that. In fact, he distinctly remembered Carmen wearing something black and silky that she must have picked up during their visit to the mall. What there was of it clung to her curves and apparently elicited the appropriate reaction from Ryan, because a triumphant smile played at Carmen's lips before she crawled in to the other bed and shut off the light.

Ryan forced himself back to the present. Like the previous morning, he moved his arm up and around to find her bare back. Yup, she was naked. And like before, when he put his arm around her, she snuggled closer against him, only this morning there was an associated murmur of contentment.

Sometime later she began to stir by his side and Ryan realized that he had been absent-mindedly trailing his fingers down the back of her body. The movement must have woken her, but he remembered how good she looked before going to bed that morning, and he let his fingers continue to roam.

The first time he allowed his hand to stray as far as the small of her back before changing its direction. Each subsequent time he let his hand stray a little bit further before calling it off and sending it on its way towards her neck....

She was definitely awake now, surprised, but not complaining. She had abandoned the other bed several hours ago, giving up on sleep after being slowly pushed to the edge of the mattress. She thought she'd get a decent day's rest in this one, but had no idea it would culminate in an even better afternoon!

Ryan had been a blissfully unmoving sleeper, and she had been resting soundly until she felt his hand move out from between them, only to come back and wrap around, her pulling her close.

His hand began to caress her back, almost tender in its exploration. The sensation caused her to purr as she moved her arm slowly across his chest, her hand opening so its entire surface traveled over his body to take in the firm chest, careful to avoid his injury in case it wasn't fully healed.

Ryan's hand began to stray from its path. Sometimes it veered off down her side, but each time it went lower than it had before. When she felt his calluses move all the way down her hip, that was enough of a signal for her. The guy seriously sent out some mixed ones, but she wasn't going to look a gift horse in the mouth. After yesterday she could stand to let off a little tension, and she bet Ryan had the stamina to help her do just that.

Her blood had already begun to fade from his system, but Ryan still felt her heat building as she ran her hand across his chest. The emotion felt slightly off. Empty? He couldn't place it, and stopped trying when her hand ventured down from his chest, not stopping until it was below his waist.

He sucked in a breath, shock mingled with excitement. She was on fire. He could feel her desire burning through him. Without it he might have resisted. But between her desire and the memory of how good she had looked before bed, Ryan came to the uncomfortable realization that he wanted her.

Ryan turned, pulling her to him. His mind was reeling, alarm bells went off, and almost two decades of hatred screamed as their lips found each other.

Then he was doing the unthinkable: kissing a vampire. Their tongues met. One of her legs moved over his and she began to slowly undulate against him. She had most certainly shaved this time; her body was soft and smooth. And wet….

For a drone, the guy could kiss. She almost felt guilty, almost had second thoughts about continuing, but when he snaked his arm underneath her, grabbed her ass, and hoisted her on top of him, the doubts evaporated in a wave of passion. She grinded against his lean body, feeling him hard against her pelvis.

At first she had planned on drawing it out and making him wait, but to hell with that! She moved forward, then back, welcoming him inside.

She let out a gasp as he entered her. His eyes fixed on the shadow of her form as she arched her back and rocked on top of him. Her lust washed over him, laced with jealousy and grief. His mind twisted over the strange mix of emotions as his hands went up to cup her ample breasts.

Ryan froze under her, each hand holding a large soft weight. He twisted so suddenly that she toppled sideways onto the bed.

"Sylvia! What the hell do you think you're doing?" Ryan hollered. He was out of the bed and standing the next instant. He tugged on his sweats with one hand as the other fumbled at the base of the lamp.

"I think you had a pretty good idea," Sylvia said lazily, rolling over.

"I thought you were Carmen!"

"Oh, did you now?"

Only after Sylvia pointedly paused did Ryan realize that he might not have wanted to say that.

"That's not what I meant! You're a vampire!" Ryan finally found the button. He blinked as Sylvia came into focus in all her glory. And it was centerfold worthy.

"So is Carmen, by the way. Maybe it would help if she joined us?"

"No! Would you please put something on?"

Sylvia took the edge of the sheet and half-heartedly pulled it in front of her. "Why the sudden change of heart? You seemed to be pretty qualm-free a moment ago."

"That's because I didn't realize who you were!" Ryan snapped.

The hole he was digging himself was getting bigger. *Go on the attack*, Ryan thought wildly. "What were you doing in my bed?"

"Carmen's a bed hog. I was in danger of being pushed off the edge, so I decided to join you. You don't seem to move. And you're so warm, like a furnace. It's wonderful."

"It comes from being warm blooded. And alive."

"It's nice."

"I'm rather fond of it."

"Me too!"

"You can't just co-opt my bed, not to mention my body, without asking!"

"Why not? You didn't even notice me sleeping with you — and as for the body, well, you started it."

"*Why not?* Because you're a vampire! And I only started it because—" Ryan stopped himself this time.

"Because you thought I was someone else?" Sylvia urged, looking at him with wide blue eyes.

122

Ryan was wresting with a jumble of thoughts and emotions. She was indeed a vampire. But there was no denying that he hadn't felt that good in more years than he cared to remember. There was also no denying that he had been the initiator.

Why had he done it?

He knew that answer. Because he thought it was Carmen who had crawled in bed with him. He glanced at where Carmen was sleeping. But she wasn't, of course. She lay on the other bed, resting on one arm, watching them. She was the source of the other emotions he had felt mixed with Sylvia's lust. The jealousy and the grief. Those were gone now. Other emotions had taken their place.

"It doesn't matter. You're a vampire," Ryan accused lamely, unable to think of anything better to say.

Sylvia nodded slowly, pulling the white sheet up as she got to all fours. She began to crawl across the bed towards Ryan, one hand keeping the sheet more or less as a barrier of decency, at least for half of her body.

When she got to the edge of the bed Sylvia, dropped the sheet and sat up on her knees. "I might be a vampire, but I'm also a woman. Or hadn't you noticed?"

Ryan started turning away the second the sheet dropped. He had his back to her when he felt the soft cool breath against his neck, her hand draped gently over his shoulder as she whispered. "Dibs on the shower."

Then her hand vanished, and moments later the bathroom door closed. All Ryan could think to say was, "Didn't she just take one eight hours ago?"

"She likes showers," Carmen replied.

Ryan grunted. Carmen's emotions still accompanied Ryan, though her grief and jealousy had been replaced by something more troubling. Satisfaction. Ryan decided not to dwell on the implications of her new feelings, and decided instead to set to work checking his gear.

He was happy to see someone had retrieved his rifle. Not only was the gun covered in his prints, it had set him back a lot of money. He sat at the table and began field stripping it, pointedly remaining fixed on his task even after Carmen joined him at the table. He was proud of himself for not even noticing that she was still wearing the black nightie.

Carmen watched him work while they waited for Sylvia. He methodically took the gun apart, cleaned each piece, oiled it, and then reassembled the parts. She helped, handing him whatever he needed.

Carmen doubted that Ryan was going to say anything, and she was content to sit there with him. She could feel his emotion, and it was the opposite of the lust that had woken her up. This emotion, which she guessed Ryan was less familiar with, was more like apprehension.

She told herself that the satisfaction she felt came from bending a vampire hunter, making him want her despite knowing what she was. Ryan made it abundantly clear that she was the one he wanted, and she had done it without pushing him.

Carmen forgave Sylvia; it was her nature. She would never have slept with Ryan if she knew Carmen had been interested in him. Not that she was, of course. Carmen knew the jealousy she experienced watching the two of them together had nothing to do with Ryan. How could it?

No, the jealousy came from the act in general. Carmen had always been jealous of how Sylvia could gain all the satisfaction she needed from only carnal pleasures, while she wanted more. Needed more.

Still, the idea of sex with Ryan stirred something within her. Another pang of jealousy surfaced, but Carmen quickly squashed it down. Sylvia had said that Ryan was the one to start it, and Ryan hadn't denied her claim. So her friend couldn't be blamed for seducing him. Ryan had started it, been the one to seduce her friend. It was Ryan's fault! But, he had only made a move because he believed she was the one lying there with him.

"Rag," Ryan said.

Carmen handed him the white cloth. "Thanks." Ryan's eyes flicked up to Carmen as he said it.

When their eyes met Carmen felt the briefest surge of another emotion. It dissipated quickly, drowned out by her own apprehension. But there was no denying it. It was the same powerful emotion that had woken her up. Lust. And she couldn't tell who it had come from.

Ryan was relieved when Sylvia came into the room. After what had happened he found himself more nervous being alone with Carmen than he had been when he first found out she was a vampire.

Both of the girls acted as if they had forgotten all about what had transpired earlier, and Ryan had no intention of ever bringing it up again. They sent Ryan to purchase a new deck of cards from the hotel lobby, Ryan's deck being deemed too worn for use, and the three of them played Hearts for an hour until the sun set.

As soon as the truck was loaded Ryan ran across the parking lot and grabbed a quick meal from a fast food restaurant. That was the problem with road trips, Ryan thought as he emptied his tray into the trash: he tended to eat a lot of crap. Then when the trip was over, he had to make up for it by eating nothing but rabbit food. It was a vicious cycle.

Ryan climbed up into the semi hoping that the two vampires would sit in back and keep each other company, but Sylvia cut in front of Carmen just as she was gripping the handle. Sylvia hopped into the front seat and settled down right next to Ryan on the wide bench.

Ryan didn't need to see Carmen's expression at Sylvia's action to feel the displeasure radiating off of her as she shut the door, crossed her arms, flicked off her shoes, and put her bare feet up on the dashboard.

It was seven o'clock when they pulled out of the hotel parking lot, the trucks GPS showed they had roughly 1200 miles to go. Twenty hours, give or take. Despite the drama that occurred both before and after he slept, Ryan had managed to get a solid ten hours of sleep in.

He felt great, though he grudgingly admitted some of it was probably due to the vampire blood in his veins. Still, the bottom line was that Ryan was confident he could drive it straight through. The sleeper cab had both tinted windows and curtains. The girls could stay back there safely, and he'd be in Chicago tomorrow afternoon. The nightmare would be over.

The thought brightened his mood so much that he managed to remain happy despite being overruled two-to-one when it came to the music selection. Sylvia had brought an mp3 player with an extensive collection of songs that she felt needed to be shared. After the first hour Ryan wasn't sure if Sylvia actually liked crooners, or if she was just punishing him for cutting their tryst short back in the hotel room.

Sylvia finally switched the musical genre to show tunes after Ryan half-heartedly agreed to play the license plate game. That lasted an hour, until *Hello Dolly* gave the girls the idea of a sing-along.

Ryan balked, despite Carmen reminding him that he brought up the idea of a sing-along back in the restaurant where they had first met. Ryan wouldn't capitulate, refusing to take part in the musical merriment. Sylvia, however, was thrilled by the idea and Ryan was forced to endure being serenaded by various bad renditions of countless Broadway musical melodies until they reached the middle of Nebraska.

# Chapter 10

When the vampires were ready to eat, Ryan was almost eager to pull over and let them drain some unsuspecting victim just for the moment's peace it would buy him. He suggested they take their time and enjoy their meal so as not to get indigestion.

While the women hunted down their prey, Ryan gassed up the truck, going into shock when the meter read $345 after only two of the tanks had been filled. He decided that would do.

Finding himself with not only some time to kill, but the first privacy he had in a while, Ryan climbed in the back of the cab and rifled through his bag until he found one of the burner phones. He fought with the clamshell for a minute until finally hacking the stubborn plastic to pieces with a knife.

First he called the Sanctuary and talked with David, one of the zoo keepers. Everything was going okay, though one of the tigers was sick and had required an emergency house call from the vet that was going to cost Ryan an arm and a leg. And there had been another home invasion in the neighborhood. It was the third armed robbery in a month and the small rural community was getting anxious.

Next he dialed up Bill. It was a call Ryan needed to make, but one he had been putting off out of dread.

The phone rang once, twice, three times. Ryan breathed a sigh of relief when he was confident it would drop to voice mail, but at the last minute he heard a click, and Bill's voice answered.

"Hello?"

"Bill, it's Ryan."

"Ryan! Thank God, I was getting worried. I thought for sure I would have heard from you by now. Is everything okay?"

"Oh yeah, if I was doing any better I wouldn't be able to stand it."

"Is she okay?"

"She?"

"Carmen. Is she okay?"

"No Bill, she isn't. She's dead."

"Dead?" His friend's voice held a mixture of shock and disbelief.

"Yes, has been for quite some time apparently."

Bill's familiar warm chuckle came over the line. "Now Ryan, it's not nice to mess with an old man like that."

"Bill, when you said she was a handful, you didn't exactly give me the whole picture did you?"

"I thought it would be better if you found that out for yourself. Otherwise how is she?"

"Otherwise? Well, Bill, other than being an undead creature that exists by consuming human blood, she's just peachy."

"I see she hasn't rubbed off on you yet."

"No, but her friend has."

"I don't quite follow."

"Never mind. Look. Bill. I'm going to give you the benefit of the doubt and assume that there was a good reason you had for not telling me the truth about Carmen."

"I see she *has* rubbed off on you"

"What are you talking about?"

"You called her Carmen."

"Of course I did. That's her name." Ryan was growing exasperated.

"I know, and you used it rather than monster, blood-sucker, thing, creature, or any of the other colorful monikers by which you usually refer to vampires."

Ryan frowned, unsure what his friend's point was. "Bill, Carmen *is* a vampire. And you knew it."

"Of course I did."

"What's so important about her? Why do you want her alive? More importantly, how on earth did you get this job, and why the hell did you send her to me?"

His friend let out an audible breath before answering. "Well, let's see…. If she hasn't told you why she's important, than I'm not at liberty to do so. I didn't get the job, I created it. And because you're the best there is at killing vampires, and that's what's after her. You and Carmen are the only ones left I can fully trust. And I needed someone I could trust."

"You trust her?" Pieces were falling into place, pieces that Ryan was not ready for. He blocked them out the same way he did too many things he didn't want to deal with. Walled them off. He was good at it.

"Implicitly," said Bill.

Ryan's voice took on a tone of resignation as he filled in his friend. "Bill, it's not only vampires that are after her. We got hit by a team of hunters outside of Vegas. They were already there, expecting us. We hadn't been followed to the city. They knew we were coming."

"Vegas? I assumed you would use the Northern route."

"I would have, but we were attacked at the initial meeting, and I wanted to lose whoever it was."

"That's most unfortunate." Bill seemed genuinely surprised and concerned by the news. "It seems they're getting more desperate."

"Who is *they*? Because it seems to me the easiest way to end this is to tell me who *they* are."

"Oh, I quite agree, and as soon as I'm absolutely sure who it is, you will be the first to know, my boy. I promise you that. And then I expect you to do what you do best."

"Well, hurry up and figure it out," Ryan said.

"Rest assured it's the only thing I'm working on. Until then you have to keep her safe."

"You know I will," Ryan grunted.

"Of course I do. It's why I entrusted her to you. So tell me honestly, what do you think of Carmen?" Bill's question surprised Ryan.

"What am I supposed to think of her? She's—" Ryan's voice trailed off as his mind continued, *beautiful, compassionate, classy, intelligent, funny, self-confident*. Out loud he said, "Bill, she's a vampire!"

Again the chuckle. "You really need to work on that, Ryan. You always were bad at poker. Everything plays right across your face like a book."

"What are you talking about? You can't see me; we're on the phone."

Bill started to answer but his words were cut off by a clicking sound. "It seems that I'm quite the hot commodity tonight. I have a call coming in. I don't recognize the number, but given recent events I can't afford to ignore any of them. Goodbye, Ryan. And keep her safe. Please."

"Yeah, fine. Oh, Bill?"

"Yes?"

"Next time I see you I am going to knock you on your ass."

"Yes, I suspect you will." A chuckle and then a dial tone as the call dropped.

Ryan sat back in the truck, taking the opportunity to search through Sylvia's music player. As it turned out at least half of her music was decent. Ryan queued up the Beatles, closed his eyes, and listened to "Paperback Writer" while he waited for the girls to return.

# # #

For dinner, Carmen and Silvia settled on a pair of college kids who were on a road trip to see a Paramore concert. The icing on the cake was that they were driving a minivan, which probably belonged to one of their parents. It was not only roomy, but the deeply tinted rear windows provided privacy for their meal.

Sylvia wanted to enjoy her food. After her earlier encounter with Ryan was cut short, she was looking forward to the carnal pleasures the two young men could offer almost more than the nourishment they would provide.

Carmen, however, was in a hurry. She fed off of one of the boys quickly and then excused herself, leaving Sylvia to take her time quenching both of her hungers.

Carmen wanted to make a phone call. It was the first time she was really alone since she had met Ryan. She searched her purse in vain for her cell phone, then cursed when she remembered Ryan's orders to toss her phone out on the road. She was about to go back to the van to take one of the boy's phones when she spied a rare sight. One of the last pay phones in America sat in front of the restaurant. The phone looked operational, despite the battered and tagged glass box that surrounded it.

She briefly questioned the wisdom of making her call from a payphone. Ryan had warned them about phone taps and people tracing their calls. But what would it get them if they did? By the time anyone got here, she would be hundreds of miles away in a truck the killers had no hope of identifying.

Carmen fed the payphone with the change at the bottom of her purse and placed the call. The phone rang repeatedly, until she had almost given up, but finally there was a click and Charles's voice answered. "Hello?"

"It's me," Carmen said. She didn't bother saying who *me* was; she knew Charles would identify her voice instantly.

"Hello, my dear. I trust everything is okay?"

"Everything is most certainly *not* okay," Carmen snapped at his tone. He actually had the gall to sound amused.

"Are you hurt?" Charles asked, suddenly concerned.

"Not at the moment. But I've been attacked twice. Charles, they know who we are. They're trying to kill us."

"I know, my dear, and by going through Las Vegas you only made it easier for them. You knew they would be watching Sylvia; the woman is too arrogant to hide. You can't imagine my relief when I learned you were safe."

"Wait, how did you know I was in Vegas?"

"I have my sources."

"Charles...." Carmen knew she had to ask, but she struggled to form the words.

"Yes?" he asked.

"Why did you send a hunter after me?"

"I didn't. I would never harm you. You must know that."

"So you're denying that you sent a hunter after me?" Carmen said, not hiding her incredulous tone.

"I assure you that I had nothing to do with what happened outside of Vegas — or any of these attacks for that matter. After knowing me all of these years I can't believe you could think I could harm you."

"So you deny that you sent a hunter after me?" Carmen pressed, wondering how Charles could possibly have been ignorant about Ryan's profession, yet hoping somehow that was the case.

"Of course I am! I find it deeply troubling that whoever is trying to kill us has resorted to using hunters. It shows they have no scruples. You're lucky to be alive. Please try to keep it that way. No more taking unnecessary risks, like you did by going through Las Vegas. Listen to Ryan, he'll keep you safe."

"He was the hunter I was referring to!" Carmen said, waiting for Charles to deny the obvious.

"Who? Ryan?" While his questions were innocent, his tone said otherwise, and Carmen knew instantly that Charles was aware of exactly what Ryan was.

"Yes, Ryan. Don't play with me. You knew very well that Ryan was a hunter when you sent him to protect me!"

"Did he harm you? Threaten you in any way? Do anything other than keep you safe?"

"Well, no."

"Then I'm not seeing a problem. Carmen, I sent Ryan to you because I knew he would protect you. He is the best at what he does."

"What he does is kill vampires!"

"And in this case, that meets our needs perfectly."

"Wait, didn't you just say you were troubled by the fact that whoever is trying to kill us has resorted to using hunters, and now here you admit to doing the very same thing?"

"That's different," Charles said.

Carmen wasn't buying it. She guessed that what troubled Charles the most was someone else actually stooping down to his level by using their own hunters. "So, how did you know Ryan wouldn't kill me? He had no idea what I was. He still has no idea who I am."

"I had faith."

"That's a poor answer."

"It's the only one I have. So tell me, my dear, what do you think of Ryan?"

"What do you mean, what do I think of him? You mean other than his being on the wrong side of the IQ bell curve, being dangerously stubborn, having awful taste in clothes, and his obnoxiously bad manners? Charles — he's a vampire hunter!"

Charles chuckled. "If I hadn't known you for however many hundreds of years, *you* I would have believed."

"Charles, when I get to Chicago we're going to have words."

"I suspect you may have to take a number, my dear."

Carmen hung up.

# Chapter 11

By the time they reached a truck stop an hour outside the Chicago city limits, Ryan was bleary eyed and had to pee. He had been nursing a 32-ounce coffee he picked up at a gas station six hours before. The half that was not sitting stone cold in the bottom of the cup was sloshing around in his bladder desperately wanting out.

A couple of hours remained before sunset when Ryan parked the truck alongside a line of other semis behind a road-side diner, then hurried in to use the facilities and grab a blue plate special. The girls had stayed up late gossiping and were still asleep, tucked safely out of the sunlight in the back of the sleeper cab. They had spent hours talking about fashion and trading gossip on people Ryan assumed were vampires. He tried to remember the names he heard and any bits of information that could be useful in the future, but the conversation had been, intentionally or not, sparse on those types of details.

Ryan ate quickly at the counter, expecting the vampires to still be asleep when he returned. But when he climbed back inside the truck he found them awake playing cards and chatting. Ryan sat in front for a few minutes before boredom overtook him, then he climbed back to join the game until the sun had safely set.

When Sylvia asked Ryan why they weren't back on the road, Ryan informed her that there was no way he was taking a tractor trailer into the city of Chicago. Ryan then demanded that she commandeer them a vehicle, with the stipulation that no one get hurt in the process.

Sylvia agreed with a huff, though as punishment for being forced to give up her semi she brought back an aging minivan from a couple on a road trip to Canada.

The idea of driving straight through to Chicago had lost its appeal hours before, and Ryan hoped Sylvia would volunteer to drive the rest of the way, but apparently the Honda Odyssey lacked the appeal of the big rig and Ryan was forced to put in the remaining hour to their destination.

While Sylvia sat in the passenger seat next to Ryan and navigated, Carmen sat in the back of the van collecting her thoughts. She stared out the window at the buildings, noting that little had changed since the last time she was here three years ago. She sighed reflexively. It was Thursday evening and they were in Chicago. True to Ryan's word, he had delivered her safely. They had made it with a day to spare. But made it where, exactly?

Carmen had been so busy worrying about other things that she had forgotten that one small detail. Chicago was a major hub in the vampire government, along with New Orleans and New York. It had been like that for over a hundred years. She had lobbied for California repeatedly, reminding everyone that the West Coast had grown up to become a major player over the last century. But it had been to no avail. Vampires hated to travel for logistical reasons, and she was outnumbered. So the Convocation continued to rotate its location between the same three cities it always had.

Because of the annual journey, both Carmen and Sylvia had residences in Chicago, along with New Orleans and New York. The question was, did she really want a vampire hunter knowing where hers was? Carmen had purchased the townhouse in the Gold Coast district in the early 1900s. She was fond of the house, and hated to have to abandon it.

Would she have to? Would Ryan really come after her? She remembered the look that came across his face a few days before. At that time she had been certain that's exactly what he had planned. Delivering her safely to Chicago to satisfy his promise, and then killing her right afterwards.

She wasn't so sure those intentions remained, but she hadn't lived this long without playing it safe, and she really, really liked that house.

"Turn right up here on to West, then take a left on Lakeview," Carmen instructed Ryan. Sylvia's place was a pretentious high-rise condo in Streeterville. Carmen reasoned that it was more easily replaced than her historic town home.

"Um, no, turn left up here then go three blocks to Marshall. It's the fifth house on the right. 1341," said Sylvia.

*That bitch!* thought Carmen, furious. "Wouldn't you rather go to your place, Sylvia? I mean the view of the lake that you have from the penthouse of the Stratum building is simply to *die* for."

Sylvia turned around in her seat so she could scowl at Carmen. Ryan stopped car at the intersection and stared bleary eyed at the green light while the two women bickered and the angry divers behind him honked.

When there was no sign the argument would end any time soon, and at least one driver behind him was close to having a coronary, Ryan made the decision for them. He would like to think that he had made the left-hand turn at random, and that it had nothing to do with wanting to see where Carmen lived, wanting to know what type of place she would pick out for herself.

The exterior of the three-story townhouse was pleasant, cheery even in the dark. The stone façade was well-kept and there were even flowers growing in window boxes. Ryan assumed they had to be recently planted given the near freezing temperatures of the fading Chicago winter.

"Um, you passed it," Sylvia said as Ryan drove by the townhouse.

"I know," Ryan said, circling the block. He was looking for any obvious surveillance: out of place cars, utility vans, a window with open blinds facing the town home.

Parking was scarce. After circling the block once without finding any spaces Ryan stopped the van in front of a fire hydrant. He wasn't worried about a ticket; he didn't own the car. Besides, he wouldn't be staying long. This was it. He had delivered Carmen safe and sound to Chicago by the desired date, as promised. He was done.

Carmen looked at her house with a mixture of happiness and apprehension. She always liked it here; it was cozy and comfortable. Though she could only take so much of the big city before she started craving the peace that only rural living could offer.

So why the apprehension? She couldn't deny it any longer. She would likely never see Ryan again, and it bothered her.

Carmen had already decided she would let him live. She owed the man her life. It was the least she could do. So what if he knew about the Council's existence? He didn't know who or where they were. Carmen hadn't told him anything he hadn't already known, and in all of his years as a hunter he hadn't found them yet, and she didn't see that changing.

As Carmen got out of the car the full implications dawned on her. She had made it! She was in Chicago. Whatever was driving the murders had to do with the Convocation, and that event started tomorrow, at least unofficially. One week's festivities, followed by one week's worth of work. Then it was over. She only had to live through two more weeks — or less if they could find out who was behind the killings.

"Be a darling and get the bags," Sylvia called over her shoulder to Ryan as she walked up the steps to join Carmen at the front door.

Carmen glanced back to see Ryan struggling under a pile of suitcases and department store bags. It was the last time she would see him. In a minute he would gone forever.

The two friends stood at the front door as Ryan huffed and puffed behind them, a vision in luggage. Carmen unlocked the door and called for Jeffrey, her butler. She had sent him ahead several weeks ago to prepare the house.

Both the alarm and the lights were off, which was strange. She flipped on the light and revealed the cheerfully decorated foyer looking just the way she remembered it. There was even a fresh bouquet of yellow daisies, her favorite flowers, set in an opaque blue vase. Nothing seemed out of place.

Ryan staggered into the house and dumped the bags in the center of a large sitting room. He straightened up, stretching out his back while he surveyed the home. It was tastefully decorated in furniture that would have been made around the same time as the house, and therefore would now be called antique.

He was wondering if Carmen had picked everything out herself, or paid someone to do it for her. His eyes rested on a comfortable looking sofa in the next room, and thoughts of sleep called to him. He walked over and contemplated crashing right there when something caught his attention. Laying on the couch was a square pillow with an amazingly intricate scene embroidered on it. Ryan picked it up and studied it. It was the skyline of an old coastal European town.

Carmen gave a brief smile as she saw Ryan holding a pillow she had sewn almost a century ago. She had recreated her hometown of Valencia as it had been when she had left it over two hundred years before.

She pulled herself back to the present and called for Jeffrey again, and when he didn't come she raised her voice and tried for Mary. Mary was the part-time housekeeper. A human, she lived elsewhere and checked on the house periodically during Carmen's absence. With Carmen's imminent arrival, she should have been here helping Charles prepare the house for occupation.

At least one of them should have been there. They knew Carmen would be arriving this week. Carmen frowned before calling each of their names again, even louder this time. No answer.

Something was nagging Ryan, and it wasn't that the pillow was too pretty to rest his head on. It was the house. Something wasn't right. He knew vampires kept their lairs as closely guarded secrets, but it was obvious that at least Sylvia knew where's Carmen's was. He had a feeling other vampires might know as well, and it was vampires that wanted Carmen dead.

When only silence answered Carmen's calls, the alarm bells in Ryan's head became too loud to ignore.

"We've got to go. Now!" Ryan said, dropping the pillow and rushing up to the girls. He grabbed each one by the arm just as they were about to go off and search the house.

Ryan pulled and to his relief they didn't resist, which was a good thing because Ryan doubted his ability to pull a vampire, let alone two, where it didn't want to go. They simply followed him, each wearing the same questioning expression.

He tugged them behind himself, turned, and pushed them hard out the door. They were almost through the threshold, Carmen tripping in surprise at being suddenly shoved, when the house exploded.

# Chapter 12

Carmen pulled herself up from the sidewalk. Her scorched back radiated pain, and a piece of something-or-other had imbedded itself deep in her thigh, but otherwise she would live. Sylvia bent down to give her a hand up.

*Ryan*, Carmen thought.

She looked back at her house. Ryan lay sprawled across the doorway, smoke billowing over him. Behind him a fire raged in her house. She ran up the stairs, grabbed him under the arms, and dragged him to the sidewalk, away from the heat. He was a mess, but she could feel his heartbeat. He was alive.

"Fine, we'll take the hero, but maybe we should pick him up. Being hauled across the cement can't be good for him." Sylvia picked up Ryan's legs and together they carried him into the van. His weight wasn't an issue, but his size was problematic. It took some shoving, and a little cursing, but between the two of them Ryan was finally shoved into the middle row of the Odyssey.

Carmen climbed in next to him and Sylvia lit up the front tires as she pulled away from the house. Neighbors had already started spilling out onto the street to see what happened. A few shouted in vain for the van to stop.

Sylvia took them in a roundabout way, doing her best to make sure they weren't followed, before finally pulling the van up to a row of warehouses in southeast Chicago. It was questionable area of the city, though this particular location was more industrial than seedy.

No one knew Sylvia had this place, not even Carmen. The building had never been in her name in all of the sixty years she had owned it. It was just an old warehouse squished amidst a row of other old warehouses near a canal.

Sylvia got out of the car and punched the code into the keypad she had installed about a decade ago, the last time she used the house with any regularity. The rolling door squeaked in protest as it raised.

She keyed the alarm code into a second console immediately inside of the doorway. Once the alarm switched red to green she went back and pulled the van in, next to a dusty Karmann Ghia parked amidst piles of crates and boxes. Safely inside the first level of the building, Sylvia pushed a button on the console and the door began to close.

Before it shut, Carmen had already begun to pull Ryan out of the car. Sylvia hurried to help, and the two vampires carried him into a freight elevator which, not to be outdone by the roll-up door, emitted its own cacophony of nails-on-chalkboard sounds as it shook its way up to the second floor loft.

Sylvia flipped on the lights, which shone over furniture that was several decades out of date. She cringed. She hadn't remembered her flat being quite so tacky.

Both Sylvia and Carmen had fed from the owners of the van when they had picked it up outside of Chicago. With the exception of the burns, which were the most difficult injury for a vampire to overcome, they would heal quickly without any additional blood. But Ryan wouldn't. At least not any time soon.

The girls set him down on an orange leather sofa. Then they carefully peeled off yet another of Ryan's ruined shirts. It was identical to all the others he wore, though in a different shade of dark fabric. The tattered vest had stopped some of the explosion's debris, anything that might have been immediately fatal. But the back of his neck and scalp were burned and bloody, and his arms and legs were almost as bad off.

Carmen looked down at him. Given proper medical care it would all heal, but it would be a slow painful process, and the burns would visibly scar. Though apparently Ryan collected scars, so he might not mind.

Carmen rolled him over. She was glad he was unconscious, because the pain might have been unbearable as open wounds and burned flesh rubbed against the sofa. Ryan probably wouldn't forgive her, but she had no time for pandering to his hang-ups. She brought her wrist to his mouth and, once again, slit her wrist and fed him her blood.

She had to be careful. This was the second — no, third — time in as many days that he had consumed their blood. He would certainly turn if she gave him too much, or he could be injured and possibly disfigured if she gave him too little. Carmen was unsure as she watched the blood flow into him. She hadn't turned anyone in almost a century and was a little out of practice where dosages were concerned.

Sylvia wasn't, however, and pulled her wrist away long before Carmen had planned to. "Let's spare ourselves any more drama than absolutely necessary. God, Carmen, could you imagine if Ryan became one of us? If he didn't commit suicide immediately he would give new meaning to the term Emo."

Carmen gave a soft laugh despite herself, as she absentmindedly stroked Ryan's cheek. While she held her wrist, staunching the blood for the few seconds it would take it to stop, she imagined Ryan as a brooding vampire. He would be a romance novel's wet dream. Turned against his will, destined to feed off the humans he once protected, a man of few words and many scowls. The only thing he was missing was long flowing hair, which she supposed he could grow out in time.

"He'll live," Sylvia proclaimed after ten minutes had passed. Ryan had not shown any signs of spasms, which would have indicated an overdose of vampire blood, certain death, and subsequent reanimation.

"Now if you're finished pining over GI Joe, let's get cleaned up and see what else has happened while we were gone. We can't be the only ones who have been attacked." Sylvia went to check the clothes inventory in her closet. She was discouraged to see that what the garments lacked in style they made up for in numbers. She had a lot of outdated clothing here.

"Nice carpet, by the way," Carmen said as she cast off her ruined shoes. She wouldn't admit it, but the long shag felt good between her toes. She tried concentrating on the thick orange fabric cushioning her feet rather than the most recent, and almost very successful, attempt on her life.

"Yeah, yeah, I haven't been here in a year or twenty. I don't even think it has cable, and I'm positive it doesn't have internet. If we survive remind me to have it updated, or maybe just replaced." Sylvia picked up the apartment phone, a model sporting a rotary dial.

Satisfied by the dial tone, Sylvia was about to place a call when she remembered Ryan's warning about phones. She replaced the handle in its cradle and walked over to fish through Ryan's bags until she found one of his disposable burner phones he had talked about. She struggled for a bit with the plastic casing before finally tearing it open with her teeth.

"If Ryan were conscious he would say we were learning," said Carmen.

Sylvia scowled, spit out a piece of plastic, and then dialed a number. When it rang through to voicemail she hung up and tried another. Again it went to voicemail. The third call was picked up by a tentative voice that had no useful information.

Between them the two women made almost two dozen calls before giving up an hour later. Most everyone was either in hiding and not answering their phones, or had nothing to offer except wild speculation.

In the end Sylvia got out a pack of playing cards and sat down to a game of solitaire at the kitchen table, while Carmen paced the living room floor until her frustration finally got the best of her. She grabbed the car keys and made a run to the nearest twenty-four hour big box store.

Carmen returned a short while later with a bag bursting with skeins of yarn and a pair of knitting needles. She had been fully prepared to start working on a scarf, which she had subconsciously pegged as a gift for Ryan, when she noticed the man in question looked sick. "What happened to Ryan? Sylvia, what did you do? I was only gone for half an hour!"

"Huh?" Sylvia glanced up from her cards to look at Carmen, then over to where Ryan lay shivering on the sofa. "I'm not sure."

Carmen went to the sofa and leaned down to examine him. Ryan had a faint blue tinge. "Please tell me I didn't turn him!"

"I don't think so. Maybe…." said Sylvia, joining the examination.

"Do you think he's sick? Maybe he's sick," Carmen said uncertainly. She had several humans on her staff, but it had been more years than she could remember since she had actually had to deal with a sick human herself. And with her blood in Ryan's system she didn't think it was possible for him to catch any regular sickness.

Sylvia bent down, opening his eyelids. "Are you sick?" she asked loudly.

Ryan blinked, his mouth opened and the words that came out were hardly a whisper. "I'm not sick. I'm freezing."

"Oh!" Sylvia found a blanket for Ryan and then went to the HVAC control to turn on the heat. Within a few minutes, a thick musty smell filled the apartment. "Sorry about the odor. It hasn't been used in a few years. I forget about temperature sometimes."

"When was the last time anyone was here?" Carmen asked her. She pulled the blanket over Ryan, then sat at the edge of the couch and ran her hands through his hair until his eyes closed. She decided an afghan would be a more suitable gift than a scarf, and made a mental note to pick up more yarn when she had the chance.

"Remember the Convocation about ten years ago, when Thomas first got it in his head to start stalking me?" Sylvia asked. "I stayed here for almost a week hiding from him."

Ryan's eyes popped open. "Who's Thomas? A Hunter?" Ryan wracked his mind trying to remember a hunter named Thomas. He wondered if Sylvia had killed the guy. He came up blank, unable to think of any hunters with that name, though ten years was a little before his time.

"No, worse," Sylvia said, but she didn't bother to elaborate.

# Chapter 13

Ryan was freezing again. At first he thought it was the cold slab of the morgue, but would an autopsy table be so soft? He opened his eyes. And orange?

Ryan discovered that he was lying on a sofa that was tragically out of date. A flimsy blanket covered him. In addition to the blanket a miniscule afghan covered his feet: two lines of yarn trailed off the couch to a pair of depleted skeins that rested on the coffee table.

He was in a large loft. The ceiling where he lay towered twenty feet above him. Off to one side the ceiling dropped to ten feet. Under it was a kitchen, and a walled-off area with a door that Ryan assumed was the bathroom. Above them was an open space surrounded by a chrome railing that Ryan guessed was the bedroom. It was accessed via a chrome circular staircase to the right of the kitchen.

Opposite the kitchen was a row of shuttered windows that ran the length of the lower section of the tall wall. The shutters stopped halfway to the ceiling. Ryan saw that there had once been a second row of windows that ran the upper length of the wall, but those had all been bricked up.

Ryan rose from the couch with a groan, and after a brief search of the downstairs found the thermostat. It had been set to sixty. Ryan gave a shiver and cranked it up ten degrees. Then he shuffled along the carpet, building a growing charge of electricity before shocking himself on the zipper of his duffel bag and cursing. He pulled out a change of clothes. This was his last one. He hadn't expected to be at this job for the better part of a week.

With the handful of clothes he shuffled over to the large, equally out of date bathroom. When he flipped the light switch he was greeted by the most amazing selection of cosmetics he had ever seen assembled in one place. Lipstick, nail polish, and plastic cases containing who knows what filled almost every inch of the long counter.

This had to be Sylvia's place, Ryan thought as he stuffed his clothes in between a towel bar and the wall. He paused, considering.

It couldn't be Sylvia's penthouse; two vampires who had managed to live for as long as they had weren't that stupid. It was obvious that whoever was behind the killings knew the two women were friends. If Carmen's place blew up then Sylvia's penthouse would at the very least be under surveillance.

Ryan ran out of the bathroom to the closest window. He opened the shutter, waving away the cloud of dust that rose, and squinted at the bright light that met him. He closed the slats most of the way, then peered back out under furrowed brows. Not only was it morning on the wrong side of the tracks, but he was too low for this to be considered a penthouse by any but the most generous sense of the word.

Ryan closed the shutter. This wasn't Sylvia's penthouse. It was a safe house.

Relieved, Ryan shuffled back to the bathroom and took a long shower. He sighed in contentment as the warm water beat down from the blissfully hi-flow shower head. He turned around, and winced as a sudden pain flared up on the back of his neck. He immediately turned to remove the burnt area from the water.

He pondered his curious state of non-death. He was injured, but only inconveniently so. Nothing was life threatening, or even serious. He closed his eyes and searched inside himself for any unnatural cravings for human blood, but found none despite the definite taste of it in his mouth.

Fifteen minutes after he had gotten clean he turned off the shower. He had concluded that the vampires had done it to him again — made him drink their blood, though apparently not enough to turn him. Yet. Ryan knew he had to be close.

It was hard for Ryan to remain angry. He suspected that if they hadn't given him their blood he wouldn't be nearly as mobile as he was, or maybe not at all. He remembered the explosion. Remembered the pain before losing consciousness. He decided it was possible he might have died from his wounds.

Ryan wiped the steam from the mirror then examined his naked body. Nothing unusual. He turned and glanced over his shoulder. The burns on the back of his neck were already fading, though he still seemed to be missing a patch of hair. Otherwise there was nothing to betray the events of the past week. Not a single mark or scar that he didn't remember having before he met Carmen. Even the gunshot wounds on his chest and back made by the sniper rifle were gone.

He wondered how close he was to turning, and figured dangerously so. He drank blood three times from vampires in the last couple of days. And these weren't newly made vampires, they were old. At least Carmen was, and he suspected Sylvia was as well. He knew they had metered his intake, but even so… with their potent blood, three small doses was definitely pushing it.

Ryan swore to himself that he was finished with vampire blood. He was getting sloppy. He worried that he was getting reliant on it. Like a crutch. Somewhere in the back of his mind he now knew that if he got hurt he could simply use Carmen to heal him.

Ryan shook his head. The next time he was injured he would have to heal the natural way. If it was fatal, then it would be his death. He would not succumb to the alternative. Of course if that happened sooner, rather than later, while traces of the blood remained in his system, he might turn anyway. Or worse, he might become a zombie.

Ryan glanced at the mirror. An intense icy shock coursed through him when he didn't see the expected reflection. Then he realized he had been ruminating there for so long the mirror had fogged again. He smiled at his reaction. He knew the reflection thing was a myth. He gave into temptation and drew a large smiley face in the dew then got dressed.

The next order of business was to forage for food. The kitchen was a disappointment. The orange appliances hid no food, not even for a vampire. The fridge was completely bare: no blood, no condiments. Not even an old pizza box. In fact its sterile white interior didn't look like it had ever been used.

After a thorough search of the cupboards Ryan concluded that the only thing consumable in the entire apartment was him (if you happened to be a vampire), water from the tap, or the contents of the very old bottles of booze that stocked a bar in the living room.

The only thing of interest that his search of the kitchen uncovered was a note on the counter. It was written in beautiful cursive that Ryan admired. He always wished he could write like that, instead his slowly printed letters.

*Ryan,*

*First of all, relax, you are not a vampire. However if you still feel the need to kill yourself please don't use a gun; we are tired and it would wake us up. Use the oven instead: it's gas.*

*There is no food here. The kitchen is not only ugly, but bare. Feel free to order something to be delivered.*

*I have some clothing ready at the following address here in Chicago: 1431 Crown Street. I would appreciate it if you would please pick up the garments and bring them here to the loft before you leave the city. They are already paid for.*

*The door code is: 332471*

*The alarm code is: 332472*

*When you are ready to leave you are welcome to take the van. Have a safe trip back to California, or wherever you are headed.*

*Carmen*

*PS – Thank you for saving my life.*

In the bottom right hand corner of the letter was a kiss in deep red lipstick. Next to the note were the keys to the Honda. Ryan smiled at the lips, until he realized Sylvia had probably planted them there after the letter was written, without Carmen's knowledge.

On a whim Ryan climbed the stairs to the bedroom. The centerpiece of the upstairs portion of the loft was a king-sized waterbed. Both behind the bed and above it were large mirrors. A tall dresser stood against the wall, as well as a long dresser with yet another mirror, but there was no closet or bathroom.

Enough light rose up from downstairs for Ryan to see two forms laying in the bed, a satin tiger-striped sheet their only cover. One was dead center of the bed, doing an impression of a starfish. The other had been forced all the way to one side and teetered precariously at the edge, only kept from falling over by the lip of the waterbed's frame. Neither figure made any move when Ryan came to the foot of the bed.

Ryan was standing before two sleeping vampires. He knew he could kill them both. In a not so distant past he would have, without hesitation. Instead, he carefully crept back down the stairs so as to not wake them, grabbed the keys to the minivan, and headed down to the garage.

His plans changed when he saw the white VW. The state it was in was criminal, and could not be ignored. It took Ryan two trips to a nearby auto parts store and four hours of knuckle-scraping work to get the car running. The car itself was in mint condition, only six thousand miles showing on its odometer. But twenty years of neglect had taken their toll on various gaskets and filters.

By one o'clock he and the old car were happily puttering down the road on their way to pick up Carmen's laundry. She certainly had chosen a dry cleaner that was the farthest away from the safe house as possible.

That's because it wasn't a dry cleaner, Ryan realized as he came to a stop in front of D'Oliveira Brothers Tailors. He double checked the address to be sure. He wondered how many days he had been unconscious if Carmen was able to purchase something and then drop it off to be tailored.

Ryan walked into a small front room. Aside from some fabric swatches piled atop a table to the right, and magazines stacked on a coffee table in front of an old worn couch, the room was empty.

There was a window with a small office behind it. He rang the bell in the window and waited. A short time later an elderly man wandered out of the hallway that led to the back of the business. He was short, balding, and had a measuring tape draped over his neck.

"Can I help you?" He had a thick accent that Ryan didn't recognize.

Ryan instinctively put his hand in his front pocket, then realized he didn't have a ticket. "I'm here to pick up clothing for Carmen. Uh, Maria del Carmen de Luna."

The man smiled. "Of course. They have been ready for a week." He went in back and emerged a few minutes later with a mountain of garment bags.

"I give you Miss D'Anchemant's also. All paid for. She called. Leave message." He looked at the tag, then at Ryan, then back at the tag. His smile turned upside down. He pulled out one of the garment bags and unzipped it, then let out a loud sigh.

"Slight problem. Wrong measurements."

"I can come back if you want," Ryan suggested.

"No, no. No time. Dance tonight. I fix it while you wait. Come."

Ryan followed the man down the hall to a room with a pedestal. Surrounding it were three full-length mirrors. To one side of the room were rows of oversized shoes, both men's and women's with various heel lengths.

The tailor motioned to the pedestal. "Please."

"Oh, no, you don't understand," Ryan said, realizing the mistake.

"No, no. Very minor. I fix it." He waved his hand indicating that he would not be taking no for an answer.

Ryan tried unsuccessfully several more times to convince the man that the outfit he was picking up wasn't for him. It was no use. Finally he succumbed to the measurements. Then was ushered back into the lobby and instructed to sit on the sofa, which turned out to be surprisingly comfy.

Ryan was still waiting in the lobby two hours later, fighting back a growing sense of unease, when another gentleman came into the store. He was dressed in a fine gray suit and smelled of too much cologne. He bore a striking resemblance to the tailor who had taken Ryan's measurements. Ryan guessed the guy had to be the other brother in D'Oliveira Brothers.

"Can I help you?" the man asked Ryan in accented, but perfect English.

"I came here to pick up some clothing and I believe there's been a mistake — your brother is making alterations to one of the outfits."

"I understand, I will check on his work immediately," the man said, then promptly disappeared into the back of the store.

"You don't get it. The mistake isn't that he's doing a bad job, it's that the outfit is not for me!" Ryan called after him, but it was too late.

Ryan sat back down on the couch. Carmen's date would be none too happy when he found out his suit didn't fit, but Ryan didn't find himself particularly caring about the guy's impending wardrobe malfunction.

He sat listening to the distant sound of a sewing machine interlaced with bickering in a language he didn't understand. By the time both men emerged an hour later, sweat beading on both of their foreheads, Ryan's unease had become a raging panic. It had become obvious the emotions Ryan was experiencing were not his own, but he was having trouble ignoring them.

"Come this way, please," said the brother in the suit, motioning for Ryan to follow him. Ryan reluctantly complied and entered the dressing room to be greeted by a freshly altered ensemble.

When Ryan was dressed and examining himself in the mirror a short time later, he asked, "Just what kind of dance is this?"

"Hopefully a costume ball, or you are going to look silly!" said the man. "And I don't say that lightly as you'll be wearing my design."

"Wonderful."

"At least you'll have company." He nodded at the two other garment bags hanging on a hook nearby.

Ryan turned to the side, deciding he made a pretty good Sherlock Holmes. The costume even came with the cool hat and pipe, same as had seen in the old movies. Ryan placed the pipe between his lips, put his right hand underneath it, and struck a pose. Not bad at all if he did say so himself. The tailors had done a hell of a job.

The brothers circled Ryan smiling, obviously agreeing with Ryan's own assessment.

It was after four o'clock when Ryan pulled the VW into the safe room garage. He would have made it sooner, but he made extra sure no one was following him.

Ryan was feeling good as he pressed the button in the elevator. He had fixed a car, picked up the laundry, and completed the strangest job of his monster hunting career. Plus, Carmen's panicked feeling, which he had been enduring for several hours, had finally subsided to a dull dread which he found easier to tune out. He thought about grabbing a ticket to a game before he headed home.

# Chapter 14

"If you're trying to wear my carpet down to a more fashionable level, at least alter your path a bit," Sylvia suggested as she studied the neat rows of playing cards arranged in front of her and tried to find a place for the three of clubs she had turned up.

Carmen stopped. She had been pacing back and forth for half an hour. "It's almost four o'clock. Where is he? What could have happened to him?"

"I'd say he's probably 500 miles away. What did you expect, Carmen? He delivered you as promised. What possible reason would he have for staying? Unless you think he's going to come back and try to kill us? Or do you imagine there is some other motivating factor keeping him here? Did you really think the guy was going to pick up your clothes for you?"

"He left his bags." Carmen motioned to where Ryan's two duffel bags lay on the floor.

"I'm sure he can replace them. Tell you what, let me call D'Oliveira's and see if he's been there." She was dialing the tailor's number into the burner phone when they heard the roll-up door opening below them.

"Delivery!" Ryan hollered when the elevator door opened a minute later. He strode into the loft carrying several large garment bags.

"Where have you been?" Carmen demanded. Ryan felt her dread pass, to be replaced by a rush of relief-tinged anger.

Deciding the answer was too obvious to warrant a verbal response, Ryan held up the garment bags. The feeling of anger grew. Apparently he had been mistaken.

Sylvia went over and opened a coat closet. "Hang them there."

"Yes, ma'am." Ryan did so, and then stopped in front of Sylvia with his palm open.

Sylvia patted the pockets of her velour robe. "Why, I'm sorry sir, but I seem to be all out of cash. Perhaps I can offer you some other form of payment." She made a motion to open her robe.

Instead of the stricken reaction Sylvia had expected, Ryan raised his eyebrows and crossed his arms. "Maybe. Let's see what you got."

Sylvia pushed the robe back into place. "It learns. Amazing."

"There were only three costumes; the rest were business suits. So which one of you is going stag?" Ryan asked, hanging up the bags. He was only a teensy bit disappointed that Sylvia hadn't carried through with her offer.

"Both of us," said Carmen.

"Given recent events, my date remembered he had to wax his car," Sylvia supplied.

Ryan looked to Carmen.

"Mine was killed two weeks ago." Carmen felt a wince of remorse. She had been planning to attend with Henry.

"Oh, sorry."

"It's okay, we weren't that close. More acquaintances and occasional colleagues than friends," she said, too quickly.

Ryan thought Carmen might be downplaying her relationship with the deceased a bit, but knew better than to press the issue. "So what's with this dance?" he asked. "Please don't tell me it's why you had to come to Chicago."

Carmen nodded. "Part of it. And it's not a dance, it's a costume ball."

"You have got to be kidding me. We just risked our lives driving half way across the country, dodging killers, so you two could attend a *dance*?"

"I told you — it's not a dance, it's a ball."

Ryan was almost vibrating with anger. "Yeah, I gathered that much. The outfits kind of gave it away. Please tell me it's for some worthwhile special event. Saving an orphanage so you can eat the orphans later? Blood drive? Raising money for the Red Cross?"

Carmen and Sylvia shared a look.

"Oh, for crying out loud. You're not going to tell me what's up? After what we've been through? Really?"

"It's an annual dance," Carmen offered.

"I thought you said it was a ball!" Ryan shouted.

"Think of it as a vampire family reunion," tried Sylvia.

"What, so every vampire in the U.S. goes? Are there sack races?"

"A lot of us do, yes, but this year I have a feeling attendance will be low," Carmen said.

"Murder tends to be a downer," said Sylvia.

"But you two are going anyway, I assume?"

Carmen nodded.

"And everyone will know you two will be there?" Ryan asked, though he knew the answer. It meant there was a good chance there would be another attack, and if there was Ryan wouldn't be around to protect them. And Carmen would die. After everything he had gone through to get her here. What a waste.

He remembered his intentions had always been to kill Carmen as soon as they made it to Chicago, but he was damned if he was going to let someone else do it.

The girls watched as Ryan went through some internal struggle. Finally he said, "I fixed your car."

"What car?" Carmen asked, surprised. She thought she was good at reading him, but that was not what she had been expecting him to say.

"The Karmann Ghia."

"I wasn't aware that it was broken," said Sylvia.

"You left it sitting for I don't know how long. You can't do that with a car. They need to be driven at least once a week. It needed freshening up. It still needs a new gas tank and tires, but at least it's running."

"It's yours."

"What?" Ryan said, taken aback by the offer.

"The car. You can have it. Consider it payment rendered for the last couple of days. You can drive it back home. Don't worry — it's legal. I bought it new. The pink slip is somewhere in the top drawer of the desk. If I remember correctly there is even some cash in that drawer. Use it to buy yourself some new tires and a gas tank."

"Thanks, but I'm charging you the same rate for bringing you here as I did Carmen."

Both Carmen and Sylvia looked at him inquisitively. Finally Sylvia spoke. "You were paid? I thought you did it for free."

"I most certainly did not! I brought Carmen here as a personal favor, which a friend of mine paid on her behalf." He stared at Sylvia, letting the implication sink in.

"Fat chance. Take the car and get out of here before I decide to make you supper," Sylvia said.

"I'll take the car if you're so eager to get rid of it, but you owe me. One personal favor. And, *not* a small one."

"And when do you propose to collect?" asked Sylvia. "You're riding off into the sunset any minute now, never to be seen again."

"Then what would it hurt to owe me?"

"No dice. You're going to ask me to give up a vampire. Betray someone I know, someone I may care about, so that you can kill them," Sylvia said.

Ryan did his best to look affronted. "What do you think I am? A monster? I promise I will not ask you to betray anyone."

Sylvia stood there staring at him, arms crossed. At last she said, "Fine. I owe you *one* personal favor so long as it doesn't involve betraying anyone I care about. Happy?"

Ryan nodded, looking quite pleased with himself. He had expected nothing and was glad that his quick thinking managed to net him something for all of his trouble. He had no idea what to do with a favor, but a vampire owing you one had to be worth something. At the very least he could have her push the cops into forgiving his next speeding ticket.

Once the deal was struck, Carmen walked up to Ryan and placed her hands on his arms. She had rather enjoyed watching Sylvia squirm a little. Her friend had been right, of course: it was an empty bargain. They wouldn't be seeing Ryan again so Sylvia had nothing to lose by agreeing to it.

Saddened, Carmen looked up at him. "Thank you for looking after me. I probably would have had a more difficult time making it here without you."

"Probably? More difficult? Try definitely not made it here at all." Ryan looked back at her, unflinchingly meeting her deep brown eyes with his steely gray ones.

He knew his mind had already been made up. His course of action had been inevitable before he even woke up that morning, set even before they had entered Carmen's house and been blown back out of it. Had Ryan been entirely honest with himself, he would say it had been decided when he had first laid eyes on her that night in the restaurant bar, when his heart put his brain in checkmate.

But it wasn't until that very moment that he finally admitted it to himself.

Carmen's brows furrowed as she watched the display on Ryan's face, wondering if he was going to start talking about car repairs again.

"So, when is this dance?" Ryan asked.

"At nine. But shouldn't you be going? I would have thought you'd be half way to California by now," Carmen said.

"He couldn't leave without his bags, remember? And he had to deliver your clothes," Sylvia teased.

"That anxious to get rid of me, huh?" Ryan asked.

"Of course not. I mean, I don't care when you leave. Leave whenever you want," Carmen said, letting her hands fall to her sides and taking a half step back.

"I planned on it. I figure maybe I'll take off after the dance, depending on how things go."

"What do you mean? You're not going to the ball," said Carmen.

"Yes I am. I need to look after my investment." Ryan nodded over at Sylvia.

"You can't," Carmen insisted.

Sylvia said, "Technically he *can*, assuming he had a date with an invitation. Which he doesn't. So it would have been more appropriate for you to say he *won't* be going."

"Yes, I will. I'll go with Carmen. You have an invitation, right?" Ryan asked.

Carmen shook her head. "I do, but you won't. Not only is it presumptuous to think I would accompany you, but your obligation to me is finished."

"You're right, it is. To be honest with you, I had planned on catching a Sox game my first night in town, but then again I planned on being here two days ago. But since someone doesn't fly, I missed my game. Since I can't do what I want, I figured I'd check out this shindig of yours instead. And seeing as you're the one that made me miss my game in the first place, it's only fair you take me to the dance make up for it."

"You don't have anything to wear. It's a costume ball, and there's no time to get something appropriate," Carmen protested.

"We can stick an apple in his mouth and he can go as dinner," suggested Sylvia. "Or he can wear nothing at all and go as dessert."

Ryan ignored her. "I can wear the Sherlock outfit in the closet."

Again Carmen shook her head. "No, you can't. The man it was made for was a couple of inches shorter than you and not as…big. It would take a tailor hours to alter it to fit you."

Ryan nodded. "Two and a half to be exact. I'm bigger than you think."

"I'm liking my dessert idea better and better," said Sylvia.

"You want to go to the ball so you can take us all out at once," accused Carmen, but she didn't believe it. She had been reduced to grasping at straws, and she briefly wondered why that was, when she secretly wanted him there with her.

"Wow, that would make me a pretty lame date. Besides, I understand someone else already has that plan. I'd hate to be a copycat. I'm more of an innovator when it comes to killing your type. So, are you going you take me to this dance or what?"

Now it was Carmen's turn for an internal struggle. She found that she wanted nothing more than to take him, and that bothered her. A lot. She needed to prove to herself that this was some misplaced desire that stemmed from the emotional rollercoaster ride they had been on together. A want born out of the close proximity she had spent with Ryan. Like how hostages can feel a connection with their kidnappers.

Ryan shrugged off Carmen's refusal to give him an answer. "No problem. I never had the time to ask many women out, but a buddy of mine back in the army told me that it's all about the law of averages. Ask enough chicks out, and sooner or later you're bound to get lucky."

He turned, extending his hand to Sylvia. "Miss D'Anchemant, would you do me the honor of taking me to the dance?"

Sylvia gave a wicked smile and moved to take Ryan's hand in hers. "Why, Ryan, I would love to accompany—"

Carmen literally jumped between them, batting their hands down. Ryan blinked at the speed at which she moved.

Carmen turned to Sylvia, "Oh, no you don't." Then to Ryan, "Fine, I will go to the ball with you."

"Fine?" Ryan shook his head. "Honestly Carmen, if your heart's not in it I would rather go with Sylvia. She actually seems to have a good time when we're together."

Sylvia nodded. "It's true. Why, just yesterday afternoon Ryan and I were—"

"I *want* to go to the ball with you," said Carmen.

"I'm not feeling it," said Ryan.

"*Please* let me take you to the ball." Carmen's eyes had narrowed and her voice had lowered, taking on a dangerous quality.

Ryan decided not to push it any further. "Yeah, all right, I guess I'll go with you."

Carmen glared at him before storming off. Ryan let out a gentle laugh as he watched her go. His moment was cut short by a hand on his shoulder and a whisper in his ear. "You're learning. But you had better be careful; she may decide to keep you."

# Chapter 15

They were going to be late.

Apparently getting ready for a ball was an all-evening event, and two women sharing the same bathroom exponentially increased the time it took.

Ryan was annoyed. The emotion was evenly split between his own and Carmen's. He tried to content himself with the fact that it was Carmen's emotions he was sharing tonight as opposed to Sylvia's. He would hate to have to endure Sylvia's emotions at a dance, especially if any grinding was involved. He would be forced to lock himself in a bathroom.

Speaking of bathrooms, it was eight thirty and the loft's single bathroom had been occupied without interruption for hours.

Ryan finally gave up waiting, figuring his chances for a turn were slim to none. He grabbed his costume and changed upstairs. He was ready to go five minutes later, and spent the next fifteen minutes after that alternating between fidgeting and checking the time on the wall clock, which he had verified and corrected using both his watch and a local news station.

Carmen exited first. Her dress was dark red velvet, as was its matching cap. The ensemble was form-fitting on top, with a row of brass buttons that ran down to the waist, where the skirt bubbled out in pleats. Black lace ruffles lined the hem and she wore black lace gloves that ended at her wrists.

Ryan had assumed that, because Carmen's date had been killed, his own costume was paired with Sylvia's. But no — Ryan was Sherlock Holmes to Carmen's Irene Adler.

Ryan couldn't help but stare. Carmen was stunning. Flawless. A Spanish beauty without equal. His heart skipped the same beat it had when he first laid eyes upon her. He corralled it and forced his mind to take over, moving on to something more productive.

"So, do you guys pick your outfits based on when you died?" he asked her. That would be useful identifying who might be on the Council, assuming any of them were going to attend the dance. They would certainly be among the oldest vampires there. All he had to do was keep an eye out for cavemen or togas.

"We prefer the terms *turned* or *made*. *Died* is somewhat rude, though not entirely untrue. And, no, the last time we tried that it didn't go over well. Most of the people didn't want to divulge their age. The women all ended up being someone from the twentieth century, and we had four Napoleons and two Moses. There were squabbles."

Ryan smiled. "So who did you go as?"

"Sylvia was right: you *are* learning." Carmen smiled back at him.

Ryan checked the clock again. Two minutes to nine. "We're going to be late."

"If you're going to spend time around Sylvia, get used to it."

"You can't entirely lay the blame on her. We would be late even if we didn't wait for her to finish," Ryan pointed out.

"I'm only late because I had to share a bathroom with Sylvia. Left to my own devices I am never late."

"Me either. I keep reminding myself that some people actually consider it fashionable to arrive late to things. I bet this dance is like that," Ryan offered.

"Of course it is. The ball officially began at eight. Nine is fashionably late. Nine thirty is simply late."

Carmen crossed her arms and stared at the bathroom door as if willing it to open. Ryan could have told her that didn't work; he had tried it for an hour and a half earlier.

He found himself studying Carmen again, marveling that he found her just as attractive when she was mad as when she was happy. Before Ryan met her he thought love at first sight was a thing people made up for books and TV shows. But now he wasn't so sure.

Not that he loved her, of course. He couldn't. She was a monster. He could never love her. But still, he could finally understand how that might happen to someone else. Two people who were compatible.

Ryan felt an unease creep over himself as he watched her.

Carmen began to fret; Ryan had been staring at her for the last minute. Was something out of place? Smudged? Maybe a detail of her costume wasn't right? Not that Ryan would notice that — she doubted he even realized who she was dressed as. Still, something must be wrong. But it couldn't be! Sylvia had assured her everything was perfect. Sylvia wouldn't lie to her. Not tonight.

Finally, after another full minute under his scrutiny, when Carmen couldn't stand it any longer, she whirled on Ryan. "Is something wrong?"

"You mean besides us being late? No, why?" Ryan asked.

"Because you're staring at me."

"No, I wasn't."

"Yes, you were."

"I wasn't."

"You were."

"It's just that...." Ryan looked away, obviously uncomfortable talking about what had been bothering him so much.

Carmen was close to panicking. She was going to start to perspire. It was a nervous tick she had, one she had been able to control for almost a century, ever since her once-storybook relationship had crumbled to dust.

Vampires didn't perspire to cool off, because they didn't overheat. Carmen did it out of some remembered habit she had when alive, and it frustrated her to no end. To make matters worse she didn't have sufficient moisture in her to sweat very much, so the perspiration was cut with blood. Which stained. Now she started to panic, which only made things worse.

Clearly something was very wrong with her appearance. She made a moderate attempt most of the time to look presentable, but for the Convocation she had gone all out. It was expected. She would be on display at least part of the time. People would be looking to find fault with her, spread rumors, create gossip. She needed to look fantastic and act perfectly.

"Well, what is it?" Carmen screamed. If Ryan told her this dress made her ass look fat, god help her, she would kill him right there and go to the ball by herself.

Ryan took one of his deep breaths, letting it out slowly before moving closer to her. Carmen faced him, her anxiety bathing both of them.

"Well, out with it! Tell me what's wrong with me now, while there's still time to fix it." Carmen pulled out a small mirror from a pocket in her dress and double-checked her face, thankful for the thousandth time that the vampire reflection thing was a myth.

Ryan placed a hand on each of her shoulders as if preparing to impart some terrible news. As his annoyance had grown over the last hour or so while he waited for the girls to finish he actually had planned to tell Carmen that her costume made her ass look fat. He'd decided that for maximum impact he would let the comment slip as she got out of the car, after they had arrived. However, seeing as she was asking for it now….

But looking into Carmen's worried eyes, with her fear washing over him, Ryan felt his mind change. He couldn't do that to her. He could tell this meant too much to her. Not only could he not do that, but he found himself wanting to do something else entirely.

Ryan's mind rebelled at what he was about to do. The fact that he had been willingly helping a vampire was almost too much for him. Wanting a vampire was far too alien for him to come to terms with.

He tried to stop it, but she was the most beautiful woman he had ever seen, and his next action was a forgone conclusion.

"The problem with you is that you're too perfect." Ryan bent down. A foot apart. Then inches apart. Then less. He could see the golden flecks in her eyes. Smell her perfume. The scent of her makeup. Her earthy breath.

He kissed her, just light peck on the lips. He withdrew after the first gentle contact. He didn't trust himself with anything else, and she would never forgive him if he marred the cosmetics she had spent so long applying. The makeup really was impeccable. If he smudged it he didn't think he could endure another hour of waiting around for it to be put right.

Ryan was proud of himself. Not only had he showed restraint, proving that he could resist a vampire's wiles, succumbing only as far as he wanted to and no more — but he had startled Carmen. Shock was plainly evident in her wide eyes and parted lips as he started to pull away.

He was surprised to learn that, when properly motivated, Carmen's emotions could change faster than Sylvia's, and when they did they could be far more intense. His face had withdrawn to almost a foot away from hers when Carmen leapt at it.

There was no time for him to react. Ryan's own eyes went wide as Carmen's lips crushed against his. Then he was lost in the most wonderful kiss he had ever experienced. His hands acted of their own accord, wrapping themselves around her slender figure, bringing her to him.

Carmen told herself to stop, but found she wasn't listening. Her mind replayed the instant he leaned close to her. When she felt his warmth approaching, the scent of him filling her senses. The knowledge that he was going to kiss her hit a split second before it happened. The thrill set her on fire.

She was alarmed to realize that she had wanted this to happen for quite some time, and now that it had started, she was completely disinclined to desist. She clung to him, eager to feel his heat through the many layers of their clothing. Their tongues sparred playfully, and she wondered if the world would truly end if she missed the opening Ball of the Convocation.

"Everyone ready to go?" came Sylvia's airy voice as she exited the bathroom. A solid black mermaid dress clung to her. Black feline ears poked out of her hair, each with a pale pink center. If possible, the ensemble made her even more slinky than she normally was.

"Apparently not," Sylvia said, dropping the feline mask she had been holding up to her face by its slender wire.

Sylvia folded her hands in front of her and leaned against the kitchen counter, watching the epic embrace displayed before her. "Typically we reserve these types of escapades until after the ball has concluded, or at the very least until everyone is so drunk they won't remember them."

The couple abruptly broke apart. Carmen was equal parts embarrassed and flustered at being caught. Ryan was mostly horrified by what they had done, and more horrified that he wanted to do it again.

"Now that is a 'morning after' moment I wish I had a camera handy to capture," Sylvia said. Then she spotted the wall clock and frowned. "We're going to be late. You'll just have to fix yourselves in the car."

Sylvia grabbed her purse and the keys to the Odyssey and hurried to the elevator, making it clear that any reason for their late arrival was now completely transferred from herself to the offending couple.

Carmen checked herself in the mirror. It would take some work, and it would never be as good as it was, but she thought she could repair most of the damage before they reached the Manor.

Then she looked at Ryan and frowned. She pulled out a handkerchief, wet it with her tongue, and begun to wipe the red smear from his mouth. Ryan immediately recoiled, forcing Carmen to grab his chin with her other hand. "Hold still," she said, continuing the unrelenting assault.

Ryan hadn't endured anything like it since he was a child. He stood motionless as the wet cloth accosted him, and not gently. Finally, sometime after the elevator doors had already parted open in the garage, after Sylvia had gotten in the back seat of the Honda, Carmen stopped the damp attack, looked at him appraisingly, and said, "That will have to do."

After Sylvia relayed the initial directions to Ryan the car ride was spent in silence. Occasionally Ryan stole a glimpse of his passengers in the review mirror.

Carmen spent the ride busily applying makeup. Ryan was thankful she could see in the dark. Somehow Sylvia always managed to return his clandestine looks with either wink and a smirk or a kissy-face that sent Ryan's eyes back to the road.

Ryan was pleased to note that they weren't the last ones to arrive, but unhappy that their ride stuck out like a sore thumb in the small line of limousines, Bentleys, and Rolls Royces that were entering the guarded gates to a gigantic estate.

Their Honda van crept along the driveway until it was their turn to stop in front of the massive house. An attendant opened each of their doors, and thankfully had the decency to not comment on their vehicle.

Not everyone was as tactful. At a whisper that was loud enough for even a human to hear, a lady said to a man, "Did you see what Carmen and Sylvia pulled up in?" to which her date promptly responded, "You mean the vehicle that wouldn't draw attention to themselves? Really, Margaret, I told you we should not have come in the Bentley. That car made us an obvious target the entire trip here."

Irked by her companion's response to the scandal, the lady immediately repeated it to a nearby woman who she found more receptive.

# Chapter 16

The huge ebony doors were wide enough to allow all three of them to enter the massive foyer together with room to spare. Ryan was in the middle, flanked by Carmen and Sylvia. Glistening white marble floors led up to a huge double staircase that ascended to the second floor. Costumed guests were milling about the room, though most were gradually joining the procession to the left that headed through an archway and down a second wide hall that went in the direction of the grand ballroom.

Ryan glanced about the room, taking in all of the vampires. There were more of them just in the entry of the mansion than he had ever seen in one place. He was surrounded. The thought made him more than a little uncomfortable.

To make matters worse, he was garnering more than his fair share of looks. Ryan wasn't sure if it was because they somehow recognized him as human, or if it was because he was monopolizing two beautiful women. But it wasn't his imagination. He noticed the glances, some sly, some open, and the ensuing whispers that accompanied them.

A well-groomed musketeer strode up to the trio and greeted them enthusiastically. "It seems my luck has changed!"

"Hello, Thomas." Sylvia didn't sound happy to see the approaching gentleman, and she pointedly switched sides, placing both Carmen and Ryan between her and the smiling man.

Ryan gave him the once-over. He was extremely handsome. Dark hair, dark eyes, and a knowing grin. The only thing he was missing in the standard equation was tall. The man could only be generously referred to as being of average height.

"Sylvia, Carmen — you are both absolutely beautiful as usual! And this fine gentleman is...?" Thomas's voice trailed off as he inclined his head to Ryan.

"Ryan," he replied, and stuck his hand out. Thomas was quick to shake it with a firm hand and a wide smile that didn't pretend to hide the elongated canines that were a vampire's trademark. Even though Ryan knew this man was a vampire, there was something about the guy he couldn't help but like. After a moment Ryan concluded that it was because Thomas made absolutely no apologies for what he was.

"It seems we might be able to do ourselves a mutual favor," Thomas said, addressing the three of them together. "I find myself a date short, while you appear to be a date tall, as it were."

"Thomas, without a date? Why, perhaps the reason for tonight's celebration should be shifted?" suggested Sylvia.

"I was supposed to be accompanied by Gretchen but, alas, she got cold feet. Something about recent events and possible death. Honestly, I stopped listening to her early on in the conversation. She always has been more looks than lady to be honest. I'm afraid some women are not fortunate enough to possess both qualities like you, dear Sylvia."

Ryan stood there uncomfortably as Thomas tried inching around him to get closer to Sylvia. But as Thomas moved towards Sylvia, she inched away from him, causing a kind of slow motion circling that was threatening to make Ryan dizzy.

"We'd be delighted to help you out Thomas, wouldn't we Sylvia?" Carmen said to her friend with an innocent smile, but with her eyes narrowing in sly pleasure. She placed her body in Sylvia's way, preventing her escape from Thomas.

Sylvia did not share Carmen's joy, but was only too happy to turn the tables. "Of course we would. I'm sure Carmen would love to accom—"

"It's settled!" Thomas said, cutting Sylvia off and taking a very surprised Ryan by the arm and leading him away.

"Wait!" Startled, Carmen lurched forward to grab for Ryan, but it was too late, the men were off in the crowd.

"Thomas, you come back here with him right this instant!" Sylvia hissed after the retreating couple.

Ryan was desperately trying to think of a way out of his predicament. He decided his only course of action was to attempt to pry the man's hand from his arm. But before he could start, Thomas had settled them down in line, slickly cutting in front of a couple that had turned to chat with someone in line behind them.

When the distracted couple turned back to glare at the line hoppers, Thomas simply flashed them his smile and then said to Ryan, while letting go of his arm, "I owe you for helping to perpetuate the romantic tension between Sylvia and me. Don't worry — I will give you back to them before the first dance."

Dancing and food were two things Ryan had no plans to partake in that night. "Romantic tension? I think she was giving off more of a gentle disdain for you," Ryan said.

"That's what she wants everyone to think. I constantly pursue, while she constantly avoids. But the results are inevitable. She can't run forever. Sooner or later she will give in to my pursuit. Do you know she's the only woman who has successfully resisted my ample charms?"

Ryan glanced around. There was no question that there were more vampires here than he had ever witnessed in one place, dozens and dozens more, and they still had yet to enter the actual ballroom. "That's quite a statement."

Thomas laughed as he watched Ryan making a mental tally. "I meant the only women I *pursued*, not on the planet!"

"Women. So, you're not gay?" Ryan wanted to make sure. Despite Thomas's words, the guy's vibes were all over the place.

"When you have been around as long as I have, you tend not to let petty things like gender get in the way of a relationship. That being said, I am generally more interested in the fairer sex. However, I would be happy to make an exception for you."

"No thanks. So, um, is it common then? I mean, we won't create any problems going in like this?" Ryan didn't see any other same-sex couples, but the line was long, and he didn't exactly want to call attention to himself by stepping outside of the queue to stare at everyone.

"Well, if it does, at least we won't be alone; I hear there's a pair of women somewhere behind us." Thomas chuckled.

It took Ryan a second to get it and when he did, he gave Thomas a sour expression.

"Relax, Ryan. There will be several same-sex couples. In fact it wouldn't surprise me if Viktor and Hector arrive together. They claim to be brothers, but if you ask me the love going on between them is a bit more than brotherly, if you catch my meaning. Besides, bringing a member of one's own sex to the Ball is certainly no rarer than one of us taking a human."

"Wonderful."

"You should be happy; you are guaranteed to be one of the topics of conversation tonight. Many people would relish your place."

"So, are human dates really that uncommon?" Ryan took another look around. He had assumed a lot of the guests were humans. Dates first, food sources later. If all of these people were vampires Ryan had sorely misjudged the number of creatures he was surrounded by. It was not a comforting thought.

"Of course not. There will be plenty of your kind here tonight. Companions that are waiting for the right time to be turned: a birthday, or certain date they have a fondness for, or what have you. When I said one of us, what I meant was: you will be the only human on the arm of a *Council* member. I daresay, we tend to be held to a higher standard and, much like human celebrities, are the prime topics for gossip and slander. Some of it actually untrue. As such, we tend to take what you would call safe bets as dates to these types of functions. So much propriety... it all gets rather dull."

Ice shot through Ryan's veins. He was walking next to a member of the elusive vampire Council! Ryan anticipated that at least some of them would be at the dance, if not all of them. He had expected it. He just hadn't thought he'd be striking up a conversation with one, let alone going as their date.

Thomas misinterpreted his companion's reaction. "No need to worry, my man. It's one of the few benefits of being on the Council. Despite any stir something might cause, no one can actually stop you from doing things like taking scandalous dates to a Ball, or cutting in line."

"I take it you enjoy bucking the standard?" Ryan asked.

"Oh, I live for it really. Is this your first time at a Convocation?"

"A convo-what?"

"I'll take that as a yes. I've attended all of them, and I would have remembered you. Let's see, the first thing you need to know is that they will announce us by our formal names." Thomas cast a sideways glance at Ryan, "So you might want to come up with something if you don't care to use your real one. If you decide to go that route I suggest something long and difficult to pronounce. Simon takes pride in his excellent elocution and delivery. And he will also not risk embarrassment by asking you to repeat yourself."

Ryan thought about it. There was no way he was going to use his real name, so when it was their turn in line, and a tuxedo-clad man of serious disposition signaled for them to come forward, Ryan was prepared.

The announcer put his hand out to stop Ryan and Thomas right before the entrance to the ballroom. "Baroni." He inclined his head to Thomas, and then looked at Ryan expectantly.

"Ryan Jürgen Schiaparelli," Ryan mumbled out his own first name, tacking on the two most difficult names he had encountered.

"Oh, nice one," said Thomas, as they waited to be announced.

Simon turned to the room. "Baroni Thomas de Castrocario and Mr. Ryan Jürgen Schiaparelli."

To Thomas's disappointment, Simon's pronunciation was impeccable. "Ah well, there's always next year," he said to Ryan, and then the vampire hunter and his new Council companion descended the staircase to a wave of stares and murmured speculation. Thomas beamed at the attention while Ryan looked uncomfortable enough for the both of them.

Once the pair reached the swirl of the polished floor, the next pair of guests was announced and the fickle room's topic of conversation switched to greet them.

"I'm afraid the main course for tonight will be rather liquid for your taste. However, the wine is always excellent, and I recommend drinking as much as you possibly can. I always do," Thomas said as they were quickly engulfed in the crowd.

A smattering of waiters circled the room like an army of vigilant penguins, holding trays of crystal wine glasses sparkling with a selection of both clear and opaque liquids. Three sides of the room were lined in floor-to-ceiling French windows that overlooked a terrace surrounded by a spectacular garden. An actual orchestra was elevated in a corner and played classical music at a soft volume. To one side of the main entrance, along the windowless wall, was a long bar.

Ryan looked to see if there were people suspended upside down behind it with stints or taps stuck into them.

But there was nothing so crass. In fact, if one ignored the large blood-filled Lalique crystal decanters, kept at a specific temperature by special heaters beneath them, the only thing remarkable about the bar was its massive inventory. In addition to wine and champagne was a mind-boggling selection of other alcohol. Spirits from dozens of countries, spanning several centuries, sat in rows waiting to be consumed.

Thomas led Ryan purposefully to the bar, and upon arriving ordered himself a red wine before looking at Ryan expectantly.

"I'll have a Seven-Up," Ryan said.

"A soda? Really? With nothing else in it?" Thomas was aghast by the prospect.

"You know, you're right. I should live a little. Throw in some ice," Ryan told the bartender.

Thomas looked horrified as the bartender handed Ryan his drink, on the rocks, not bothering to wait for Thomas to relay the order.

"I don't drink while I'm on duty," Ryan explained to the vampire.

"On duty? Do you mean Sylvia paid for you? Oh wonderful! Please tell me how much!" Thomas looked genuinely pleased by the revelation.

"I'm not a gigolo."

"I suspected not," Thomas said, trying to hide his disappointment, "but one could always hope."

"Besides, I came with Carmen, not Sylvia."

"You don't say?" The news perked Thomas up a bit. "That's potentially even more scandalous. Given the recent turn of events am I to assume you're a bodyguard?"

"Yup."

"And you're protecting Carmen? I hope your fee reflects the level of discomfort you will encounter. She's been — how do I put this delicately? — *bitchy* for quite a few years now."

"That's what I hear. Sylvia gave me some insight into why a couple of days ago."

"A couple of days? So the three of you have been together?"

"Not by choice. I was originally hired to protect Carmen, but it seems I've been roped into protecting both of 'em."

"That happens with those two. You'll learn that where one is, the other is usually not far away. I recommend you charge double. Putting up with that pair should be worth a fortune."

Ryan nodded in agreement. "Already taken care of. I can't complain about the pay, but they are quite a handful."

"Now, see, that's what I've been dying to do: get a hold of Sylvia to find out how much of a handful she really is."

Ryan reflected briefly on the time when he had two pleasant handfuls of Sylvia before answering. "You won't be disappointed. But I'm surprised you've found her a difficult conquest." Ryan was no expert, but it was obvious Thomas was a ladies' man and Sylvia was, well, more or less a lady... assuming one used the term loosely.

"That is the frustrating part. Not only is she the first woman to ever refuse me, but as you alluded to, she doesn't have a history of being particularly selective. It's rather embarrassing."

Ryan wasn't sure if he should be offended by that, but decided not to dwell on it. "So what's up?"

"I'm not really sure. The harder I try, the less receptive she becomes."

"So stop trying."

"I can't. That's the troubling part. I keep getting drawn back to her, like a moth to the flame. Giving up on the hunt goes against my nature."

Ryan understood. "Mine too." Ryan considered for a bit before continuing, "So, Sylvia is really the first woman to refuse you, huh? That's quite a statement. I'm not saying I don't believe it, but...."

"Well, not to undersell myself, but I choose my targets wisely. Which is why Sylvia was so promising!"

"Ah. So... Carmen?" Ryan knew he shouldn't ask a question when the answer was likely to bother him.

Thomas chuckled. "Oh, heavens no. Didn't I just say I choose my targets wisely? I don't mind playing with fire occasionally, but wrestling with dynamite? I'll pass."

"Dynamite?"

"Yes, you see, I like my women smoldering. Not too hot to burn, but not completely cold either. And you know what they call Carmen, of course?"

Ryan didn't, but he nodded anyway. "I got you, but I'm still not seeing how dynamite fits in."

"Seeing as you've been hired to guard her, you obviously have had a chance to get a good look at the goods, so to speak. Needless to say Carmen has countless suitors. Yet she has selected none of them in decades. Why is that, you ask? Well, I'll tell you.

"When you encounter a piece of unexploded ordinance there are only two possible outcomes: Either it's dead, and will never be brought back to life. Or the fuse is simmering below the surface, and the ensuing explosion will bring devastation and ruin to whoever is unlucky enough to be nearby when it goes off."

"Devastation and ruin?" Not only was the guy a little longwinded, he made no sense. Ryan happened to know firsthand that Carmen wasn't dead — at least not in that way, and though Ryan believed any type of a relationship with a vampire was ruinous, he didn't think Thomas held the same view.

"Commitment, my dear man. Or worse, marriage! Carmen strikes me as the type of person who is extremely selective, but once she decides on a fellow she will trap the poor man and beat him into lifelong submission before he can escape." Thomas shuddered. "Marriage! Can you only imagine? One woman for the rest of your life? For you it might not be so bad — what is the worst you could be burdened with, a handful of decades? But for us? Perish the thought. It could last an eternity."

Ryan chuckled. "I'm with you. Never had a serious relationship in my life, don't plan on starting one any time soon. No advantage to one that I can think of, lots of downside."

Thomas beamed at him. "Well said! I think that calls for another drink!"

The two of them went for seconds, then leaned back against the bar to survey the room. Ryan tried to calm his nerves, but it was difficult given his surroundings. If even a small percentage of these vampires turned on him he had no chance. And a small nagging thought insisted that this was all some set up. That at the end of the night he, and all of the other humans in attendance, would end up as dessert.

Ryan's apprehension lessened as he let himself get caught up listening to Thomas, who had started relating the between-the-sheets ratings of a good portion of the vampire who's-who.

"And that is Sorry Sophie." Thomas pointed out a blonde woman who, though she must have been turned into a vampire in her early twenties, managed to seem much older as she stood there alone.

"Sorry Sophie?" asked Ryan. He studied her. She was undoubtedly attractive, with perfect posture, a slightly upturned nose, and a haughty demeanor that radiated formality. She was by herself, and, on the whole, appeared to be quite content. Except for her fan. She held it angled upwards, an inch away from her face, its blades moving back and forth at incredible speed. Ryan could only guess it was a habit picked up a long time ago that either betrayed uncomfortable nervousness or displeasure.

"Yes, Sophie Eaton. Everyone calls her Sorry Sophie because she's obsessively sorry for herself. There was an unfortunate incident back in Europe that resulted in the loss of her territory. She came to this continent a few hundred years ago expecting to find something here. No luck, I'm afraid."

"Why not?" Ryan asked.

"Because no one particularly likes her. She's old fashioned and a dreadful bore, not to mention a prude."

"Sounds like an aunt I once had. Alright, so no one likes her, and because of that she doesn't get a territory?"

"That sums it up. Though you can't say she isn't persistent. She's been petitioning the Council for a territory of her own ever since she arrived."

"And she keeps on asking, even after being denied? How many times has she pleaded her case?" Ryan had heard somewhere that the definition of insanity was doing the same thing over and over again, expecting a different result.

"Technically, none. To be honest I don't believe we've ever granted her an audience for fear she might have a compelling argument."

"Wow, that's messed up."

"Yes, though between you and me, I think this may be her year. She *is* old, and with the recent murders there will be movement in the Council. We may have no choice but to give her something."

Ryan said, feeling irrationally sorry for the lonely vampire, "So she's not one of your conquests, I take it?"

"Sorry Sophie? Oh heavens no! Even *I* have standards. But do you see that one over there?" Thomas pointed to a group of guests engaged in an animated discussion.

"The one dressed as Cleopatra?" Ryan saw her. She was a comely woman, with olive skin and jet black hair that made her look every bit the part of the famous queen.

"Hailey? No, no, not her. Keep away from her. She's crazy — literally. I believe she is the first case of vampire Alzheimer's."

"Hailey?" Ryan asked. The name seemed too modern for a vampire, let alone one old enough to have dementia.

"It's not her real name. No one knows what her real name is; she changes it whenever she finds one she likes better. It's impossible to keep track of, so I no longer bother to try. I was referring to the other one."

"Elizabeth?" A beautiful redhead with alabaster skin and bright green eyes was giving Cleopatra what, to Ryan, seemed like a forced smile.

"You know her?"

Ryan shook his head. "No."

"But you know her name?" Thomas frowned.

"Not her real one, but I'm pretty sure she's supposed to be Queen Elizabeth."

"Ah, dear Elizabeth is suffering from delusions of grandeur, I see. I apologize; I was confused because her name is, in fact, Elizabeth. Though I daresay she was a Hungarian countess, not an English queen.

"Anyway, she and I spent three solid days in a room in Barcelona. 1895. She never let me come up for air — not that I wanted to mind you. Now *her* I would consider having again. Not marriage, of course, but I could see a week, maybe two."

"So why don't you?" The lady was certainly pretty enough. Ryan watched as she brushed a lock of hair behind her ear and tried to detach herself from the conversation with Cleopatra.

"Apparently when you wait a few days to call them back they get upset… a few years even more so. The fact that telephones were not in regular circulation at the time doesn't seem to make a difference."

"I've been there."

"Haven't we all? Alas, I might not have many second dates, but I do enjoy the first ones."

"Still, if she's that good she might be worth another go," said Ryan.

"I tried, but she's been distracted lately. Seems a hunter has been chasing her all over the country."

Ryan was all ears. "How long has this been going on?"

"Fifteen years, and neither has managed to kill the other. It's quite curious." The way Thomas said it hinted that he had already come to his own conclusions regarding the reason for the prolonged chase.

Ryan felt a shock. He knew exactly which Elizabeth this was, and exactly who had been chasing her all of this time. An associate of Ryan's had been obsessed with tracking the Blood Countess for as long as Ryan could remember. Jack let the vampire slip away over a decade ago and had been dogging her heels ever since. The thing was, every time he got close to her, she would manage to escape — but each time a clue was left behind as to where she was going. It's as if they were playing some strange form of tag, one where he didn't really want to catch her, and she didn't really want to lose him.

Ryan made himself a mental note to see what he could find out about Elizabeth and her regular whereabouts. Maybe he could help his buddy out, or at least determine if the guy really did want to kill this redheaded vamp.

Thomas was watching Ryan. "You're a terrible liar. You *do* know her."

"Know *of* her maybe, but I've never met her before, I promise. Who's the bruiser next to her?" Ryan asked. Elizabeth's date looked like he could handle himself. Ryan wasn't sure if the guy was a vampire or human, but from the way he held himself Ryan was positive the guy was trained. Probably ex-special forces.

"I have no idea who the gentleman is," Thomas said, not even bothering to feign interest. "Never seen him before. I imagine you're not the only bodyguard here. Frankly I'm surprised I didn't see anyone trying to sneak in something more exotic to protect them, like a pack of werewolves."

"I take it that would be frowned upon?" Ryan decided it was best to forget the Blood Countess and focus on the big guy. He was unusually large. Ryan hoped he wasn't a troll, but it was possible. He had tangled with them once or twice before. Nasty creatures. He'd take a fight with a vampire over a troll any day.

"Vampires only, I'm afraid. And the occasional human, of course. Trolls might be an exception, considering recent events, but werewolves are right out."

"It looks like you could use all the help you can get," Ryan said, glancing around the room.

"You're overreacting. Security here is normally tight, and I am sure that tonight it is beyond that."

Ryan couldn't hide his look of disbelief. "Tight? You're joking? Not only were there no metal detectors at the door, but I walked right in without being searched."

"Well, true, but of course they couldn't search the *guests* — that would be bad form."

"I thought it was vampires who were causing all the problems? How can you be sure the killer isn't one of your guests?"

"Hmmm... you do have a point. They seem to be rather focused on keeping out *uninvited* guests. It is possible, though unpalatable, that someone with an invitation is to blame for the murders." Thomas looked around the room with a new mindset before adding, "I begin to see the flaw in our security's plan."

"It's negligent, is what it is," Ryan said. He continued scanning the room, performing a mental assessment of its security, until Simon announced the next couple. Their names brought Ryan's attention to the room's entrance. "Maria del Carmen de Luna and Sylvia D'Anchemant."

# Chapter 17

Carmen spotted them by the bar. Rather than wearing his usual smarmy smile, Thomas was frowning over something. Ryan also looked annoyed as he took in the room with a scowl of disapproval. At first she thought Ryan was angry at being surrounded by vampires, or maybe he and Thomas had a row, but when Carmen followed Ryan's darting eyes she realized his dispute seemed to be with the staff.

She wondered what they had done to offend him. The service at these events was normally impeccable. Had they accidentally offered him blood? She didn't think that would offend Ryan. Disgust maybe, but not offend.

She gave up on her speculation as she reached the ballroom floor. She would find out what the problem was directly from Ryan, and then speak to their hosts about correcting it.

Carmen did her best to thread her way through the crowd towards the two men, gracefully dodging small talk as people tried to engage her. Sylvia was making Carmen's attempt at haste rather difficult, as she seemed only too happy to chat with anyone, and everyone, they encountered.

First up were their hosts, Isabel and Hugo, dressed as Punch and Judy. "Carmen! Sylvia! We're so glad you made it. With everything that's been going on we were worried." Hugo beamed at them.

"We wouldn't miss this for the world," Carmen said.

"Tell me honestly: do you think the attendance is really that terrible, all things considered?" asked Isabel, concern marring the blonde's otherwise perfect features.

"On the contrary, given recent events I think it's marvelous," said Carmen.

"Of course it is," nodded Hugo. "I told Isabel not to worry; we're all perfectly safe here. We even procured a pair of trolls to bolster our security. While you're in Chicago, you two should stay with us until this mess gets sorted out."

"I agree," said Isabel. "We heard about the attempts on your lives from Charles. How dreadful! First Johannes, and then Henry, and they almost got Peter and Elizabeth, and now the two of you!"

"It does put a damper on the festivities," said Sylvia dryly.

"Have you any idea what they're after, or are they simply trying to kill us all?" Carmen asked the couple. If anyone had an inkling as to what was driving these murders, they would.

"I doubt they want to kill us all." Hugo's expression contorted with thought as he prepared to voice the theory that had crossed everyone's mind. "It's more likely this has to do with next week's convening of the Council. Someone is trying to swing a vote in their favor."

"But whatever for?" asked Carmen. She thought about the suggestion and struggled to come up with a connection between the two had been killed, and those who had narrowly escaped death.

"Seriously," Sylvia chimed in, "who would kill so many of us just for a vote? What law could possibly be so important that they would murder us over it?"

"That's the crux of the matter, isn't it? We don't know. All we can do is wildly speculate," said Hugo before speculating. "Whatever it is has to be controversial. If I had to guess, it's one of two things: Either an attempt to bring back the old ways, when we hunted for our food and didn't get it out of bags, or they want to out us — to become known to the humans."

"Don't be an alarmist, dear," said Isabel. "Why would anyone want to do either of those things? No one in their right mind would make our rules any more lax. They protect us, and have served us well for decades. Especially in this era, with all of its new technology. Between cell phones with digital cameras and social media we can't be too careful. Hunting is dangerous. Even if one leaves one's prey alive, there are risks. And why hunt at all when, thanks to entrepreneurs like Carmen, we have a ready supply of blood provided to us?"

"Thank you." Carmen's smile of acknowledgement hid her inner flinch. Her supply chain had been anything but adequate lately, and she realized if it weren't for their friendship, both Isabel and Sylvia would have long since gone to another supplier.

"Don't be naïve, Isabel. Many want to go back to the days of hunting. Some even enjoy the thrill of the kill. Catch and release doesn't sate their desires," Hugo stated.

Isabel didn't bat an eye as she continued, not acknowledging her husband's disagreement with her assertion. "And as far as the other is concerned, it's simply inconceivable that anyone could be so foolish as to think we'd be better off if our existence were known to mortals."

"There are always the radicals that want humans to know us, and fear us," said Hugo.

"I wouldn't go that far. Everyone knows that announcing our existence to humans wouldn't end well for any of us," Carmen said. "But I agree with what you said about being able to hunt again. That's something I know some of us want."

"I miss it sometimes, not having to be so careful," Sylvia lamented.

"We all do, if only a little, but it simply isn't practical anymore," said Isabel.

"There is always the possibility that whoever is behind this is an outsider," said Hugo, though he didn't sound convinced.

"But how would they know about us?" Carmen asked, her skeptical tone echoing Hugo's.

"I don't know, maybe they got to someone. Maybe they're blackmailing one of us into giving the rest away?" Hugo said, one hand going to his chin.

Sylvia shrugged and said, "It could be the Europeans. You know they've been desperate to get their hooks back into us."

Isabel nodded. "That's true. They've been desperate to get us back under their thumb ever since they realized they no longer controlled us."

It was clear to Carmen that everyone was guessing, and their guesses were no better than her own. She wanted to talk to Charles, but she wanted to find Ryan more. She felt a little uneasy throwing him to the wolves. "We really should be going. I need to talk with Charles before the first dance," Carmen said, signaling that it was time for them to move on.

"Of course, but please consider our offer. I mean it when I say that you are welcome to stay with us here," said Hugo.

"Thank you. We will definitely consider it, Hugo," Carmen said before resuming her journey toward the bar.

Thankfully they managed to escape Elizabeth and Hailey with only a cordial nod and a smile, mostly because Sylvia and Elizabeth didn't get along. They were two piranhas in one small pond, even if Elizabeth had removed herself from the hunt lately. Carmen was relieved to avoid them. Elizabeth could be tedious, and conversations with Hailey tended to be odd and unsettling. Carmen knew they would have to do something about the odd vampire at some point soon; her idiosyncrasies were getting worse with each passing year.

Carmen and Sylvia managed to meet Charles right on the way to the bar. Charles, with his immaculately groomed gray hair and dapper mustache, was looking as distinguished as ever dressed as Al Capone. He was talking with three other Council members: Peter, and the brothers Hector and Viktor.

Carmen noted that all three of the Council members were with their dates. The blonde standing with Charles was named Rose. She was an odd duck, hard to pin down. On one hand she preferred living on the fringes of society, almost a street vampire. On the other, she never missed any of the major social functions. Rose didn't talk much, preferring to keep to herself, but that didn't stop her from being a smash hit with anything male, and a few things that weren't. She attracted men seemingly without trying.

Carmen didn't trust her.

"My dear Carmen, you look ravishing." The muscular Peter bent down and kissed her proffered hand, holding onto it a second too long. He was dressed as Romeo. Carmen decided it was wishful thinking on his part.

Peter was attractive. Gorgeous, really. But Carmen found him even more slimy than Thomas, mostly because at least Thomas never hid his intentions. Peter, on the other hand, was a snake in the grass. He claimed to have been a commander in the Roman army, supposedly leading a legion for Octavian in the war against Antony and Cleopatra. Peter claimed a lot of things, including that he was the oldest vampire in North America.

"Carmen, I'm sorry to hear about Henry. Recent events have shocked us all," said Viktor. The short man was almost as wide as he was tall, but none of his girth was fat. Viktor was built like a barge. Huge muscles bulged over every part of him. Tonight he was dressed as a pirate, with an eye patch and sporting a beautifully taxidermied parrot on his shoulder. The only thing missing from his ensemble was a peg leg.

Carmen knew that Hector and Viktor were almost as ancient as Peter. Probably even more so, though they never discounted Peter's claim to the title of oldest vampire in North America.

The rumor had it that Viktor and his brother Hector had been famous gladiators in Ancient Rome. Carmen knew the truth: they had been Vandal soldiers, though they had been turned during the chaos of the sacking of

Rome. Hector had told her the story of their making, long ago.

"Thank you, Viktor. We'll all miss Henry," said Carmen. Rumors had started the moment she agreed to accompany Henry to the Ball. She had only agreed to go with the old recluse because she needed a date. It was basically required that you bring a date to the Ball. Carmen had been putting off suitors for months, and finally had run out of time. Henry had been the least annoying, most harmless prospect she could think of at the time. He cared more about spending his nights amidst nature with actual birds and bees than he did about pursuing the metaphorical ones.

A recluse, Henry kept to himself and rarely got involved with the petty squabbles of the Council members, or the hangers-on that surrounded them. He was more than content wandering the hundreds of acres of his estate in Maine. That's what had been so shocking when he had been killed. Henry kept such a low profile that no one could imagine him attracting the attention of hunters.

When it was discovered that vampires had a hand in the murders, it became even more unlikely that Henry was a target. Henry had a knack for getting along with people and had no real enemies. He wasn't weak by any stretch, he was simply neutral — the Switzerland of the Council. He may have lived long enough to have crossed some people, but Carmen couldn't think of anyone who disliked Henry enough to kill him.

"His death was a tragic loss," Hector added.

Hector and Viktor claimed to be brothers, and you could see the resemblance if you squinted. They both had the dark hair and swarthy features associated with the people who lived along the Mediterranean. But that's where the resemblance stopped.

Unlike his brother, Hector was tall and thin. He would be strikingly handsome if it weren't for his large nose, which looked like it had been broken and never quite set right. Even so, he caught one's eye.

Tonight Hector had chosen to come as the Grim Reaper. It was fitting, Carmen thought. Something about the man had always reminded her of death. He was the epitome of manners and politeness, but something lurked underneath that he did his best to keep hidden.

They had been together once, before Carmen knew better. Their relationship lasted for more years than she cared to remember. She had allowed herself to become so used to life with him that she hadn't realized how miserable she had become. Until finally, one day, he did something that was inexcusable and she left. It was only then, after the weight of his presence had been lifted, that Carmen realized how unhappy she had become, and how happy she was once she shed his shadow.

Hector had been displeased when Carmen broke it off, furious really, but he had always maintained his composure. Hector was an incurably stoic man, or at least appeared to be. He prided himself in his outward lack of emotion.

Since the breakup, Hector had never been anything but cordial to Carmen. Even so, she always watched her back around him. She knew the man had both a vicious streak and a long memory. Hector was one you didn't want to cross.

Each of the brothers was accompanied by a trophy. Viktor was with a girl named Colette who had been no more than fourteen when she was turned sometime in the early nineteenth century in an alley off of Place Pigalle in Paris. She was dressed as a harlequin, and the tight-fitting costume accentuated all that she had to offer.

Hector had brought Margaret. The Swan Princess looked delicate enough to be broken with a breath. It was deceiving. Carmen knew her well. Margaret was a nasty piece of work whose main pleasure in life was to spread rumors, true or not, to see what trouble she could stir up. Then she would sit back and laugh at the destruction she had wrought, not caring if the world crumbled around her.

The only thing Margaret liked better than gossip was meddling with happy couples, especially if it involved her orchestrating the relationship's demise by being the 'other woman.'

"How nice that the two of you came together," said Margaret, showing her dimpled smile. "I understand Carmen would be mourning the loss of Henry, and it is only proper that she wouldn't replace him so soon. But whatever happened to you, Sylvia? Were you unable to get a date? You poor thing... it was only a matter of time before your reputation preceded you."

Sylvia took a half step toward the girl, who ever so slightly nestled herself back into the crook of Hector's arm.

"And what reputation might that be?" Carmen asked. She knew Margaret was baiting Sylvia, but it was time someone taught the skinny little wench a lesson.

Hector did his part to rein in his date, albeit in a backhanded way. "Now, Margaret, we don't talk ill of Council members in their company, no matter how much validity it may have."

"Seeing as Margaret isn't a Council member, would it be ill manners for me to ask if the plotting little bitch was behind the recent attacks? They seem like something that would be right up her alley," said Sylvia.

"That is quite enough, Sylvia. We don't make accusations without proof," Peter said, putting a hand out to catch Margaret, who had managed to escape Hector's grasp in a frenzied attempt to get to Sylvia.

Sensing impending disaster, or at least an epic cat fight, the always-proper Charles stepped in before it could escalate further. "Did you see that giant fellow Elizabeth came with? He used to be a professional football player, if you can believe that. Turned less than a decade ago. And here I thought Elizabeth was with Joseph."

It was a transparent lie. Everyone knew Elizabeth had left Joseph fifteen years ago. Even Charles, who was woefully behind the times when it came to gossip, knew that. Margaret, however, took the bait. Forgetting her murderous intentions, she leapt at the opportunity to fill Charles in on Elizabeth's relationship woes.

Having expertly diverted Margaret's attention by providing her the chance to gab, Charles was then forced to listen to her.

"Haven't you heard? Elizabeth threw Joseph over. It seems that she's been fixated on a hunter…."

Charles bore Margaret with stoic heroism until the first opportunity for extraction from the unpleasant girl presented itself. By that time Margaret had finished vomiting all she knew about Elizabeth, the hunter she was allegedly playing cat-and-mouse with, and her current athlete of the week.

She had taken a rare breath, getting ready to spurt out a whopper about Sylvia, when Charles gave a little bow and excused himself.

"Gentleman, ladies, I really should be going. A friend of mine is attending his first Convocation and I feel that I should welcome him."

Carmen took the opportunity and broke away with him, but then had to immediately take a half step back and drag Sylvia by the arm, hauling her away from the stare-off she and Margaret were suddenly engaged in after Margaret had unloaded with her little gem.

# Chapter 18

Ryan recognized the man headed his way despite the gangster outfit he was wearing, though he didn't recognize the Hollywood pinup attached to him. The absolutely stunning blonde on Bill's arm looked just this side of legal. Of course, at a dance full of vampires that was both common and misleading.

The other two ladies walking with Bill were intimately familiar to Ryan.

Thomas's smile broadened as the four people approached them. "Charles!" he said, extending his hand.

Ryan was fast for a human. He cut in front of Thomas, the right jab he sent to the face of his friend taking everyone by surprise. Ryan hadn't pulled the punch, seeing no reason for it. In fact he put everything he had into it.

Bill's head snapped back at the blow. A gasp could be heard rippling through the nearby witnesses as silence spread around them. It was cut by a hearty chuckle as he held up a hand to signal it was okay, while rubbing his jaw reflexively with his other.

"I believe I deserved that," Bill said with a bloody smile. The blonde next to him was not so forgiving. Her blue eyes shot daggers at Ryan, and Bill was forced to place a hand on her arm to halt her advance.

"Well, Charles, I see that you and Ryan have already met," said Thomas taking the exchange in stride.

"We go way back," said Ryan.

Bill dabbed his lip with a handkerchief. "Indeed we do. I have to say, Ryan: despite your pugilistic greeting I am pleased to see you here. I was hoping you might make an appearance."

Carmen had started to suspect that Charles and Bill were the same person some time ago. Charles simply wouldn't have trusted a recommendation for Carmen's personal security from anyone but a good friend, and Carmen knew all of his good friends.

Still, she was more than a little surprised that not only had Ryan belted Charles in the middle of the Ball, but that Charles had instantly forgiven him for it. She had a sudden feeling that the two men's relationship went a little deeper than she initially suspected.

"Hoping or intending?" Ryan asked.

"A little of both really," his friend confessed.

"I need to talk to you," Ryan demanded.

"Certainly you do. Maybe we could step outside?" He motioned to the nearest set of double doors that led onto the patio that surrounded the ballroom. A handful of people were out there, and Ryan suspected that as the evening progressed the moderate sense of privacy it offered would become more popular.

But the reunion was cut short before it began by Simon's booming, yet perfect, oration. "It is time for the two hundred and thirty second annual Masquerade Ball to begin. Please clear the floor so that our most honorable Council may have the pleasure of the first dance."

Thomas smoothly stepped across the group and threaded his arm through Sylvia's. She had been too busy watching the exchange between Ryan and Charles to see it coming and was already being whisked toward the floor before she could extricate herself with any hope of decorum.

Bill gave a slight bow. To Ryan he said, "You will have my undivided attention after the dance, my friend, but right now, duty calls." To the blonde, he extended the same arm that he had used to restrain her, and said, "Shall we?"

The blonde gave Ryan one last look that promised a painful death, then she was all smiles, allowing herself to be escorted to the center of the ballroom by her strutting date.

That left a reeling Ryan alone with Carmen. Bill was a member of the Council? Or was it his blonde date? No, not her, it was Bill. Ryan was sure of it.

The suspicion that Bill was a vampire had been growing in Ryan's mind ever since he found out that Carmen was one. When Ryan thought back over their relationship it made sense. While he talked to Bill on the phone or email at all times of the day and night, the infrequent times they actual spent together had always been in the evening. There was always a legitimate excuse for this of course: Bill had come straight from a meeting, or had a few hours' layover between flights, or wanted to watch a nighttime sporting event.

Still, looking back on it now it was obvious. Or should have been, if such a thought could have even entered Ryan's mind. But how could it have? How could Ryan suspect the very man who had saved him from vampires of being one himself? How could he suspect the man who had killed the vampires that had slaughtered his family?

It was hard enough for Ryan to finally, undeniably, admit Bill was a vampire. To realize he was a member of the Council? Ryan couldn't believe it.

Ryan remembered telling Bill about the Council after he had heard about them from Jacob. The two of them speculated about the possibilities: Where it was, how many vampires were in it, what the Council's purpose was. Did they wear hoods and meet in some dank cellar? Or was it business suits and boardrooms? Ryan went on to his friend about how amazing it would be to kill one of them, to strike a blow to the vampire hierarchy. Disrupt their government.

Ryan's thoughts drifted back to the night that Bill saved him. The night his family had been murdered. He turned to Carmen, a whole series of questions he wanted to ask bubbling up. But he stopped at her look.

"Well?" Carmen said. She was clearly expecting something, but Ryan had no idea what it was.

"Well, what?"

"It's the first dance," Carmen said, her eyes moving to where the Council members were assembling on the floor.

"Yeah, but it's for the Council members." Ryan shook his head in wonder as he followed Carmen's eyes out to the center of the room.

There they were right in front of him, the entire vampire Council standing a grenade's throw away. There weren't many of them. He tried to sweep aside malicious thoughts, forcing himself to dream, rather than act out, what he would have done given this opportunity at any other time.

"Yesss..." Carmen drew out the word like it was supposed to mean something very obvious.

"Yes what?" Ryan had no idea what she was alluding to, but he did know this was a good opportunity to get some information out of her.

When she didn't immediately expand on her point, Ryan decided it was question time. "So I had some stuff I wanted to ask you. I need your help straightening some things out."

"Wonderful. We can do it out there. But we need to hurry; if we keep them waiting much longer we'll be adding scandal to the things we need to straighten out."

"What?" Ryan's look was blank.

"They're waiting for us, and it's customary for the gentleman to lead the lady onto the floor." Carmen waited for him, crooking her arm so he might get the hint.

"What are you talking about? This dance is for Council members," Ryan said.

Carmen stared at him, a smile playing on her lips. She waited for it, knowing it would come. She would know the exact moment that it did. Ryan was easier to read than a picture book. There it was! The light went on behind Ryan's eyes. And with it came the comprehension, the full implications, of who he had spent the last several days with.

A stunned Ryan took Carmen's arm and led her onto the dance floor.

Once the last couple had joined the others the music began. Ryan had almost regained his composure, only to lose it again at the first notes. "I can't dance."

"Now is not the time to make that kind of confession. Fortunately for you, I can dance well enough for the both of us. Just follow my lead and try not to trip, or to step on me too often," Carmen said.

Ryan stood terrified.

"Relax, it's a waltz. It's not hard." Carmen moved his hands into the open position.

Maybe for someone who had been doing it for a hundred plus years, Ryan thought. But with little choice he began to dance. He did his best, and though he sold himself a little short on his capabilities, he really wasn't a seasoned dancer, and certainly not intimately familiar with the Viennese waltz. But Carmen was, and she managed to keep him from seeming too awful.

Despite Ryan's intent to talk to Carmen he found himself lost in thought. The woman in his arms was part of the Council. The woman he had spent the last several days with was a member of the vampire's ruling body. One of their royalty.

He could have killed her; he had countless opportunities. As far as he knew killing a Council member would have been something no other hunter had done. But instead he had protected her. He counted the times he had saved her life as they danced.

And what about Sylvia? It was possible that even she was a member. Certainly Bill was, or Charles, or whatever his real name turned out to be.

That was the hardest thing of all to understand. Bill. The man who had rescued him so many years ago from the vampires that murdered his parents, his brother, his sisters — all of them. The man who had whisked the newly orphaned Ryan away to safety, becoming something like his guardian angel.

As Carmen guided them in to a spin, Ryan took in the couples dancing around them. They were all there, the entire vampire Council. Ryan wondered how many members there were in the Council. He began to do the calculations in his head. He knew he wasn't one of them, and there were only nine couples dancing, meaning there could be a maximum of seventeen Council members left, every last one of them here in this room.

And watching them were perhaps two hundred more vampires. Ryan had no idea what percentage of the United States vampire population was here, but it was not insignificant. This was the bulk of vampire society, or at least its movers and shakers, the master vampires.

He now knew that it was the Council members who had been targeted; that's why Carmen feared she would be a victim, even before she had been attacked. Why she had gone to Charles for protection.

Given the sad state of their security, had Ryan known about this event in advance, he could have taken them all out right now. Granted, he would have died in the processes, along with most of his team. But imagine — the entire vampire hierarchy destroyed in one fell swoop! It would have been easy, just one large bomb. The thought both excited and troubled him. Because if he could do it, so could someone else.

Carmen cleared her throat. "Less plotting, more smiling. Or, if you insist on spending time with us, you'll need to learn how to smile and plot at the same time. It's convention."

"Sorry. Just thinking."

"That was obvious; there was steam. About what, might I ask?"

"The attacks on the Council. That's why you knew you were a target. The murders have all been Council members, right?"

There was no reason to deny it anymore. Ryan was literally standing in the middle of it now. "Yes."

"So, tell me," Ryan said.

"Tell you what, exactly?"

"Everything. Why a vampire would want to kill their own Council members? How many have they killed so far? How many are left? What do the ones that have been attacked have in common?" He paused. "Please don't tell me that at the end of the ball you elect a king and queen, and it gets hyper-competitive?"

Carmen smiled. "No. If they did that, Sylvia and Elizabeth would have killed each other long ago. I can answer your questions, though. Let's see: probably to swing a vote, they have killed two, tried to kill half a dozen more, there are eleven of us left, and nothing. That is the problem. They have attacked both the conservatives and liberals among us."

Ryan frowned at the terms Carmen used, trying and failing to come up with what differentiated a liberal vampire from a conservative one.

"Eleven of you left?" he repeated.

Carmen nodded.

"Thomas?"

"Yes."

"Sylvia?"

A nod.

"Bill?"

Carmen smiled. "Charles William Garret. Yes."

"The feisty little blonde attached to him?"

"No, thank god. Rose is creepy. I don't know what he sees in her."

Ryan knew what he *saw* in her, he just thought Bill would have been a little more resistant to her obvious assets given the nasty package they were wrapped up in. And just how bad did you have to be for a vampire to call you creepy? He added a mental note to include Bill's taste in women to the other topics Ryan planned on discussing with him after the dance.

When Ryan's face scrunched back up in thought, Carmen decided to step on *his* foot for once.

"Ow!" Ryan said.

"You're doing it again."

Ryan closed his eyes for a brief instant. He cleared his mind, took a deep breath, and then opened them. "You're right, I was. Here I am dancing with the most beautiful woman at the ball and I'm thinking about work."

Carmen lit up like a Christmas tree, which made Ryan smile. She stared into his eyes as they whirled, pleased that he met her gaze with abandon. She liked his eyes and relished the opportunity to become lost in them. She was disappointed that the Ball's convention required them to stay at a respectable distance.

There were three main dances at the Convocation. The first two were balls, and very formal. The third, the one that celebrated the conclusion, was more of a party, and was anything but formal. She wished they were at that one now.

Or did she? What outcome could there possibly be in this? Her and a human? Her and a hunter? A hunter that knew far too much about them. Especially now, after everything Ryan had seen. The entire Council. There was only one possible fate for him once this was over. The best Ryan could hope for was a head start followed by a quick death.

"Now who's all doom and gloom?" teased Ryan. Carmen's smile was still perfectly in place, but traces of her blood still flowed through him. He felt a shadow of what she did, and her emotions had taken a dark bent.

Carmen started at Ryan's words. He had seen through her! She prided herself on her impregnable mask. She had always been skilled at hiding her emotions.

She worried she was slipping until she remembered the blood she had given him. She had forgotten about that. She had given him a lot during the past days. Ryan could sense her feelings, of course. It was one of the reasons vampires only rarely gave their blood to humans. In fact, if you weren't planning on turning one, the gift of blood was almost unheard of. It opened you up to someone completely. It made you vulnerable.

Ryan shook his head. "Nope, still grumpy. Whatever you're thinking about it's not working. You need to take some lessons from Sylvia."

"Oh *do* I now? And exactly *what* things could Sylvia teach me?"

"Yes, tell us!" Thomas said as he spun by, reminding Ryan that with all the vampire ears around, he might as well be belting out his conversation on a bullhorn. Well, maybe not that bad, but anyone in the immediate vicinity could certainly hear him if they were bothering to listen in.

"I can't," said Ryan. "Sylvia mentioned on the ride over that she'd hoped you'd be here so she could give you a private demonstration of her skills later this evening. I don't want to spoil the surprise."

Thomas beamed while Sylvia fumed. Carmen smiled, her heart feeling a little bit lighter.

"You're an amazing dancer," Ryan said, his attention drawn back to her after Thomas and Sylvia had passed by.

"Thanks. I'd like to say you weren't so bad yourself."

"Hey!" It was true, though. On the dance floor Ryan needed serious help. At least with the classical music he was less likely to bust out with the white man's overbite. "So how long *have* you been dancing anyway?"

"Nice try. And don't worry about it; we'll practice before the next one," Carmen said.

"The next one? I only barely decided to ask you to this one. How do you know I'm going to decide to keep you around for an entire year?" Ryan asked with faux offense. He realized Carmen had been making an off-hand remark, but he couldn't help but capitalize on it. It seemed like she was planning on keeping him around for the foreseeable future. For the most part that horrified Ryan, but a small piece of him reveled in the possibility that he would continue to see her after the evening ended.

Carmen was stunned! Ryan was right; he had caught her assuming that they would go to the next event together. Granted, she had been talking about the one next week, not anything as far off as next year's Convocation, but still. Even to assume Ryan would be around a week from now to take her to the Black and White Ball, and that they would be practicing together beforehand, was a big assumption.

"The next dance is a week from now," Carmen said, trying desperately to think of something clever to say, but in a rare occurrence she found herself at a loss for words, too flustered by her gaffe to collect herself properly.

She tried to dismiss it, telling herself it had been a throwaway line she hadn't meant. Only it hadn't been. She distinctly remembered thinking as she said it that they would have to put in a few hours of practice each day that week, or she would need new feet.

"Man, you vampires sure do like your dances," Ryan said. "Okay, we'll practice before the next one. And, who knows, maybe if you can get Sylvia to give *you* a lesson or two, I'll bring you home with me afterwards."

Carmen's eyes flared. Her grip on him tightened and Ryan, realizing he might have pushed things a little too far, remembered exactly who he was messing with.

To Ryan's intense relief the music died down. He had mapped out an escape route off the dance floor: he decided that he would lose himself in the crowd and hide from Carmen during the cooling off process. The last thing he wanted was to get caught on the dance floor when the next song started, giving Carmen an opportunity to exact her revenge.

The music ended and dozens of new couples poured onto the floor. Ryan let go of Carmen, whose glare had not diminished in any appreciable way. Yes, a rapid tactical retreat was in order. Ryan took his first step toward freedom only to find someone else in his arms; he literally blinked and she was there.

Cleopatra smiled up at him. "Hello. Did you know that Cleopatra really wasn't Egyptian? She was Greek."

"Um… My name's Ryan. I can't dance." It sounded a bit like an introduction at an AA meeting, but it was all Ryan could manage as his brain raced to pull up what he knew about the vampire before him.

This was Hailey, the vampire Thomas had said to steer clear of. What had he said about her? Crazy? Avoid at all costs? Ryan hoped Hailey didn't forget her manners and decide to drain him right there on the dance floor.

"I can," she said as she began to move to the opening chords of the Blue Danube. Ryan had remembered seeing Hailey during the first dance with an equally trapped-looking gentleman moments before. He turned his head to search for the man, hoping to see him standing somewhere alive, but he had vanished.

Ryan didn't know what to do. He looked to Carmen for help. She was no longer glaring at him, at least. She appeared even more shocked than he was by this development. Ryan watched as Carmen backpedaled off of the dance floor helplessly, then waited on the fringe of the crowd, hands wringing in front of her.

So Ryan did what he had to do: he danced. If anything Hailey was a better dancer than Carmen, but she had no interest in helping him. Meaning that as a couple, they did a lot worse.

Hailey didn't seem to care. "I met her once. Cleopatra? History has been kind to her. She was quite homely in person."

Ryan smiled and nodded. He decided that would be his strategy until the nightmare was over.

# # #

"Oh my," Thomas said in genuine astonishment as he and Sylvia came to stand next to Carmen. The three of them watched as Hailey led a distraught and stumbling Ryan along with the flow of otherwise elegantly waltzing couples.

"Poor Ryan," said Sylvia. "And I had just grown to tolerate him."

"He'll be fine. Hailey is harmless," said Carmen, more for her own comfort than anything.

A smiling Charles came up, blissfully unattached to Rose. "Did everyone enjoy the first dance? Where is Ryan?" He followed Carmen's finger. "Oh dear. I see he's met Hailey. We really need to do something about her."

"I had been thinking the same thing," said Carmen.

"I'll go rescue the boy." Charles said stoically, as if he were volunteering to lead the Light Brigade into the mouth of the roaring cannons. The group watched as Charles strode purposefully up to the couple, halted them, bowed, and obviously requested to cut in.

Relief washed over Ryan when Charles offered to cut in. Ryan wasn't sure if his friend intended to dance with Hailey or himself, but at that point he didn't care.

Things had started with Hailey having a one-sided conversation about parrots, brought on when she noticed the stuffed one on some short guy's shoulder. Somehow she had maneuvered Ryan into responding back, and they were now talking about taxidermy and how it related to the ancient Egyptian practice of embalming. It didn't, according to Hailey. She explained something about souls and technique.

"No thanks!" Hailey told Charles before she moved Ryan into a rapid spin, narrowly missing a couple dressed as Death and a swan. A befuddled Charles William Garrett was left standing alone and slightly open-mouthed on the dance floor.

"I do believe she declined," said Thomas. "I wasn't aware you could do that. In fact, I rather counted on the fact that you couldn't. It's how I get most of my dances."

"You can't," said Carmen.

"Apparently you can," said Sylvia. "If this gets out, filling your dance card will be a bleak proposition, Thomas."

Three dances later Hailey got distracted by a man dressed as a legionnaire, giving Ryan the opportunity to escape her clutches and start for his friends. He was so relieved to not be dancing, he didn't even realize that his subconscious had classified that group of vampires as such.

Hailey herself actually hadn't been so bad, Ryan thought. The crazy vampire seemed more like a child than a monster. A little strange, sure, but almost refreshingly so. He wouldn't say she had Alzheimer's, like Thomas had suggested. Ryan had a feeling Hailey's problem was that she had so much knowledge stored in her mind that it had gotten jumbled, like a full hard drive desperately in need of de-fragmenting. Perhaps it had even started writing over itself.

Her knowledge of animals was remarkable. She knew more about them than any of Ryan's keepers back at the Sanctuary. And Hailey had seen so many species that were gone: the Tasmanian tiger, the dodo, the passenger pigeon. Hailey claimed to have seen them all, first hand.

Ryan returned the four friendly greetings as he stopped next to Carmen, forgetting she was annoyed with him. He was reminded when he bent sideways to make a comment to her about Hailey and was met with an icy expression.

Charles had smiled as his friend walked up to them and noted the distance, or lack thereof, that Ryan chose to put between himself and Carmen. They were practically touching, almost like a couple.

Ryan leaned over to say something to her, and oh boy! Charles was familiar with that look, though a little shocked to see it directed at someone other than himself. Ryan was in for it, all right. Charles felt the slightest pang of jealousy that some else had received Carmen's certain stare — the particular look that, up until this night, had been reserved for him alone. But it was quickly swept aside by the tide of satisfaction and joy he felt at seeing the two people he cared most about together.

# Chapter 19

After what had happened earlier with Hailey, Carmen was hesitant to leave Ryan alone. Though she was confident that no one would harm him at the ball, she was worried that he might spook and do something rash.

She had been babysitting him for the last several hours, even managing to get him out on the dance floor a few more times, to the detriment of her feet, when an opportunity presented itself to get Charles alone.

She jumped at it. After all, how much trouble could Ryan possibly get into? Sylvia and Thomas were with him. In fact, they probably wouldn't even notice that Carmen was gone. The three of them had been largely ignoring her for the past half hour as they critiqued costumes and the people within them.

Charles stood nearby engaged in conversation with Sorry Sophie. Carmen saw that Sophie was clearly agitated, and Charles was wearing his patient expression. Charles would welcome the interruption.

Sophie was a broken record, and Carmen knew the conversation had to do with her title and territory, or lack thereof. Sophie knew her chances at something were negligible, and yet every year she kept trying to petition the Council to hear her claim.

Carmen walked up and took Charles's hand. "Lady Sophie," Carmen said, inclining her head politely. "I'm so sorry, but Charles had promised he would talk with

Hector and Viktor about an upcoming vote, and they are waiting for him outside."

"Of course," said Sorry Sophie, her smile plastic. She knew she was getting the brush off, but had little recourse.

Charles had turned when his hand was grabbed, thinking Rose had found him. He was relieved to see Carmen, and only too eager to follow her out to the patio and away from Sophie. He was almost prepared to hear the petition and grant her some piece of territory just to shut her up.

"How are you enjoying the ball, my dear? You haven't danced as much as you normally do. Is everything okay?" Charles asked her.

"I decided to remain ambulatory. If Ryan steps on my feet one more time I will have to be carried out."

"I'm sure there are other gentlemen who would love an opportunity to dance with you," Charles said with a smile.

"And leave Ryan to the sharks? I don't think so."

"Oh, don't worry about him; Ryan is quite capable of taking care of himself."

"He is, I suppose."

"And *sharks* is too harsh of a word. It would be good for Ryan to get to know other vampires, maybe start thinking of us as something other than monsters. And what better place to expand his experiences than at the Ball?"

"How so?" asked Carmen.

"The charm and elegance of a Ball is hard to resist, even for someone like Ryan. There's something magical about it. I'm sure some of the ladies would love to take the time to expand Ryan's horizons, get him thinking of us as friends instead of enemies. Don't you think?"

Carmen saw the trap from a mile away, and refused to step in it. She only nodded absently and asked, "Where did you meet him?"

"I met Ryan in Massachusetts exactly twenty years ago," Charles said. Carmen might not have taken his bait, but her question had betrayed her mind nonetheless. It was obvious that Ryan was the reason Carmen had pulled him out here to talk, and not the attempts on her life as one would expect.

"Tell me about him. How did you meet?"

"There's not much to tell," Charles shrugged, knowing Carmen would see through his lie. "I met him as a boy. He was eight. I've kept an eye on him ever since. I'm afraid Ryan will have to be the one to tell you anything more — it's not my story."

Carmen was not giving up. She redoubled her efforts and began using all the tricks she knew to pry information out of Charles. And Charles, with over half a millennia of experience dealing with Carmen's tricks, spent the next half hour deftly fending her off.

# # #

"Uh-oh, look who's headed this way." Thomas nodded to a couple in the crowd. Though they were bouncing between guests, the pair was undeniably working their way toward them. The ravishing, powerfully built man was dressed as Punch, his beautiful blonde wife as Judy.

"Who are they?" Ryan asked.

"If we had a king and queen, they would be it."

"They're the two oldest," Ryan said, testing his understanding that in the vampire world, age was power.

"Actually, they're not the oldest; they're simply the social butterflies. They're glue that holds us all together, if you will. They're also sticklers for propriety. If you have ever met someone who follows the letter of the law, regardless of intent, you've met their soulmate. I find them a bit dull," said Thomas.

"Have they been a couple long?" Ryan asked.

Sylvia nodded. "They've been married for centuries. Almost as long as Christian and Eleanor had been."

"Who are Christian and Eleanor?" asked Ryan.

"Christian was a former Council member. His wife, Eleanor, was killed by hunters a few decades ago. Christian died recently," said Sylvia.

"Hunters killed a Councilmember?" Ryan repeated, unable to hide his surprise.

"And here you thought you would be the first." Sylvia gave Ryan a mock-sympathy pout.

"First what?" asked Thomas.

"Nothing," said Ryan.

Thomas paused, hoping an elaboration would come. When it didn't he moved on with a slight shrug. "Well then, to answer your question: no, hunters didn't kill a Council member. Eleanor was never a member of the Council, and Christian stepped down after his family was murdered. He was no longer a part of the Council when he was killed."

"So his death wasn't part of this? These recent murders?" Ryan asked.

"We don't think so," Sylvia said. "There's an uppity master out in Texas that we think might have had a hand in Christian's death. Apparently Christian was trying to usurp her place. She maintains it was hunters, and swears it had nothing to do with her. Despite Christian and all of his followers dying in the middle of her house, while she and hers miraculously survived."

Ryan wanted to press them on the death of this Christian. Find out which hunter had killed a former Council member. See if he knew them. But Sylvia had gone silent at the imminent arrival of the married vampires, and the moment was gone.

"Oh, look! They seem to have picked up Elizabeth. Well, Ryan, you're in for a treat!" Thomas said, nudging Ryan and pointing shamelessly at the lovely Queen Elizabeth.

Sylvia snorted. "More like a tart."

Ryan had a theory about Sylvia, and he decided to test it. "Thomas, is *that* the Elizabeth you were telling me about? The 'three solid days you spent in a room in Barcelona' Elizabeth? She's even prettier than you said she was." When Ryan said it he was looking at Sylvia, not Thomas.

Thomas's smile disappeared as Sylvia got whiplash turning towards the Musketeer. "You and Elizabeth!" Shock and pain were mixed in with the accusation. Sylvia wasn't anywhere near as inept as Ryan in hiding her emotions, but she wasn't up to Carmen's level, and the revelation had clearly surprised her.

"Now, Sylvia, it was a long time ago. I can assure you I have no interest in Elizabeth anymore," said Thomas, his hurried answer devoid of any of its usual humor.

Ryan could get used to this — lobbing a verbal grenade and then watching the destruction it wreaked. It was almost as satisfying as staking a vampire.

"Three days?" said Sylvia.

"It *was* rather impressive," Thomas replied, his bravado creeping back.

"You misunderstand me. I had thought, given the opportunity, Elizabeth would do better. But then again, she never could keep up with me. I'm sure the poor performance wasn't a reflection on yourself."

And then, just like that, both Thomas and Sylvia plastered on the biggest, most genuine smiles imaginable.

"Sylvia, Thomas, you must introduce me to your friend here! I don't believe we've had the pleasure." The blonde woman extended her hand to Ryan, but it was turned the wrong way.

"I'd be delighted to," said Thomas with a bow. "Isabel, may I present Ryan, a personal friend of both Carmen and Charles?"

As Ryan reached to shake her hand, Thomas whispered out of the side of his mouth, "You're expected to kiss it. No tongue."

It was a new one for Ryan, but he did his best. Bending down, he planted a light kiss on the back of the vampire's hand. He probably flubbed the whole thing, but Isabel was tactful enough to not comment.

"This is the Countess Bathory," said Isabel, indicating the Queen at her side.

"You may call me Elizabeth," said the redhead, extending her hand to Ryan palm down, in the same manner Isabel had.

"She prefers to be kissed too," said Sylvia, "with tongue."

Elizabeth glowered at the comment, and even Ryan could tell there was no love lost between these two. He felt himself naturally siding with Sylvia, even though he had no information regarding the squabble between the two vampires. Ryan had come to grudgingly like Sylvia. And though he didn't know Elizabeth personally, he knew of her. The Blood Countess had killed hundreds of innocents during her lifetime, and countless more since her death.

Ryan took Elizabeth's hand and repeated the gesture he had made with Isabel, pleased that he pulled it off with slightly more flair than the first time. He looked up at Elizabeth as he rose, but the vampire's brilliant green eyes were fixed on Sylvia. Only at the last moment did they flick to acknowledge Ryan.

"Charmed," she said in a voice devoid of any sincerity.

"Hugo," said the man at Isabel's side, holding out his hand. Ryan was relieved that all he had to do was shake it.

Between Isabel and Hugo it was instantly clear who was the talker of the couple. Hugo stood there, grinning with the best of them, but Ryan suspected if the vampire had his choice he would be somewhere else, away from the crowds. He had a feeling the guy preferred to be by himself, or maybe with his wife indulging in something more low key.

Isabel, however, was social enough for the both of them. "Tell me, Ryan — why is it we haven't seen you before? Being a good friend of both Charles and Carmen, I'm surprised we haven't run into each other before now."

"I'm more of a recent acquaintance of Carmen's. Actually Charles asked me to look after her."

At both Isabel and Elizabeth's raised eyebrows, Thomas interjected, "Ryan is a bodyguard."

"Oh, I see." Isabel's tone indicated that Ryan's importance had been instantly reduced a number of ranks, from "human friend and likely future vampire" to "staff" ...and possibly "future meal."

"Be honest, Hugo. If you had to guard a body, Carmen's wouldn't be a bad one, huh?" prodded Thomas tactlessly.

His sense of self-preservation strong, Hugo refused to acknowledge Thomas's comment. Isabel rolled her eyes, apparently both used to, and bored by, Thomas. Elizabeth and Sylvia had different reactions.

"Poor Thomas," said Elizabeth. "Always wanting what he can't have."

Sylvia nodded in agreement with Elizabeth. Her eyes were fixed pointedly on the redhead when she spoke, "Yes, it's tragic that all he's ever managed to bed are cheap whores."

Elizabeth's hand was a blur. By the time Ryan had even registered the slap, it was back by her side.

Isabel looked horrified as she turned to her husband with a *do something* look. Hugo's shoulders slumped and his expression was that of a man just told to step between two charging rhinos.

Before Ryan had a chance to think through the logical results of his action, he instinctively placed himself between the two women. Hugo perked up at having someone take what was apparently his usual place: in the line of fire. Hugo hastily retracted the half step forward he had just taken.

Sylvia was readying her response, and it looked like it was going to be something in the haymaker family.

Thomas took a drink from his glass as he watched, far more amused by the spectacle than he was insulted by Sylvia's statement about his conquests.

Elizabeth had backed off a step herself, satisfied that she had gotten in the last word, as it were. Sylvia advanced, going on the offensive, and it was all Ryan could do to keep her off the redhead.

There was an overly loud jovial chuckle as Charles joined them, Carmen at his side. "Ryan, I see that you are getting to know some of the Council better!"

"Biblically, from what I understand. Or haven't you heard Charles? Ryan's become *intimately* familiar with some of us," said Sylvia, her eyes momentarily resting on Carmen so that no one missed who she had been referring to.

Sylvia was fuming, desperate to lash out at someone. Apparently by interceding before Sylvia could unleash her ire at Elizabeth, Charles had diverted her wrath onto himself.

Charles was astonished by the statement. Surely he had misinterpreted Sylvia's innuendo. But then he noticed the horrified looks her comments garnered from both Ryan and Carmen, and there could be no mistake.

"My, my," Charles said.

He admitted he hoped getting the two of them together might have some sort of a happy ending, at the very least keeping Carmen alive. Maybe even bringing Ryan to the realization that not all vampires were the evil monsters he had thought they were. And yes, he had a distant wish that there might be a spark between the two of them, something that might simmer for a while, to be realized at some far off date. In fact, when Charles realized Carmen had pulled him aside to ask about Ryan and not the murders, he was sure the spark had happened.

But Charles had assumed it was a spark, not a bonfire. He hadn't dreamed it would have reached its current state so quickly. Poor Carmen; this would be quite the scandal now that it was out.

Of course no one knew that Ryan was a vampire hunter. Neither Carmen nor he would ever tell. But Ryan was a human. Not only a human, but he had been labeled as a bodyguard. A servant. He was a member of her staff.

Council members were held to a higher standard than others, like royalty. They weren't so nepotistic as to confine themselves to only spend time with other Council members — it was much too small of a pool. But they normally kept their relationships to the social elite. Humans were acceptable if they were a movie star, a powerful businessman, or an heiress. *Not* acceptable was a chauffeur or security guard. These affairs happened, of course, but they were hidden, not admitted to in public, and certainly not announced at a Ball.

Elizabeth glanced over at Isabel. "I don't know about you, but I may look up Mr. Ryan's services after he night is over. It's been awhile since I've had a good bodyguard. If he can wake up our frigid little Carmen…"

The hanging comment prompted Hugo to tactfully remind his wife that they should be preparing for the speech. At this point Isabel seemed as eager as her husband to leave the distasteful display, and the two strode hurriedly into the crowd.

Carmen was speechless. She couldn't believe what Sylvia had said about her and Ryan. Not only was it scandalous, it was a lie! She was going to stake her friend. The only thing keeping her from doing it right now was Elizabeth's last comment. Carmen couldn't decide who to kill first.

Carmen was well aware what they called her behind her back. She had picked up the nickname in the last century. She told herself it was perpetuated by hunters who feared her mercilessness, but deep down she knew the reality was the name had come from one of her own.

She didn't know who created the moniker. It might have been Margaret, or perhaps Elizabeth, that tagged Carmen the Ice Queen. Carmen knew it was not her mercilessness, nor her impressive self-control, but her perpetual spinster status since the Big Breakup with Hector almost a century ago.

After Sylvia's proclamation that Carmen was sleeping with her security guard, there wouldn't be a hole in the city small enough for Carmen to hide in. If it had been only Charles who had heard the comment it would have been horrifying, but controlled. But with Thomas standing there grinning like an idiot, and Elizabeth, and Isabel, and— Oh, this was a disaster!

By tomorrow everyone would know. Or think they knew. Her. With a human. And not even a lover, or a potential mate, but the hired help! It would be the talk of the Convocation. Carmen could feel herself beginning to perspire, which only made her more distraught.

Thomas continued to gape and grin, and he made the inappropriate gesture of extending his hand to Ryan in congratulations, while saying, "You and Carmen! The next time we're alone you have to tell me all about it. *Excruciating* details are encouraged."

# Chapter 20

Ryan stared down at his alcohol-free glass of soda with disappointment. He reconsidered amending his rule regarding no booze on the job right then and there.

He had been abandoned. The others had left soon after Sylvia's bombshell. Most of them wanted to stay, hungry for more gossip and slander, but the Council had to give a closing speech and they had to prepare for their entrance.

Ryan had watched them go. Carmen was the last to leave, still wearing a look of murder on her face directed at Sylvia's retreating back.

Now that he was alone, Ryan was getting an awful lot of predatory looks from the ladies. He liked to think it was because of his ruggedly handsome looks, but he suspected that rumors spread around this room faster than a California wildfire in a wind storm.

A particularly pretty Marie Antoinette caught his eye with a wink. He found himself smiling back and had to force himself to stop. A week ago not a single thought other than how he could kill all of the creatures in the room would have entered Ryan's mind. He certainly wouldn't have been thinking about what a wonderfully poor job Miss Antoinette's dress was doing containing her generous bosom.

Ryan reminded himself that every woman in the room was a dangerous predator, and sex with one was likely to end with him being a post-dance snack.

Ryan forced himself back to the real reason he was here: protecting Carmen. The dance was an obvious place for another attempt on the Council, and it would likely be a successful one. All of the Council members were here, and security was nonexistent if you had an invitation.

Ryan had a feeling that those pieces of paper had been easy to come by. Even if people knew they were not the targets, no one would want to be collateral damage. So the more cautious among the usual guests would not be attending the ball. Which meant that if the hosts wanted to keep their event from looking like a ghost town, they would have been forced to extend invitations to people who might normally not have received them. Ryan suspected that this year, if you were a vampire you were in.

Given the circumstances Ryan knew the killer was at the dance. He was sure of it. What he didn't know was who it was. No one was telling Ryan anything, which made divining the attacker's identity difficult. Which made protecting Carmen impossible, especially if she was going to insist on attending public functions.

Ryan took a sip of his 7-Up and tried to work backwards. Who were the targets? Well, the vampire Council. But the real question was: were all of the Council targets or simply a subset of them?

He examined the limited facts. The main one was that the easiest time to strike, if you wanted to kill the entire Council, would have been this dance. That's what Ryan would have done. They would all be gathered together. There would have been the element of surprise. No one on their guard.

But whoever it was hadn't waited until the dance. Instead they had tried to pick them off one by one.

That meant the killer wanted a subset dead, not the entire Council. Ryan couldn't get much farther along that avenue. He didn't know the members well enough to know what they had in common.

He couldn't define a narrow motive, but what about a broad one?

What were the possible motives? Ryan had been asked to ensure that Carmen made it to Chicago in time for the dance, but was this the event people were worried about? A masquerade ball? He doubted it. Carmen had said something about a vote. That made more sense.

There was some sort of vote happening after the dance. Since everyone clammed up around him, Ryan didn't know what the vote was, but he did know the Council was the ruling body for all vampires in the United States. That meant they made important decisions.

He took another drink, keeping an ice cube in his mouth to suck on while he thought. A decision was going to be made, and someone wanted awfully badly for it to come out in their favor.

Ryan mulled over what it could be. Were they going to pass judgment on an alleged criminal? Was this criminal bumping off the Council members likely would rule against them? That seemed like a stretch.

What about power? Ryan knew that master vampires controlled territories. Some of these territories consisted of an entire state, while others were parts of one like Northern and Southern California.

Ryan used to think that the master vampires got their turf through murder and intimidation, the same way as street gangs, but after hearing about Sorry Sophie and how territories could be awarded by the Council, an obvious motive came to mind. A land grab.

Another possibility for the murders was to get a law changed. Most of the vampires Ryan killed were Street, not Society. They had been solo, or living in small nests. They were living outside of the society he was currently standing in, outside of the law. The ones here, the so-called Society vampires, lived by a code of laws. There were punishments for breaking them. Maybe there was some rule that someone wanted to repeal or enact.

There was no way for Ryan to know. All he knew was that they had killed two members already, and judging by the attempt on Carmen and Sylvia, needed to kill at least one more. This dance would be the prime place to do it, yet the night was almost over and there had been no signs of foul play. Ryan looked through the bottom of his glass, disappointed there was no cherry.

# # #

"You're right; you can almost see the smoke," Thomas noted. He stood with Carmen and Sylvia on the fringe of the pack of Council members, all waiting for the closing speech to begin. The three of them observed Ryan's expressions morph as he mulled over something in his head.

"It's kind of fun," said Carmen.

"If you ask me the man has indigestion," said Sylvia.

"No one asked you," said Carmen, still miffed at Sylvia's allegations.

"Oops, looks like we're up!" said Isabel, motioning everyone to advance.

Simon introduced each member as they filed into the open area of the floor that the crowd had made for them. The eleven members fanned out around a wooden podium that had been carried out a moment before.

Ryan was so lost in thought he almost missed the applause. Actually he would have missed their entrance entirely if it weren't for a nudge from a lady to his left who pointedly looked at Ryan, then to the row of Council members, then back at Ryan as she clapped her hands appreciatively.

Ryan smiled apologetically at the woman, and began to clap until the woman was mollified and focused her attention back on the Council members.

Ryan did the same. The eleven members stood in a semi-circle, Isabel and Hugo in the center. Hugo smiled and raised a hand to quiet the crowd as his wife walked up to the podium. Her pearly white grin and perfect features reminded Ryan of a government spokesperson, or a corporate shill, about to address an audience.

"We are all so glad to welcome you to the beginning of the two hundred and eighteenth Convocation," Isabel began. "We hope you have enjoyed this year's Masquerade Ball and will continue to enjoy the week's festivities, which culminate next Friday evening with the Black and White Ball, to be hosted by our very own Sir Charles William Garrett!"

Isabel continued, but Ryan tuned her out. The remaining ten Council members stood in a row behind her, all wearing plastered-on smiles that would have done a tooth-paste commercial proud. All had their backs to a wall that was made entirely of floor-to-ceiling French glass windows and doors.

Ryan moved, pushing aside the lady who had nudged him earlier. This earned him a startled, "Well, I never!" But it was uttered to his back. Ryan had already reached a full sprint and was expertly weaving in and around the startled guests who were more loosely scattered in back of the denser crowd that immediately surrounded the Council.

A bullet wouldn't kill a vampire. Neither would a wooden stake. You needed to cut its head off, burn them, vaporize them, or rip out its heart. The real trick, if you only wanted a select few dead among a large crowd, would be taking out just the ones you wanted, leaving the rest alone. Explosion, too risky; decapitation, not feasible; heart removal, implausible; fire, like explosion, impossible to pick and choose.

No, you had to isolate the ones you were after *before* you killed them. The method of choice was developed by hunters decades ago. Ryan had used it himself last year to snag a vampire that had been eating his way through some Colorado ski bunnies. The monster had gotten into the habit of sitting at the same table at a swanky lodge bar to wine and dine his dates — a table right against a window.

Ryan saw them as he was sprinting toward the doors to the left of where the Council had assembled. Four waiters with two silver carts had been making a show of collecting glasses left out on the patio.

However, they had stopped their efforts at cleaning up and now milled around the two carts. Three of them bent down and pulled large crossbows known as arbalests from under the white canopies draped over the silver carts. Rather than a regular bolt, each arbalest was loaded with a specially designed metal grappling hook. At the back end of each hook was a thin, but very strong, cable.

Ryan ran as fast as he could for the doors. He didn't know how many Council members were targets, but he was sure Carmen was one of them, probably Sylvia, and maybe even Bill.

Depending on how paranoid you were, you might think that a man charging toward a group of political figures while pulling a gun from his coat was a threat. The fact that the angle the man was taking may, or may not, have taken him past the delegates rather than directly toward them could always be debated later.

So Ryan didn't really blame the two tuxedo-clad security guards from reacting the way they did. Not that it stopped him from shooting the first one in the head three times. The man had been just drawing his gun on Ryan, his weapon only partway out of the shoulder holster hidden under his jacket, when he was forced to pause and wait for his splattered cerebral cortex to try to repair itself.

Unfortunately the gunfire focused all eyes in the room on Ryan, instead of what was going on outside, behind the Council.

Security guard Number Two had been both faster, and noticeably larger, than his friend. It was only when Ryan had already committed to his course of action that he realized Thomas had been mistaken. Apparently they *had* made an exception to the "no trolls" rule at this year's Ball.

"Get away from the windows!" Ryan yelled. He had been intending to incapacitate the vampire with a stake through the heart, but that gesture would have been both futile and suicidal against a troll. Instead he adopted plan B: avoidance.

Ryan dropped to the floor, slipping under the troll's powerful swing.

The entire Council stared at the sliding man, their expressions ranging from shock to anger. The question in the back of Ryan's mind was: would they heed his warning, kill him themselves, or watch as the troll did it for them?

With nothing else he could do, Ryan slid across the polished tile past the troll, then as an afterthought used a backhanded swing to shove the stake into the monster's calf.

Ryan was strong, but trolls were unnaturally tough. The stake didn't penetrate the leg more than an inch. Ryan hoped it was enough to slow the beast down a beat and buy him time to take care of the threat outside.

Back on his feet, Ryan yanked open the door the same time the arbalests fired. Glass shattered as three grappling hooks plowed through them in search of their targets.

It was impossible to know if it was the result of the crazy man running towards them, or the words he shouted, but many of the Council members had begun to move, though a few of them were headed in Ryan's direction rather than for cover.

One of the projectiles missed its target completely and sailed through the empty space where Charles had been a second before. It instead struck the shoulder of an unfortunate gentleman. The man screamed as the large shaft plunged through his shoulder. Its arms sprang open like a four-pronged umbrella that had lost its canopy immediately upon exiting his back.

The second bolt struck a Council member in the arm, almost severing it. The third traveled right through Isabel's chest. She had been standing at the podium and realized exactly what Ryan's words had meant. But instead of fleeing, she had whirled to face her attackers.

Hunters typically used winches to pull out vampires. And that was usually to pull them into the sunlight, if available. Apparently vampires preferred to use their own power to do the pulling. It turns out it was a lot quicker. More glass shattered as Isabel exited the ballroom at the same time Ryan did. While Ryan used the door, Isabel, with her arms and legs flung out in all directions, was hauled straight through a window.

Glass, blood, and bits of wood and vampire sprayed Ryan from the side as Isabel screamed past him.

Ryan was actually hoping the attackers would be armed with flame throwers, though he would have settled for RPGs. Both were both relatively slow and clumsy weapons. He might have been able to work with those and kill or incapacitate the attackers before they could turn on him.

Unfortunately they weren't using either of the weapons favored by hunters when sunlight wasn't an option. Ryan could only assume the three vampires with the big crossbows were either fanatics, or didn't know the whole plan. Because apparently their survival had never been part of it.

The fourth guy was human, and almost definitely had been pushed into his course of action. Ryan knew he was human because the four rounds Ryan shot him with killed him instantly.

Unfortunately for Ryan and Isabel, who were now both within ten feet of the man, it turned out that he had been pushed into being a suicide bomber. The poor human had been rigged with a dead man's switch. It was a little device invented to ensure that killing a suicide bomber, such as by shooting him like Ryan had done, wouldn't stop the explosion.

Ryan suspected the man might have one and had preemptively dove to the ground. He turned his back to the bomber and used his arms to shield his head the instant after shooting him.

# # #

Hugo had started moving as soon as Carmen's crazy bodyguard screamed at them. When he had first seen the man charging, he thought Ryan was there to kill the Council and that Carmen had been behind it all. But one man with a pistol? It was a clumsy attempt.

But when the man yelled for them to get away from the windows Hugo had looked out into the patio and realized what was happening. By then it was too late. Before he could stop it, his wife was being sucked through the air towards the courtyard.

Hugo had already shifted course away from Carmen's bodyguard to follow his wife of eight hundred and thirty-one years out of the hole she had made when the fireball erupted. The flame engulfed her and threw him backwards, awash in searing flames.

# # #

Carmen experienced the whole thing in slow motion. Out of the corner of her eye, she caught Ryan running towards them, as they all had. The difference was that she knew he wasn't attacking them. She turned, following his eyes outside. She also saw what was coming.

She dove out of the way, grabbing Sylvia, who had already started moving of her own accord. Someone else had already reached for Sylvia. It was Thomas. They had a brief tug of war before a grappling hook, similar to the one that had hit Carmen the other day, almost took his arm off. A woman nearby screamed, and more glass shattered when someone was pulled outside.

Carmen rolled on the floor, a vision in petticoats. She leapt to her feet and found that Sylvia had already risen and was starting to run toward the room's main exit. Carmen hesitated. Did she escape with Sylvia, or go help Ryan?

The decision was made for her. As she started to turn back for him, fire erupted where she had seen Ryan only moments before.

The explosion was massive, blowing out all of the remaining windows in the room and showering everyone in biting, stinging glass. Carmen doubted that whichever vampire had been pulled into the fireball could have survived. She knew Ryan didn't; he was only human.

- End -
The Vampire Council, Book One

And now, a preview of the first book
of the Chance Lee series…

# *Chance in Hell*
## By Patrick Kampman

"This the corpse?" came a thick Boston accent and a tap against my side. A shoe? I was down and someone was kicking me. It was one of those days.

"Nah, he's still alive. The stiff's over there in the blue truck," came another voice. "Well, most of him is, anyway. Don't worry; you can't miss him."

The voices echoed through my aching head as I heard footsteps moving away from me. There were more voices off in the distance and I struggled through the pain to figure out what was going on. Slowly I won the battle, finally opening one of my eyes partway for a split second.

"Hey, Cassara, he's coming to!" came a new voice, female, this time from immediately above me. I managed to open both my eyes and was greeted by the blurry form of a short woman with close-cropped spiky hair. She was dressed like a paramedic.

The retreating footsteps stopped, then got louder, until a few moments later another form joined the first. They both swam in and out of focus above me. The new one was wearing a cheap blue sports coat over a white button-up that, even with blurred vision, I could tell was heavily stained around the collar. He had short dark hair combed back with some greasy-looking product and wore mirror shades a couple of decades out of fashion.

"You okay, buddy?" asked the paramedic.

"What's your name?" It was the standing guy. He had the thick Boston accent I had first heard, which was strange considering I was pretty sure I went unconscious in California.

"Uhhhh…" It took a second. "Chance?"

"Chance," the man in the blue blazer repeated back to me. "Okay, Chance. So, what happened?"

I tried to think of a good lie, but my mind wasn't cooperating, so I chose to just omit a few facts. "Dunno. I was standing here when a guy ran by me. As I watched him go, something slammed into my back and I was out."

The man grunted and asked the paramedic to get him if I remembered anything useful. "Sure thing, Detective."

The detective walked off to what I presumed was the body they had talked about earlier. The paramedic asked me a few more questions, then told me an ambulance was on its way. I unsuccessfully tried to convince them that I was fine. It looked like I was getting an ambulance ride whether I liked it or not. At least I had student insurance, crappy though it was. I hoped it would work here – I was a long way from Austin, Texas.

The last thing I actually remembered was standing in a California parking lot waiting to meet my contact. He was supposed to hand off a package that I was being paid to destroy. Unfortunately he seemed to be running for his life when I met him. He came around the minivan I was standing behind, grabbed me, gave me a terror-filled look and then he was off. It wasn't quite the meeting I had expected. I didn't even have the chance to ask him anything.

Confused, I had watched him flee, not realizing there was someone right behind him until I kind of felt something. It was like the pressure you feel when you're deep underwater, a weight surrounding and pressing in on all sides. Now, I knew what vampires felt like, at least to me: cold, like the dead things they are. This was definitely something different. I had just started to turn when he rounded the van. He was either going too fast to stop or just didn't care, because he slammed into me, knocking me out cold with the impact. In retrospect, that was probably a good thing, because then I fell face first into the pitted blacktop, which would have really hurt had I been conscious.

I was getting bored with lying there waiting for the ambulance so I tried to see what was going on, but I couldn't get a good look at anything from my vantage point. All I could make out were lots of tires and shoes. I tried to move, but the paramedic told me to stay still. So instead I listened. I heard plenty of sirens and enough snippets of conversation to piece some facts together.

Apparently the first guy, my terrified contact, only made it another twenty yards before getting himself stuffed into the front windshield of a truck. The only witnesses were the second victim (me) who was knocked unconscious and couldn't give them any details, a couple of teenagers who found the body, and an elderly lady who saw the perp running from the scene. She was being taken to the police station to give a description to a sketch artist. Before she left, she went on about how he was wearing a trench coat, which she thought very odd for August.

The teenagers were still hanging around, asking if the guy was dead (he was) and how he got that way ("Wish I knew," said the detective).

I listed to the detective become increasingly agitated with their questions until someone eventually came and put me on a stretcher and hoisted me into an ambulance. Not long after, I was outside the emergency room, where I spent the next hour lying on a gurney until a doctor finally found me. Five minutes after that, the doctor determined that I had a mild concussion and some abrasions on my face. The scrapes were dressed, and I was released into the custody of an officer who explained that I needed to give a statement at the station; then I'd be free to go.

The ride from the hospital to the police station was quick, and at least I got to ride in the front seat of the patrol car. The officer had a cousin who went to the University of Texas, so we chatted about the Longhorns' chances at a championship this year. Along the way I decided to take a look at my face.

I wasn't vain, but it was my face and I had grown attached to it. I glanced in the side view mirror and, to my relief, it wasn't as bad as I feared. On the other hand, that was probably because all I could see was the large bandage covering my left cheek, and the smaller one taped to my forehead.

The officer saw me staring at myself and said, "Don't worry about it, kid. You were lucky. The other guy...." He shook his head and didn't finish the thought, instead leaving me with the parting wisdom, "Besides, chicks dig scars."

At the station I waited around for another hour before finally giving my statement to the greasy-haired Detective Cassara from the parking lot. I had no choice but to give him my real name. I answered the questions as best I could, leaving out only why I was really there. That would have been a little complicated.

I would have had to explain that I was a vampire hunter from Texas. I had been one of five hunters in Robert's crew. We had contracted for this easy job out in California. It wasn't even killing vampires. We were just about on our way when Robert got a line on a vamp that had supposedly killed a family out at a ranch in Central Texas. We decided to take a little detour to check it out. It was a setup, and now the rest of the team was dead and I was on the run.

I panicked and decided to follow through with this job, eager to put fifteen hundred miles between me and the Texas vamps that attacked us.

Most people don't believe in monsters, at least not real ones. I wasn't interested in being locked up in some loony bin, so I told detective Cassara a modified version: I was in California to scout out graduate schools before the fall semester started. I had just parked my car and was going to visit the university campus down the street. He asked a bunch of questions several different ways and then, satisfied, said I was free to go. I gave the cops my contact information in case they needed to follow up with me.

That's when I remembered I had been holding my phone when I was hit. I needed it to check on my mom and my brother. I didn't know if the vamps knew who I was, or if they would go after my family. I quickly searched my pockets; my phone was gone. There was, however, a funny-shaped key in the pocket of my cargo shorts that hadn't been there before. My contact must have slipped it in my pocket when he bumped into me.

I asked Cassara if he had seen my phone. He said he hadn't, but that he would ask the officers at the scene. He suggested that if they hadn't found it, I should go to the wireless store across the street and get a new one in case he needed to get in touch with me about the crime. In retrospect, it was pretty good advice.

While he called about my phone, I went into the restroom, took out the key, and examined it. One end was orange and plastic with the number thirty-two in faded letters. The other end was a stubby metal key that looked like it would fit a locker. I had no idea where the locker might be, and my contact wouldn't be telling me anything, at least not without the help of a medium.

I left the bathroom and checked back in with Detective Cassara. I hoped my phone had slid under a car or something and that the officers had spotted it. It wasn't expensive, but the SIM card had all my contact numbers in it. Cassara shook his head and apologized, saying no one had found it, but that they'd take another look around the scene and I should check back with him tomorrow.

With that piece of good news I signed my statement, said goodbye to the detective and walked out of the station into downtown San Jose.

# ABOUT THE AUTHOR

A native of Northern California, Patrick Kampman moved to Central Texas in a well-meaning effort to bring culture and civility to the Lone Star State. Having accomplished that, he has taken to reviewing maps of the U.S. to identify the next region that will benefit from his benevolent influence.

When not writing or plotting the cultural makeover of cities, Patrick spends his time reading, hiking, exploring Central Texas waterways, and helplessly watching as the St. Louis Rams lose games.

He is currently writing the third Chance Lee novel, *Better Lucky Than Dead.*

# PatrickKampman.com

Sign up for Patrick's email list to keep up with the latest news and to be eligible for special offers and giveaways

## ALSO BY PATRICK KAMPMAN

Chance Lee Series
*Chance in Hell*
*Texas Hold 'Em*
*Better Lucky Than Dead (Winter 2014)*

Vampire Council Series
*Hunted*
*Sanctuary (Fall 2014)*

Pico, Texas
*Haunting in Pico*
*Full Moon Over Pico (2015)*